PRELUDE TO A SHOWDOWN

Vic studied Dave. "Man," he said quietly, "you like to trifle with sudden death, don't you?"

Dave shrugged. "That's been the story of my life since 'sixty-one." He half grinned. "Besides, none of you are going to kill good ol' Davie yet, or you'll have to do the digging yourselves."

"And after that?" Vic asked.

The two hardcase men eyed each other for a moment, then Dave turned and attacked the fill. Both of them knew the answer without speaking . . . .

HELL'S FORTY ACRES

Gordon D. Shirreffs

FAWCETT GOLD MEDAL • NEW YORK

A Fawcett Gold Medal Book
Published by Ballantine Books
Copyright © 1987 by Gordon D. Shirreffs

Library of Congress Catalog Card Number: 86-91375

ISBN: 0-449-13171-8

Manufactured in the United States of America

First Edition: April 1987

To Louisa Rudeen, friend and editor.

"There is something in a treasure that fastens upon a man's mind. He will pray and blaspheme and still persevere, and will curse the day he ever heard of it, and will let his last hour come upon him unawares, still believing that he missed it only by a foot. He will see it every time he closes his eyes. He will never forget it until he is dead—and even then—doctor, did you ever hear of the miserable gringos on Azuera, that cannot die? There is no getting away from a treasure that once fastens upon your mind."

—Joseph-Conrad, *Nostromo*

IT IS OFFICIALLY RECORDED THAT A CERTAIN CAPTAIN DON
Pedro Melgosa, commissioned by the Society of Jesus in the
year of Our Lord 1745 to make an exploratory journey to
the north where the Firebrand River[1] makes its great bend,
changing its westward course to flow south, returned after
many months to the Presidio of Tubac. There was but one
member of his party with him, a certain Bartolome Tomas
Lopez, a muleteer; the remainder of the party had been
killed, including the Jesuit representative Father José Francis Dominguez. The muleteer Lopez, a most godly man,
secretly told the authorities that a lode of almost pure silver
had been found in a hidden canyon. Captain Melgosa had
convinced Father Dominguez that the lode should be
worked for the glory of the Church and the Society of Jesus, and that he, Captain Melgosa, would take only a mi-
nor share of the profits. Thereupon Captain Melgosa, with
the spiritual aid of Father Dominguez, had forced the members of the party to work the lode. Some of them were
killed by an accident in the mine. Others were ambushed
and killed by Indians. When the lode had been only partially worked, Captain Melgosa had slain others of the
party. Father Dominguez had disappeared when the mine
had been sealed. Captain Melgosa had sworn Lopez to utmost secrecy about the matter, promising him a large share

---

*[1] The Colorado River was originally called the Rio del Tizon, or River of the
Firebrand, by the Spaniards. It was renamed the Colorado (Sp., red or reddish) by
a Father Garces in 1776.

of the treasure when it was retrieved from the mine. Lopez had agreed, intending to inform the authorities at the first opportunity. Shortly after they reached the Presidio, Captain Melgosa also disappeared. The captain was never seen again.

From Lopez's description, it is said the canyon of silver is within a maze of interlocking canyons, one hardly distinguishable from another. The entrance is so narrow that one can almost touch the two sides of it with outstretched arms. It is guarded by two tall, gaunt pillars of rock, one on each side. The entrance can only be seen at a certain time of day when the light is just right and then only from a certain spot. A variance of just a few Alicante *varas* to one side or the other, and the entrance cannot be detected. Lopez claimed that Captain Melgosa had left a marker indicating the canyon entrance, but that he, Lopez, had not been allowed to see where it was located. Lopez estimated that the canyon would be perhaps six leagues[2] or there abouts south of the east-west course of the Firebrand River and an estimated twelve leagues east of the southerly course.

When questioned thoroughly by the authorities as to the quantity of silver in the mine, Lopez was in some doubt but insisted that although there had been a great deal of silver already mined, it was beyond doubt that a far greater quantity of silver ore still remained in the lode. In his enthusiasm, Lopez claimed that it was entirely possible that the mountain itself was principally formed of silver. In any case, it is believed that an immense quantity of unmined silver ore remains within the mine.

In the past twenty years a number of expeditions sent by the Society of Jesus, as well as a number of private expeditions, have searched for a canyon of silver but have been unable to locate it. Several of the expeditions vanished into

---

[2] League: three miles.

the isolated and uninhabited area called Tomesha, or Ground Afire, by the Paiute Indians.

From the report of Don Gaspar Abeyta,
Secretary to his Excellency
the Governor General of Chihuahua
in the year of Our Lord 1765.

CHAPTER 1

DAVE HUNTER DROPPED HIS PICK AND SNATCHED UP THE fragment of rock he had broken loose from a ledge of conglomerate. He pressed strong fingers into the fragment as though he could force the silver from it. "Float," he murmured. *"Float!"* he yelled hoarsely. The heat-sodden canyon dutifully echoed his cry: *"Float! Float! Float!"* The echo died away quickly. Tomblike quiet returned to the canyon.

Dave looked up at the naked rock heights brooding on each side of him. They seemed to be moving in on him. He winced as the harsh sunlight needled into his eyes. "It's a jest," he said quietly. "A cruel joke. Damn you! Have your fun with me, but I'll beat you yet." He looked up sideways at the canyon walls. There didn't seem to be the slightest possibility that there might be silver in this particular area and yet there was the indisputable evidence of the float, a bit of silver ore detached from a larger deposit up the canyon and washed down by one of the terrifying flash floods generated by violent and sudden thunderstorms.

Dave wiped the stinging sweat from his burning face. The Colorado River was to the north and also to the west, scouring its way through solid rock and harsh earth on its journey south to the Gulf of California. Dave was somewhere within the Big Bend of the mighty river where it made its change from flowing west to flowing south. It was a hell's package of a country, arid, almost completely waterless, burned and ravaged initially by the awesome

1

fires of Earth's creation and then seared by eons of a pitiless sun from cloudless skies. The distant mountains beyond the intricate labyrinth of canyons were like islands rising from the sea, veiled by shimmering heat waves that gave them the illusion of engaging in a slow and sinuous rituallike dance. Nothing else moved in that lost and remote place of blazing sun and bright blue sky; of rock too hot to touch, deathly silence, and the long, empty distances of a land forgotten by man and likely by God as well. It was like the damned gut of all Creation. But there was a persistent legend, verified in some certainty by Mexican government and Jesuit sources, that there was a vast lode of pure silver somewhere in the Big Bend country.

Dave's horse had broken a leg three days past and he had been forced to kill it. Amiga, his patient female burro, stood on spraddled-out legs with a down-hanging head. A thin thread of yellowish saliva hung from her dry mouth. She didn't have long to live at this rate. The only living thing in sight that seemed to be able to survive the 110–degree heat was the tall, gaunt, and dun-bearded man who stood there softly touching his badly cracked lips with dirty fingertips while his squinting blue eyes scanned the upper reaches of the canyon. *"From Lopez's description, it is said the canyon of silver is within a maze of interlocking canyons, one hardly distinguishable from another. The entrance is so narrow that one can almost touch the two sides of it with outstretched arms. It is guarded by two tall, gaunt pillars of rock, one on each side."* Or so read the account of Don Gaspar Abeyta in the year 1765.

Time after time Dave had sought those two guardian pillars. This was his third trip into Hell's Forty Acres, as the area was termed, although he thought it should be called Hell's Fifty Square Miles. Hell's Forty Acres had a better ring to it, he admitted. There were extensive silver deposits in the Cerbat Mountains about forty miles south, but no one seemed to know of any in this area. Still, there were persistent rumors of the Melgosa Legend, as it had come to be called, and legends ofttimes have a basis of truth.

One story came from an 1870 issue of *The Chlorider*: A prospector known only as "Shorty" Hebdon had stumbled into a mining camp in the Cerbats, more dead than alive. He had babbled of finding positive proof of old Spanish or Mexican mining activities in a hidden canyon guarded by two rock pillars. He had then died of exposure and exhaustion. Ore samples found in his possession were said to have assayed six hundred to two thousand to the ton. That had been seven years ago.

Dave hefted the chunk of float up and down in a big, callused hand. He looked up toward a bend in the canyon. The source *had* to be there somewhere! But he was low on water. Even if there was silver, it would not matter at all if there was no water. That would be the difference between life and death. Certainly the river was up ahead somewhere to the north, but what was between him and the Colorado? Worn out, exhausted, out of water, stricken by the sun, and hopelessly lost in some damned box canyon, he'd go down to stay down. By the grace of God he just might have the wit and strength left to blow out his brains.

Dave scratched his ragged beard. He looked back at Amiga. There just might be enough water in one of his big blanket-covered canteens for him alone to survive the rough trip to the Colorado if he walked steadily for a night and a day, and quite possibly another night. He'd have to abandon her, of course. It would be better to kill her than to leave her three-quarters dead and helpless when the night predators came out from where they hid during the heat of the day. The buzzards would clean up the remains. In a day she'd be nothing but a scattered pile of neat little bones glistening white in the sunlight.

"Go on or go back," a voice seemed to whisper in Dave's brain, "but do not stand too long upon the order of your going, for the sands of your life, too, are running out fast and freely, Dave Hunter.''

He could lead Amiga on until she could go no farther, then kill her and drain the blood from her still-warm body to wet his lips and mouth if need be. He shook his shaggy head. He passed his big hands up his burning, saddle-brown face, pushing up the flesh until he could place the heels of his palms into his burning eye sockets. For a fraction of a second it seemed to ease the thudding pain that, at times, threatened to burst his skull. The heat forced its way through the thin soles of his flat-heeled boots and the holes as round as silver dollars that he had patched from the inside with the end pages and leather back of his copy of Milton's *Paradise Lost*, a legacy of his professor father.

Dave stood there, slowly lifting one foot after the other in a futile effort to ease the heat. He looked back at Amiga and then let his right hand down to rest on the worn walnut butt of his Colt revolver. It would likely be a blessing to her. He looked beyond her down the long, twisted canyon. At least he knew the way he had come. Even so, it would be a long, hard march to the nearest water. He took out the makings and absentmindedly rolled a quirly. He thumb-snapped a lucifer into flame and applied it to the tip of the cigarette. The sun was slanting to the west. Long shadows were creeping down the slopes of the heights.

''Davie, lad,'' the voice in his mind whispered, ''it's now or never. Shit or get off the pot.''

He finished the cigarette and slowly ground it out under his heel. He quickly drew his Colt, cocked it, and turned toward the burro. Amiga raised her head and looked at him with those soft, expressive eyes of hers. For a moment there seemed to be a powerful communication between them, then she lowered her head again.

''Shit!'' Dave spat out. He let down the hammer after rotating the cylinder so that the hammer rested on an empty chamber. ''All right, little lady, you rest here. I won't be long.'' He took his lariat from her packsaddle.

Dave clambered up a talus slope, then worked his way up a declivity in the almost sheer canyon wall until he reached a chimney. He went up it foot by foot, placing his back against one side and his feet on the other, shoving himself up by placing his palms on rock protuberances or by reaching up to dig his long, powerful fingers into crevices. The exertion brought a freshet of sweat to replace the old stale perspiration that soaked his thin flannel shirt. He was almost at the top when his head began to swim and he thought he might faint. He braced himself to wait it out. His legs trembled from the exertion. His head pounded and throbbed. He was afraid to look down. Rock fragments pattered and slid down the talus slope.

The weakness passed. He continued on and, at long last, managed to hook his right arm over the lip of the chimney and then pull himself up and over the rim. He lay flat, with heaving chest, feeling the rock's heat burn through his clothing. He grinned wryly. It was like lying on top of his mother's big kitchen range back in Michigan.

He got to his hands and knees, then stood up, swaying a little. He looked about himself. The mountains were still hazy from the day's heat. Far to the right and easterly was the great depression of a vast dry lake, the Grand Wash, and beyond that the unseen Lower Granite Gorge of the Colorado River. To the north was the heart of Hell's Forty Acres, unmapped, remote, and uninhabited, a vast maze of canyons, mesas, and three-thousand-foot peaks beyond which was the Colorado River. He glanced to his left, to the trend of the canyon from which he had ascended and the bend that had been ahead of him, perhaps leading into other canyons or just a dead end. He tried to follow the possible course of the canyon by studying the contours of the land. He had a fine eye for terrain. Ahead of him and slightly to the right, he seemed to sense a depression. It wasn't clearly visible, perhaps it didn't exist at all, but the sixth sense that a person must have in that type of country nagged in the back of his tired mind that there *was* something there.

Dave stood, peering through squinted blue eyes as he shaped a cigarette. "To be or not to be," he murmured. "It's not death, but the *way* of dying that is paramount." He lit the cigarette. Dave was no stranger to violent death. Four years of Civil War service in the famous "Iron Brigade" of the Army of the Potomac as a sharpshooter had exposed him many times to violent death right at his elbows. Since the war he had contributed to the virtual extinction of the vast herds of buffalo on the Great Plains. Service as a civilian scout for the army in Arizona Territory and time spent as a prospector in hostile Apache country both in Arizona and Mexico had added to his experience of death by violence. He had hardened himself to it; he had never gotten used to it.

He looked back the way he had come, up from Chloride, days ago. There was a quirk in Dave. Once committed to a course of action, he found it almost impossible to quit and turn back. It was often a dangerous course, as it was now.

Suddenly, Amiga brayed from far down in the canyon. Dave peered over the rim. She was looking up at him. "All right, all right," he said quietly. He grinned. "You're as stupid as I am, little girl."

He formed a loop in his lariat and quickly tied a sheepshank knot. He placed the loop around a boulder, then cut one of the three strands within the knot. He lowered himself down into the chimney, rapeling in the wider places, until his feet struck the talus at the bottom. He stood back and flipped the lariat vigorously a few times, releasing the sheepshank but leaving a few feet of the lariat still looped around the boulder. He coiled the lariat and slid down the talus slope in a rush of decomposed rock and dust.

Dave took up the burro's lead rope. "Come on, little lady," he said softly. "Once more into the breach." He pointed up the canyon. "*Más allá, Compañera*—on beyond . . .'' He grinned crookedly and instantly regretted it as his lower lip split. He led her up the canyon.

Dave had been looking for a strike in the Southwest and in Mexico for the past seven years. He had first stumbled across a copy of *The Account of Josef de Armijo, Archivist in the City of Mexico in the year 1765,* which related the tale of a fabulous lost canyon of silver in the Big Bend country of the Colorado River, five years past, but had put it down as one of the elusive legends of lost mines and buried treasure with which the Southwest and Mexico were rife. He had gradually drifted north to Wickenburg on the Hassayampa. While working in the Vulture mine, he had read the item about ''Shorty'' Hebdon in an old issue of *The Chlorider.* The coincidence of the canyon of silver guarded by two tall rock pillars had intrigued him. It was the first hint that the fabulous silver canyon might be real. He had earned enough money in the Vulture to grubstake himself. So for two long years he had poked his big sun-burned nose into lost and hostile country, always living on the very edge of a water scrape, and at times having hardly enough food to keep his six-foot-plus body alive. He had kept on. Many times he'd hidden by day and traveled by night. The country was haunted by Paiutes and sometimes Mohaves. Any lone white man with firearms was fair game for them.

Dave had wandered from the Peloncillo Mountains to the east, clear west to the Trigos, north and still farther north through the Hualpais and finally into the murderous Cerbats and beyond, to his present situation. He'd searched for ''color'' everywhere. With hammer, pick, and magnifying glass, he had thoroughly explored the likely places and then the unlikely places all with a common factor—a complete lack of success. He had run out of many a hard-earned grubstake and been forced to swing a doublejack in other men's mines and stopes until he could earn just enough to outfit himself once again. Then it had been back

to the lonely hills, brooding mountains, and lost canyons
to find his own bonanza—*Dave Hunter's Bonanza* . . .

Amiga lagged. Perhaps she had sensed something Dave
had not. More than a few times he had relied on that per-
ceptive sense of hers. This might be the most unlikely of
unlikely places to prospect for the elusive will-o'-the-wisp
silver, but an uncanny premonition had begun to grow
within his mind that this time success just might be within
reach of the cup of his dirty hands. The float might have
been the clue. Surely it was a sign from whatever gods
there might be!

Dave slid an arm about Amiga's neck and spoke softly
into the shaggy, dusty off ear of the patient little jenny,
"Can you hang on for a little while and yet a little while
longer? Comes the bonanza, I'll shoe your dainty little
hoofs with solid silver and put you out to pasture for the
rest of your life. There will be no more heavy loads to
carry, no, nothing but the prettiest of little girls, all curls
and smiles, with white starched dresses and huge blue rib-
bons." He grinned. "Why, you lucky little bitch!" He led
her on, slogging through the deepening shadows of that
canyon of hell, a lean lath of a man whose body fat had
long ago been burned away. He raised his hard, bronzed
face to look up the canyon, now a darkening and uninviting
place. *Más allá* . . . On beyond . . .

It was his eyes that would first draw attention to him.
Now they peered, tired but hopeful, from under the brim
of the faded black Hardee campaign hat he had worn since
his service in the war. His eyes were a light, hard blue in
absolute contrast to his brown face. There was something
in those eyes—a force and determination few men ever
possess, coupled with a lingering loneliness that perhaps
no one but an extremely sensitive woman could even partially fathom. Some had tried; all had failed. Their names
and features were but the vaguest of memories to Dave, a
charter member of the Legion of the Lost. He was one of
the solo nomads who wandered the face of the Southwest,

always probing into the unknown, seeking precious metals and perhaps something else, something indefinable, something of which they themselves had little, if any, understanding. This legion had no organization, no charter, no officers, and no dues. There were never any meetings except for fleeting ones between two members in their unceasing quest, for these lonely, dedicated, and determined men were indeed a race apart.

The rising floor of the canyon crumbled and grated under Dave's boot soles. The quiet air was still hot. He stopped looking up to see how far he had to go. He planted one foot after the other, keeping his eyes on his frayed boot toes and feeling the exhausted burro dragging back on the lead rope while its little hoofs slid and clattered on the loose rock. Gradually, the ominous thought crept into Dave's mind that each footstep, each yard of travel was taking him deeper into the unknown and farther and farther away from a safe retreat. In his time in the lonely places, he had found more than a few bleached-out, grinning skeletons in forgotten back canyons and on burning desert sands, relics of men known only to God. They were wanderers who had failed and died alone, just as they had lived.

Dave looked up and shouted fiercely, "But not for me, Amiga!" The echoes chased each other endlessly along the canyon. "But not for me, Amiga! But not for me . . . But not for . . . But not for . . . But not . . . But not . . . But . . . But . . ."

There would be chilled imported wine in tall, slender-stemmed crystal. There would be caviar and pheasant under glass. There would be soft, warm women with full red, parted lips and creamy white shoulders exposed above their silks and satins. There would be sultry invitation in their great, expressive eyes. There would be the best of everything for Dave Hunter. The lode was just up ahead! It *had* to be there! He had not come to this blazing suburb of Hell itself just to die and mummify in a place where he'd never be found until the end of eternity.

Amiga stumbled and went down. Dave turned back. He ran a quick hand along each of her legs. None broken. He held her furry jaw between his hands and looked into her eyes. He nodded. "You're tired, little friend. You've given your best and more than your best, and I won't leave you here."

He got her to her feet. He unloaded the packsaddle and cached the load behind some boulders. He took only the one canteen with some water left in it and his Sharps rifle. He led Amiga on again. She trotted somewhat briskly for a short time, as though to show her appreciation, then lagged again, although not as much as before.

The darkness came almost suddenly, plunging the canyon into obscurity. A wide ribbon of night sky showed at the top between the towering vertical walls. Dave halted. The way was too difficult to continue on through the blackness. There would be a gibbous moon that night, bright enough in that clear atmosphere to light the way. He'd have to travel all that night if no water could be found.

Dave placed his back against the warmth of a boulder and closed his eyes. There wasn't much danger of a Paiute or two creeping up on him. Paiute legend had it that this area was haunted at all times and particularly so at night. Those who entered here risked much unless they had strong medicine. Dave grinned in the darkness. "Whiskey," he murmured. That was strong medicine for white man and Paiute as well. "Or insanity," he added dryly. Amiga was as good as, or better, than any watchdog. She had saved his life once or twice that way. She had a particular dislike of Indians.

It was the furnace wind that woke him up. That was the way of the canyon country. The wind blew downslope after darkness and upslope with the coming dawn. He whistled softly for Amiga. She trotted to him, chewing something— God knows what—she had found to graze on. While he waited for the moonlight, he lighted one of his precious cigars, a dried-out long nine of dubious quality.

When the first pewter light tinted the sky, presaging the coming of the moon, Dave poured a scant two cupfuls of water into his hat and gave it to Amiga. When she was done, he filled his dry mouth from the canteen, swirled the water around luxuriously, and then let it flow back into the container. He waited patiently until the moonlight filled the great bowl of the sky. The heights became bathed in the soft translucent light and after a time the canyon lightened enough for Dave to continue on into the unknown.

A graveyard filled the land. Nothing could be heard but the steady *crunch crunch crunch* of Dave's footfalls and the irregular *patter patter patter* of Amiga's hoofs.

The canyon widened greatly. One side canyon came in from the right, or east; two others entered from the left, or west. Heavy talus slopes flowed down from the decomposing canyon walls. Here and there pillars of rock thrust themselves up from the detritus of the slopes. In some places, where the main canyon was at its widest and the walls were riven with deep gullies through which torrential rainwater from violent thunderstorms would flow and cascade down to the canyon floor to join a roaring flash flood, there were smooth slopes of finer material, thoroughly decomposed rock and soil, called *bajada arenoso* by the Mexicans and the Spaniards before them. Here, in the spring, watered by gentler rains, flowers would rise and bloom prodigiously for a short time until the killing heat of summer burned them away.

Midway up the main canyon, Dave halted. He looked back the way he had come. An artist hones his senses to *feel* rather than to see nuances and delicate shades of tone and color. He cannot explain this sensitivity to anyone else. But, he *knows*. . . . So it is with men such as Dave Hunter, who live in a perpetually hostile environment. They *feel* danger long before it is seen.

There was nothing back down the canyon that hadn't

been there when he had passed through like Dante on his journey into the Inferno. Dave shrugged. There were enough dangers in that Hell's delight of a country without him conjuring up any more. It was a Pandora's box of peril on its own—thorned, clawed, fanged, and poisonous. But the greatest danger of all, unseen and undetected until it struck, was the terrible and utter loneliness that crept up on a lone man. It was always just beyond sight and sound, but it was *always* there. It was as though someone, or *something*, was close by, never seen, yet there. Time and time again the lone wanderer would whirl, placing a tense hand on the butt of his pistol or raising a ready rifle, only to see nothing. He'd laugh foolishly and nervously, then continue on with his wandering or working, until once again the uneasiness would creep insidiously into his mind and soul. Then, too, there were the strange uncouth mumbling voices in the wind, muttering warning words never quite intelligible.

Dave shook his head hard as though to rid it of apprehension. He walked on. He glanced up at the east wall. Somewhere to his right was where he had seen, or thought he had seen the almost imperceptible depression when he had been up on the heights. There was no indication of it now, but it had to be somewhere to his right, perhaps farther along. There were pillars here, sure enough, but no two standing closely side by side, guarding, as Don Gaspar Abeyta had written, the narrow entrance to the canyon of silver.

Dave halted again, glancing back the way he had come. Nothing had changed. The moonlight gave the landscape an unearthly, almost lunar aspect. It was as though Dave and Amiga had wandered off the face of the Earth and were the only living creatures on an unknown planet.

The canyon trended somewhat right, perhaps north or north by east. Dave scanned the walls. It was the same. He shook his head. Don Gaspar Abeyta had written: "The entrance can only be seen at a certain time of day when the light is just right and then only from a certain spot. . . . ." It would be many hours before dawn light and another day of blazing sun and killing heat before that "certain time" came to detect the entrance, *"and then only from a certain spot."* It was no use. There wasn't enough water for another day. He'd have to go on to the Colorado for water, then return to take up his search again. He closed his eyes. Was it all worthwhile? He visualized a set of scales. On one side was a heap of gleaming silver, a veritable fortune; on the other side was a grinning skull. *Son of a bitch!* He'd always had too vivid an imagination.

Dave walked on, following the gentle curve of the main canyon.

Amiga brayed, awakening the dormant echoes.

Dave turned and looked at her. He scanned the canyon behind him. It was the same. She brayed again. He looked to his left, then up the canyon, then to his right. It was the same and yet . . . He scanned the looming walls again. Nothing. He closed his eyes and then opened them suddenly, a trick he had learned from a Chiricahua Apache scout at Fort Bowie. By this means one might detect some slight disturbance on the slopes that had not yet been returned by the process of nature to its original form.

"A day is twenty-four hours long," his mind's voice seemed to say.

Dave nodded.

"Therefore, a certain time of day could be either day *or* night . . ."

The moonlight was almost as bright as day.

Dave closed his eyes. He opened them and then looked to the north and east. A rectangular-shaped notch showed high on the rim, descending down into shadows.

"A variance of just a few Alicante *varas* to one side or the other, and the entrance cannot be detected," Don Gaspar had recorded.

An Alicante *vara* was 35.90544 inches. It was the standard measurement used in Alicante, Spain, Melgosa's birthplace.

Dave took a long pace forward and looked up at the notch. It seemed to him that it described a long vertical line of shadow all the way down the wall to meet the talus slope. He took half a pace and stumbled over a flat rock sunk in the earth. He looked down at it, then up and quickly down again. There was a faint, natural-seeming mark on the stone. He dropped to his knees and studied it. There was nothing unusual about it. He stood and looked up at the notch. He looked down again at the flat rock. He dropped to his knees again, drew out his heavy sheath knife, and dug around the edges of the rock. It was about three inches thick. He dug until he could put his fingers under the edge, then pulled up on it. It moved a little. He dug around its perimeter some more and then tried again. This time he lifted it and then threw it back onto the ground with its bottom side uppermost.

His eyes widened. Neatly incised in the rock was a depiction of a bell, and extending from it was the curved body of a snake with the head pointing directly toward that puzzling line of shadow. The early Spaniards and later the Mexicans, avid treasure seekers, had long ago developed a system of symbols and signs. A bell, for example, was one of the many symbols indicating that a mine or treasure was nearby. A snake, arrow, sword, or similar signs indicated the direction of the treasure or mine.

The moon was now fully up. Dave walked toward the line of shadow. Then, as though he were watching a magic lantern show, he saw the bulge on the canyon wall resolve itself into two gaunt, towering pillars of crumbling rock and between them what appeared to be a narrow slot of perhaps a passageway. It was as though the pillars were guarding whatever mystery lay within. A shout or a shot might tumble those pillars into dusty, roaring ruin and block the passageway forever.

There was an almost undetectable line ascending the

slope toward the pillars as though a trail had once been made there or the runoff water from a flash flood had poured between the pillars and down the slope to the canyon bottom.

Dave ascended the slope to stand within the shadows of the pillars. A faint warm breeze crept from between them and dried the sweat of his face. The draft indicated that the passageway was open at the other end. "Wherever the hell *that* might be," Dave said dryly.

He removed his hat and bowed his head for a moment or two in silent thanks for at least finding the pillars.

He went downslope quickly and replaced the flat rock. As he did so, he studied the curious marking on the top. It still looked natural. He picked out the dirt that filled it. Evidently, whatever it had been, it was man-made. Years of wear and erosion had reshaped it and worn part of it away. He traced the shape in the coarse sand beside the rock and continued it as he thought it might have gone. It developed into a four-pointed star.

Dave stood and looked up and down the silent, moonlighted canyon. He looked down at the star. "Grave danger," he translated quietly. He kicked the loosened earth along the edges of the rock and scuffed out his drawing. Suddenly, he grinned. "What the hell! Doesn't mean a damned thing more than I've known about this area for the past two years."

He picked up the lead rope and led Amiga up the slope toward the looming pillars.

CHAPTER 2

THE NATURAL PASSAGEWAY WAS AS WIDE AS THE SPAN of Dave's stretched-out arms, his fingertips just brushing the walls. It trended left for a time, then to the right for quite a distance. His left foot struck something. He picked it up. It was a thoroughly rusted mule shoe. How long it had lain there was a puzzler. Wind could have covered it with earth for months, perhaps years. A flash flood could have uncovered it and then covered it again. It could have been washed here from a great distance. So it was with such objects in the desert and canyon country, playthings of wind and rain like the old carnival shell game.

The passageway ran string-straight for perhaps several hundred yards. It seemed to end in a blank wall. When he reached it, he found that the corridor turned to the right in a sweeping curve and suddenly he was in the open again. He stopped, a gaunt, bearded man wearing dusty, thread-bare, and ragged clothing and carrying a heavy Sharps rifle in his left hand with the lead rope of a dainty shaggy burro in his right. His eyes widened as he surveyed the terrain ahead of him. It was a rather deep and narrow canyon with a high, precipitous wall to the left. The canyon walls had, millennia past, been riven and cracked by enormous pressures beyond the comprehension of man. To the right, the wall was lower and sloped backward, although lower was only a comparative term as opposed to the left wall. In the right one were great open crevices and deeply eroded surfaces; knife-edged ridges and narrow, crumbling ledges;

and formless jumbles of shattered and tumbled rock. Farther along were the possible mouths of branch canyons. Higher, beyond the serrated rimrock, were serried phalanxes of precipitous heights sharply outlined against the moonlit sky.

Dave uncased his battered field glasses, a relic of his wartime sharpshooting days. He focused it and studied the canyon. There was no sign of man. There was a growing certainty within him that this was the canyon of silver. But water was his first priority; only after he found it could he go after the silver. Without the first, the second was valueless. If he couldn't find water there, he'd still have to strike north for the Colorado and hope to God he'd make it.

He walked on within that gigantic panorama of colored rock, with its hues of salmon, red, yellow, and brown, like a louse crawling on the body of a giant. A mile or more from the entrance, he stopped again. The moon was on the wane. Already long shadows inked themselves on the canyon walls and in the depressed areas of the canyon floor. There was no sign of water. Still he kept on, reluctant to leave although he knew he'd have to start finding his way back through the thick darkness if he tarried too long.

Two miles from the entrance, he stopped yet again. It was tomb-quiet in the vast labyrinth of canyons. Nothing moved. It was a silent, dreamlike landscape, as though seen in one's sleep.

Amiga brayed.

Dave looked at her. "What is it?" he asked.

She pulled on the lead rope. Dave let her go. She trotted off into the growing darkness. He heard loose rock clattering ahead of him to the right. She brayed again. The echo died away. Dave reached a slope leading up into what looked like a double-branch canyon. It was indistinct in the dimness. He ascended the slope, with gravel and decomposed rock cascading down behind him. It was impossible to pierce the darkness of the canyons. The burro could not be seen.

"Amiga!" he called.

From far up the left-hand canyon, she brayed.

Dave walked on. Suddenly, his boot soles were not crunching on harsh soil or broken rock shards. It was a softer surface. He knelt and pressed his right hand on matted, wiry growth of some kind. He looked up the canyon. He knew such growth could not survive watered only by the infrequent rains of the area. But he would not run despite his torturing thirst. He climbed a side slope close to the looming canyon wall. The slope suddenly leveled. Where in hell was Amiga?

She brayed again, as though in answer, this time to his left and downslope. He walked on slowly. He tripped over a rock and fell face downward into about two feet of sun-warmed water.

Dave scrambled out of the water. He fumbled in his shirt pocket for a tin container of matches, flipped up the lid, and withdrew a lucifer. He thumb-snapped it into flame and held it high. There before him was a wide area dark with water, evidently a rock *tinaja,* or water pan. Amiga was just to his left, calmly lapping up the water.

Despite his murderous thirst, he would not drink until he was sure of the water. He led Amiga away, slapped her on the rump, and watched her trot down the slope to begin munching on the growth. Then he twisted some dry grasses together and lighted the rude torch.

There were many such *tinajas* in the Southwest, hollow places in the earth or rock where rainwater collected. The water ran down his wet clothes and into his boots. It was a blessed feeling, but it augmented his burning thirst. Christ, but he wanted to plunge his burning face into the water! He held back. He must make absolutely sure the water was palatable. He went down the slope to Amiga. She seemed all right as she munched contentedly on the vegetation.

He returned to the pool and formed another torch. He lighted it and walked along the rim. The torchlight revealed a patch of scum stippled with tiny pink bladders, floating on the far surface. Poisoned or not? Then he noticed a water skater skimming the surface. A few bird feathers floated nearby. He found a few deer droppings around the edge, and in a damp place where the water had overflowed were a few faint hoof marks and, sure enough, the paw marks of a coyote or two. It was enough evidence for Dave.

Amiga trotted up the slope and thrust her muzzle into the water. She drank daintily, then looked up at Dave with her soulful eyes. He held her long, furry ears and bent to kiss her on the nose. "Bless you, my child," he murmured.

Dave knelt beside the burro and cupped water in his dirty hands. It wasn't exactly nectar, but he was more used to this type of water than he was to nectar. Besides, who in hell's name knew what nectar tasted like, anyway? He grinned in the darkness.

Dave stood up. He unbuckled his gunbelt and dropped it on the ground. He stripped off his sweat-soaked shirt. He sat down and yanked off his worn boots and peeled off his horrible socks, or what was left of them. He stood up, clad only in his baggy longjohns, glanced upward and smiled at the heavens, opened his mouth to bellow, "Yow-eeeee!," then stripped off the underwear and hurled it away. He fell forward into the pool, then rolled over and over like a playful porpoise, raising his head to spout mouthfuls of water, submerging himself again and again as though he could never absorb enough of the blessed moisture. At last he floated on his back and stared up at the dark blue blanket of sky that was now beginning to be stippled with stars.

It wasn't easy to leave the pool, but at last he crawled out onto the bank. He shaped another torch and lighted it. He walked slowly around the pool rim and then stopped short. The level area where the pool was situated sloped downward somewhat toward a lower spot, which was thickly matted with a type of glaucous gray-green vegetation that extended off into the darkness. He looked closely at the rim. It was partially covered with earth and loose pieces of rock that had possibly washed down from the heights behind the pool during a flash flood. Beneath was a low wall of rock neatly fitted together. *Man-made*!

There was a trough set into the wall for the pool overflow that ran down the slope to water the vegetation. He circled the *tinaja* back toward the canyon wall. There was another trough evident, although it had been partially filled with soil and detritus. He pawed through the loose material and noticed a dampness in the coarse sand about a foot below the surface. Evidently, the source of the water was somewhere at the base of the towering canyon wall. The moon was gone. Further exploration could wait until daylight.

Dave dined on hard biscuit and beef jerky as tough as sole leather. He allowed himself a swallow of his precious Baconora brandy. Slowly, lethargy overcame him. He'd be safe enough with Amiga on guard. He didn't anticipate any visitors.

He was up at first light. The trough, or channel behind the pool, led to another *tinaja* that seemed more natural than the first one. It was much smaller and deeper. A beetling cliff rose above it. This *tinaja* was almost completely filled with loose rock and soil. He dug into it with his spade until he detected a dampness. The rock pan extended into the cliff base. With a few nervous glances at the towering cliff face scaled with loose rock, he attacked the blockage. He was in five or six feet when he noticed a trickle of water seeping between the rocks. He removed more rocks and earth. The trickle became a small flow and in a little while he was kneeling in half a foot of cool, fresh water. He worked his way back toward the large *tinaja*, clearing the channel to its original depth. He watched in delight as the water flowed steadily into the large *tinaja*. He cleared out most of the scum and weed. The water level rose slowly until it was lapping at the rocks rimming the pool. A little stream began to run into the outlet trough down through the vegetation. He wisely blocked off the trough; the water supply might dwindle and, in time, dry up.

He looked up at the cliff. "Who's this Moses, anyway?" he called out. "Striking the earth with his staff to bring forth a gush of water? Ol' dirty Dave Hunter did the same thing with his spade!" He paused guiltily, shot a sideways and upward glance at the sky, and mumbled apologetically, "Sorry, Lord. Just joshin'."

Somewhere within that gigantic mass of seemingly solid rock must be a reservoir of water stored over many years, perhaps hundreds and possibly thousands. It might be spring-fed, but more likely it had resulted from rainfalls. Perhaps the rain had filled another reservoir high on the cliff, then the water had seeped down into a hollow area, which in turn led to the small *tinaja*. Dave wasn't about to question it. All he was sure of was that he had found water aplenty in a place where water rightfully should not be. He looked about him, down the slopes to the main canyon, then to the right and left. To the right was a small branch canyon the floor of which was thickly matted with enough grazing to keep horses and mules alive for quite a span of time. To the left was the opening at yet another canyon. Maybe there was yet another miracle hidden in those implacable land masses comprising the terrain—*a silver lode*. The water was miracle enough; to find silver as well was more than a simple miracle, if there was such a thing.

Amiga was happy in her natural pasture. She rolled contentedly on her back. Without her, Dave might well have continued up the main canyon into a deathtrap before he'd have had enough sense to turn back.

He'd have to return here to the main canyon for their cached supplies. As long as there was water and forage here he could spend quite some time searching for the silver. Whether he found it or not, eventually he'd have to return to the outer world for more supplies.

The branch canyon held other surprises, proof that there had been silver workings here at one time. Several sizable rock huts were clustered together. A roof had caved in in one of them. There was a hut without a front wall that had evidently been used as a blacksmith shop. It held the remains of a crude bellows and a smelter for the silver. Rusted picks, spades, and other implements were lying about mingled with horse and mule shoes, drill bits, and other odds and ends. Beyond the tool hut was a level patch of ground that was paved with flat rocks in a roughly circular shape. In the center was a large rock with a hole drilled into it. The stub of a thick pole was still in the hole. It was an *arrastre* or ore crusher. A shaft would be attached to the central pole to which a team of horses or mules, or in some cases oxen, would be hitched. The ore would be thrown onto the paved area and rocks would be attached to the shaft and dragged over the ore to crush it for the smelter.

It was positive evidence that silver must have been found in abundance here and that the Spaniards, or possibly Mexicans, who had mined the area must have been there for a considerable length of time. Fine! Good! Great! *But where the hell was the mine?*

The sun was beginning to stoke up the furnace heat in the canyons. Dave studied both sides of the branch canyon with his field glasses. The fine lenses ground by that master of his craft, Vollmer of Jena, picked out each detail of the terrain. Dave was looking for even the slightest disturbance of the natural appearance of the canyon. The long years that had evidently passed since the mine had been worked had done their best to return the area to its original appearance, but nature was never static in that respect. There was constant change brought about by wind, rain, freezing temperatures at night in the winters, and hellfire by day during the summers. Rain and snow would seep into crevices and then freeze hard, splitting and cracking the surface

rock and then scaling it away to fall hundreds of feet below
to form the great talus slopes lying at an angle of repose.
Who knew whether or not the mine entrance was hidden
under tons of decomposed rock and sheets of scaled stone?

Dave walked slowly along the foot of the slope and paused
to use the field glasses again. He shook his head and continued on toward a wide area of depression. As he descended
into it, he looked back over his shoulder with the habitual
wariness of a man in an unknown and hostile country. Something rolled from under his foot. He looked down at a grinning skull. He instantly leaped backward. It was an area
where sparse grasses had sprung up through the harsh soil.
Here and there were scattered parts of a skeleton, probably
so distributed by animal predators. Shreds of cloth and leather
as hard as wood lay about. He picked up a piece of cloth. It
crumbled between his fingers. A rusted Spanish morion hel-
met lay behind a boulder. Dave picked it up and peered
into it. Faint letters had been scratched within: Do- --dr-
Me-g--a and an indecipherable date.

An eerie feeling crept through Dave. "Don Pedro Melgosa," he murmured. *Captain Melgosa had disappeared. . . . Captain Melgosa was never seen again . . .*

Dave looked at the rib cage and touched it with his toe.
Something rattled within it. He picked up the rib cage and
shook it. A foot-long piece of rusted metal fell out. There
was no question in his mind that it was a lance point. Who
had stuck Don Melgosa down? Indian or white man? An
Indian at that period of time would not have had much
access to an iron or steel lance point. Paiutes considered
most of the Hell's Forty Acres area to be haunted. Still,
the reason *for* that belief might have been the very fact that
they had slain a Spaniard there and feared the possibility
of an avenging ghost.

Dave walked on while scanning the walls. Two hundred
yards up a gentle slope he found a clue. A hollow at the
top of the slope didn't look quite natural. Below it was a
wide *bajada arenoso* of slit and fine gravel. Above the

hollow and the talus slope was another beetling cliff that was hung with scales and shards of decomposing rock, which, it seemed, a shout would bring tumbling down.

There would be time to investigate it later. If it was the site of the silver lode, it could wait until the next day or so. His first need was to establish his camp. Even if he did find the lode, could he work it alone? The Spaniards had evidently put a great deal of time and labor into their mining. Dave might need at least one partner. Even so, one man would likely not be enough. He'd try it alone first. It was always the same. Maybe the search was over; the problems, however, had likely just begun.

He reached the scattered relics of Captain Don Pedro Melgosa. He courteously touched the brim of his campaign hat with the tips of his right fingers. "No need to get up, not just yet, anyway, Captain Melgosa. I'll give you a soldier's burial soon." He walked on and then looked back over his shoulder. "Or do you walk again at night?" he asked quietly. He didn't wait for an answer.

Dave tasted the water in the *tinaja* again. He grimaced. "Coyote tea," he said. A concoction of water and coyote piss. He had drunk it many times before in his wanderings.

He led Amiga back down the main canyon and through the zigzag entrance passageway. He paused at the exit to the main canyon beyond, staying well back in the shadows, scanning the sun-filled canyon through his field glasses. There was no sign of life in the mighty, shimmering rock trough. They returned to the cache. Dave replaced the packsaddle on Amiga and loaded his gear. Then he led her back through the canyon and into the passageway. Again he studied the landscape. He hadn't realized how high he was, as the ascent in the past few days had been so gradual. He could see far to the west toward the distant, unseen Colorado.

He led Amiga back to Silver Canyon, as he called it, perhaps somewhat prematurely. By the time he had stowed his gear and prepared his camp, it was dusk. He lit his oil lamp and set about cleaning his weapons, The big, single-shot Sharps rifle was his pride and joy. During the war he had been designated a sharpshooter because of the extraordinary marksmanship he'd gained from his early teens spent as a deer hunter and the many rifle competitions he had entered in his native Michigan. There had been many Germans in the area who had brought their fine *schuetzenbund* target rifles with them from Germany and had formed shooting bands in the new country. Despite his Scottish ancestry, Dave had been made welcome in one of the bands and became one of their best marksmen. He and many of the Germans had joined the 24th Michigan Volunteers, a part of the Iron Brigade, which was famed for its fighting ability. During the war, Dave had been issued the .54-caliber percussion Sharps New Model 1859, which was loaded with a linen-covered cartridge and fired with a percussion cap. Upon his discharge he had taken the weapon with him when he'd left Michigan in his restless wanderings throughout the West and later the Southwest. With the development of the full brass cartridge with primer base, he had bought one of the new Model 1874 rifles. It weighted nine and a half pounds and was chambered for the .44-caliber, 500-grain bullet propelled by 90 grains of powder; the bullet and powder charge was contained in a lengthy $2^5/8$-inch case. Dave had taught more than one predatory Apache, American outlaw, or Mexican *bandido* that he was not safe at half a mile or more from a searching 500-grain slug. Dave's Colt was the 1872 Army issue in .44/40 caliber. He carried reloading gear for both guns with him. When he had cleaned both weapons, he cleaned and honed his sheath knife, ground from an old hoof file, to a razor-sharp edge.

Dave ate sparingly. After dark, he filled his old pipe with Lone Jack, took his rifle and field glasses, and started walking back toward the pillared entrance to the main canyon. In a little while, he heard the hard pattering of hoofs on the ground and in intermittent jangling noise. He

grinned. Amiga had jerked her picket pin from the ground
and was following him. She was better than a dog and a
hell of a lot more useful. He coiled her picket line and
slung it over his shoulder. The two of them went on, the
rangy, broad-shouldered man with a faint wraith of pipe
smoke about his lean face and the sturdy, little burro with
the flapping, dusty ears. So it had been for over three long,
hard, and profitless years.

The country to the west was softly illuminated by the
rising moon. Nothing moved. Not a sound was heard. Dave
was sitting on a rock at the canyon entrance, idly watching
the play of moonlight on the land, when he saw, or *thought*
he saw, to the southwest a tiny spark of light that flicked
on and then almost instantly off. Such a light could be seen
for a great distance in that clear atmosphere. It was difficult
to estimate how far away it had been, but Dave figured
between three and five miles. It wasn't like Paiutes or Mohaves to camp on lower ground and show a light at night.
So it had probably been a white man, or men. Whoever it
had been, if there *was* really anyone there, they'd been a
damned fool to show a light in that deadly hostile country.

Dave sucked at his pipe while covering the bowl with
his palm to prevent a flare-up. It wasn't possible that he
had been followed this far into the unknown and unmapped
canyon country. He had always made sure of that. Every
night he had back trailed several miles to see if he was
being tailed. Paiutes and Mohaves would not be seen in
any case—not until they were ready to strike. They'd not
be seen until they wanted to be seen. They'd be ultra careful if they knew he carried a long-range, large-bored rifle
like his Sharps. A careless attack might make the price of
his death too costly. Still, if he found the lode, he'd have
to go out for supplies, thus exposing himself to attack.
Silver meant nothing to the Paiutes and Mohaves. Guns,
horses, and mules were everything. That was the key to
his problem: getting back to the canyon with a fresh horse,
a pair of burros, and plenty of supplies.

Dave shrugged. He turned and walked back through the passageway. "Them's the hazards of this happy and carefree life," he said. He grinned. " 'After all, it *is* my choice of life-style," he added dryly.

He made up his bed on the floor of the largest hut, the one nearest to the *tinaja* and closest to the main canyon. He lay down, hands locked at the nape of his neck, and stared up at the low ceiling. He had a powerful feeling that he would find the silver. That was good, but throughout his musings he could not forget that tiny flicker of light in a place where logically a light should not be. Or had it been a momentary illusion in a land were illusion and delusion were commonplace?

Amiga brayed sharply.

Dave awoke, rolled sideways, automatically yanked on his boots, and got up on his knees to buckle on his gunbelt, then stood up while reaching for his rifle—all before he was fully awake. He crawled out of a rear window and crouched behind the hut. He peered around the side of the hut to look toward the *tinaja*. Amiga stood alertly in the last of the moonlight peering down toward the main canyon. She brayed again.

Dave eased down the breechblock of the Sharps and slid in a cartridge. He raised the breechblock and cocked the hammer fully. Minutes ticked past. The night wind murmured through the canyons. Dave bellied up to the hut and went to ground behind a boulder. He looked into the box canyon behind the *tinaja,* up to his right where the mine should be, then left again and down toward the main canyon. He saw nothing; he heard only the night wind. Amiga had gone back to her grazing as though she had done her duty.

It could have been a stalking mountain lion. He had never seen any in this country, but then *león fantasma* was rarely seen by man at any time. It might have been a coyote, that ubiquitous predator of the West. Still, he *had* seen what looked like mountain lion tracks near the *tinaja*.

He looked to the right again. The mine canyon was as it had been before. He started to descend to the hut. Out of the corner of his right eye he thought he saw, or perhaps sensed, a slight, almost imperceptible movement in the shadows near where the mine entrance might be. He looked quickly in that direction and saw nothing except the dying moonlight shining softly on the white bones and grinning skull of Captain Don Pedro Melgosa. Uneasiness crept into his mind. He had a powerful imagination. The isolation and brooding qualities of these remote canyons, coupled with his sensitivity and imagination, could conjure up strange and eerie thoughts at a time like this. Perhaps it had been a skulking Paiute or Mohave. He shook his head. No Indian in his right mind would come anywhere near that canyon with its baleful and silent guardian lying in his path.

Dave waited. Minute after minute ticked past. *Nothing* . . . He returned to the hut and stood just within the doorway, watching until the moonlight was gone. The darkness moved in with its thick shadows. The night wind murmured. It seemed peaceful enough.

Dave yanked off his boots, unbuckled his gunbelt, placed his Colt beside his bed, and leaned his rifle in the corner of the hut near his head. In a few minutes, he was sound asleep.

During the night, unheard by Dave, Amiga brayed twice.

CHAPTER 3

DAVE WAS AWAKENED BY THE PREDAWN BREEZE. HE got up, reveling in the comparative coolness of the air. It wouldn't last long. Once it arose, the sun would stoke the fires of Hades anew in the canyons. Dave brewed a pot of Arbuckle's Best and quickly downed three cups while gnawing on a hunk of jerky and a hard biscuit. He carried his canteen, pick and shovel, and Sharps rifle with him to the hollow area at the top of the talus slope and just below the cliff that towered above it. He looked up through the grayish light at the decomposing cliff. If something started a fall, he'd likely be buried under tons of rock. It couldn't be helped. He hadn't come this far to turn back now.

Dave stripped off his flannel shirt and undershirt, exposing his lean, long muscles, flat belly, and broad shoulders. He looked up at the cliff once more. "Ho, ho," he murmured. "Stay tight, little rocks, at least until I get some cover over my *cabeza.*"

He began to dig. By the time the sun began to strike hotly at his sweating back, he had cleared the loose soil and rock to expose the cliff face and a definite plugged-up, man-made entrance of some sort. Now and again he would hear the thud of falling rock on the talus slope and the dry hissing rush of the displaced talus. The rock and loose soil he had shoveled out might have been from a fall, or a number of falls, perhaps natural, perhaps man-made. The latter, for purposes of concealment, was most likely. If so, it would be logical to assume that if the miners had so carefully concealed the entrance, there must still be something within the mine.

The sun was well up when he was forced to quit due to the heat and near exhaustion. He had dug a depth of six feet into the entrance to find a pair of pit props and a header bar with the bark still on them. They were in comparatively good shape despite the passage of so many years. Lack of moisture and being hidden from the sun in the dry fill had preserved them. Whoever had dug the mine had invested Herculean labor in the project. The only possible place where they could have found such prop timber was along the Colorado River bottom and the heights above the river. They must have laboriously cut it and hauled it through the canyons to the mine site.

He returned to the hut still naked to the waist and plastered with sweat-streaked dust. He shook with exertion and heat exhaustion. He ate his hard biscuit and jerky and rationed himself to a good swallow of his precious brandy supply. It was difficult not to return to the mine entrance, but he knew better than to do that. If he was felled by the sun and heat, he might lie unconscious until he died. There would be no one to help him. A man needed a partner. But where to find one who could be trusted and relied upon?

Dave moved Amiga into the hot shade of the box canyon and lengthened her picket line with his lariat so that she could reach the *tinaja*. The *tinaja* was situated in such a position that the full rays of the sun never fell upon it. He drove the picket pin into a rock crevice.

One of the prices of safety in that country was constant vigilance, and the thought of that infinitesimal spark of fire he had seen the night before had never really left his mind. Dave took his rifle, field glasses, and a canteen. He walked to the passageway into his canyon. That was how he thought of it now—as *his* canyon.

He stood in the hot shade of the pillars and scanned the outer canyon with his field glasses. Suddenly, he held the glasses steady. A faint thread of dust rose beyond a sharp-angled monolith of rock three quarters of a mile away. As he watched, the dust thickened. He lowered the glasses. A sudden movement on the slope on the far side of the canyon and closer to the monolith caught his attention. He trained the glasses on the slope. A hatless head swam into view. The thick dark hair was bound about the temples with a cloth band. The head was followed by a body—an Indian carrying a Spencer repeating carbine with polished brass tack ornamentation on the fore and butt stocks that shone in the sunlight. Dave shook his head. An Indian could move silently and unseen in a country where a white man would stand out like a lump of sorefinger bread and then the damned fool would go and hammer all the shiny brass tacks he could beg, borrow, or steal into the stock of his rifle or carbine.

Dave spat. "Paiute. Damned dirt eater . . ."

The buck looked across the canyon toward Dave's side. He raised the carbine in both hands while slanting the butt toward the ground. He moved the weapon up and down rapidly.

Dave nodded. "Enemy in sight," he translated. "Cute as all hell, ain't you? You'd fill your breechclout if you knew who was watching you now. *Chihuahua!* What a shot!"

Two more Paiutes raised their heads from behind a jack-straw pile of fallen rock and thick brush to the left on Dave's side of the canyon. "Shoot 'em if they don't wear a hat," Dave murmured. It was a good rule of thumb in hostile Indian country. He had made a mistake or two in his time, but he had learned to accept the Mexicans' pious saying. "God will sort the souls . . ."

Dave drew two Sharps cartridges out and placed them on a boulder in front of him. Just as he did so, he saw a lone and hatted horseman round the pillar and start riding slowly up the canyon. The rider turned in his saddle and looked behind himself, then turned back again and began to quirt his mount. The horse didn't move any faster. Exhausted maybe, Dave thought. Damned fool, that rider. "He'll be walking before too long in this heat, providing the Paiutes don't get him first, and that, by God, is likely up to me! *Son of a bitch!* I'll give away my position and the entrance to my canyon if I do. Damned if I do and damned if I don't!" Dave said in absolute disgust.

It was really none of his concern. A fierce possessiveness had taken him over since the night before. It had taken tenacious root in the rich and fertile ground of his determination. No one, but *no one,* was going to take *his* canyon and mine away from him.

The lone buck across from Dave fired. A puff of smoke revealed his position. The gun report slammed back and forth in the canyon. The horse went down. The rider cleared the saddle and landed on his feet while jerking a rifle from his saddle scabbard. The Spencer flatted off again. The horseman dropped behind a rock ledge. The pair of Paiutes were in a good position to see behind the ledge. They opened fire. The hidden man fired once. One of the bucks jerked up and down and then dropped from sight. Dave nodded. Good shooting, a clean uphill hit from about one hundred and fifty yards.

There was nothing to see now but the downed horse and the drifting gunsmoke. Dave put the glasses on the horse. The man was bellying toward it. Damned fool! The Paiutes had that horse zeroed in! Two shots cracked out. Dirt spurted up close to the crawling man. His hat fell from his head. He got up on his knees. Long hair, freed from the confines of the hat, fell about his shoulders and almost to his waist.

Dave sighted the glasses on the figure. "Jesus Christ! A *woman*!" he exclaimed. Even as he spoke, she fell back partly behind the ledge and lay still.

Dave raised his Sharps. He set the trigger. He rested the heavy weapon on the boulder in front of him. The buck across the canyon stood up. His head and shoulders were visible. The air was hazy with heat. He raised his Spencer and aimed it at the woman.

The throaty roar of the Sharps filled the canyon. Smoke plumed from the muzzle. The butt slammed back solidly into Dave's shoulder. The Paiute had moved sideways at the very moment of Dave's shooting. Dave lowered the breechblock. The spent cartridge casing came out with a puff of smoke. He caught the hot shell before it could hit the hard ground and possible damage itself. Another cartridge was slid into the chamber. The breechblock was snapped up, hammer fully cocked, trigger set and squeezed off almost as fast as one could say it. The Sharps roared again. The Paiute had been stupid enough to stand still, staring at Dave's position. The 500-grain slug slammed him backward. He was dead before he hit the ground, with half his head missing.

Dave reloaded at once and got quickly away from the revealing cloud of smoke surrounding his position. A moment later a bullet ricocheted off the pillar closest to where he had been.

Dave worked his way down the slope toward the puff of smoke that indicated where the Paiute had fired from. It was good shooting for a Paiute or almost any other Indian except for maybe the Delaware who had been his buffalo-hunting partner in the Texas Panhandle. Delawares could shoot as well as any white man.

The canyon was deathly still again. Nothing moved. Dave had vanished into the jumble of shallow gullies, fallen rock, and tangled cat-claw brush that clothed the slopes on his side of the canyon. The pair of Paiutes were somewhere to his left and below his position. One of them might have been killed by the woman. If wounded, he could still be dangerous.

Dave moved along, taking advantage of every scrap of cover. He mentally cursed the clinging cat-claw thorns that were tearing at his clothing and stinging his sweaty flesh, as well as the sharp-edged rocks that were cutting into his knees and forearms as he crawled, cradling the heavy rifle in his arms. It was hot. Christ, but it was *hot!*

Dave paused to peer out between two boulders. Down-slope, one hundred and fifty yards from him, a Paiute was on his knees peering around the side of a boulder at the position Dave had hastily vacated. Then he vanished. Time passed. The shadow on the side of another boulder higher up the slope and closer to Dave's old position grew fatter and darker. Dave put the glasses on it. He nodded. He took in a deep breath, let out half of it, then took up the trigger slack. The shadow moved a little. The Sharps spat flame and smoke, sending a thunderous echo along the canyon. When the smoke drifted off, the Paiute lay still, smashed into instant death.

Two down, possibly one to go.

Dave cached the Sharps. He bellied like a gecko lizard downslope to where he had last seen the wounded buck. The juices in his lean body seemed to be bubbling within him from the extreme heat. The woman, if she had been wounded, would be in bad shape lying in the sun. If she had no water, it would be hell itself for her, for wounding always brings on a deep, unquenchable thirst, as Dave well knew from the first day at Gettysburg when the Iron Brigade, virtually alone, had held back a large part of Ewell's Second Corps and had suffered heavy losses in the process. Dave had caught a minié ball between his left bicep and his side, breaking three of his upper ribs.

Ordinarily, Dave had the patience of an Apache in such a situation, but the condition of the woman forced him to make his move. Usually, panic, or a rash and sudden movement, was a sure ticket to hell. He had learned that the hard way while in hostile Apache or Yaqui country. "Paiutes," he said softly. *"Shit . . ."* He crawled on toward the woman.

She was sprawled face downward. Even as he looked, she stretched a hand out toward her Winchester rifle. A gun cracked not fifty yards away. She twitched and lay still again.

Dave peered between two rocks. He heard a metallic sound. The Paiute who had just fired was trying desperately to cram a cartridge into the chamber of a battered Smith carbine. Blood dripped from his left hand. Dave stood up. The Paiute stared at him. The Colt thudded twice. The Paiute staggered backward and fell heavily. He did not get up again.

Dave rolled the woman over onto her back. The upper part of her left sleeve was soaked with blood. There was a welt along the left side of her head. He found the pressure point beneath her left arm and held it as he checked the wound. It was in the fleshy part of the arm. The slug had plowed on through. He cut off her left sleeve and bound it about the arm. He sheathed his Colt, hoisted her to his shoulders, and slogged his way up to the canyon passageway. He was gasping for breath and staggering on rubbery legs when he got her through the passageway into the inner canyon. He whistled sharply and waited.

Amiga came trotting down to Dave, braying all the way. Her broken picket line dragged behind her. Dave dumped the woman over the burro's back and led Amiga back to the hut. He placed the woman on his bed, picked up his spade, and immediately led the burro back to the outer canyon.

The woman's sorrel mare had been creased alongside the head. It now stood with splayed-out legs and down-hanging head. Two large, dry canteens hung from the saddle. There were thick cantle and pommel packs on the saddle. Dave sheathed the woman's '73 Winchester in the saddle scabbard. He thrust her Colt under his belt. He retrieved his Sharps and hung it on the sorrel's saddle.

A soft thrashing noise came to Dave. He drew his Colt and walked cautiously toward the sound. The Paiute he had shot with his pistol lay face downward, trying to overcome the unfamiliar coldness of paralysis in his legs that now bound him helplessly to the ground. He turned to stare at Dave with pleading eyes. No sound came from his lips. His spine had been injured by one of Dave's bullets. There was no hope for him.

Dave passed the back of a dirty hand across his mouth. No Indian ever commits suicide because then his soul would be eternally damned and he would wander in limbo forever. The buck's knife was still in its sheath, but he would not use it on himself.

Dave looked away. It would only be a matter of time before the combination of the heat and the wound would kill him, but it would be a living hell until then. Dave looked back at the Paiute.

The warrior had stopped moving, but his pleading eyes held Dave's.

Dave cocked his Colt. 'God have mercy on me," he murmured. He punctuated the prayer with the crashing discharge of the .44/40.

Dave turned to get the horse and burro. He looked back at the dead Paiute. "Him, too, Lord," he added quietly.

He stripped all three Paiutes of their weapons, cartridges, and whatever else he could find of use. They might have ridden into that country, but he didn't know where they had left their horses if they had had them. He loaded the gear onto the sorrel and the burro, tying Amiga's load with the woman's lariat. He led them up to the pillars and into the passageway and left them there. Then he took his spade and returned to his first kill. It wasn't sentiment that made him decide to bury the corpses as best he could. The less evidence that he and the woman were in the area, the better.

He dumped the first buck into a deep cleft, rolled rocks on top of him, and then shoveled in earth. The second one was more difficult. The best he could do was to place him between two ledges and pile earth on top of him. Already the flies were buzzing about the brave's wound. When night came, the predators would be out in force. They'd dig up the body soon enough.

Dave was reluctant to return to the last Paiute. His way of death had marked him differently in Dave's mind. It was one thing to kill from a distance; it was another to shoot a helpless man to death within a few feet of oneself. He dragged the buck to a cleft, followed by a cloud of angrily buzzing flies. He dumped him in and covered him as well as he could. Exertion sweat streamed from Dave's body and his thirst grew prodigiously. He threw earth over any bloodstains he could find and then slogged his way up the long, hot slope to the pillars.

Before he entered the passageway, he looked up at the pitiless, brassy blue sky. A scrap of charred paper seemed to be riding the updraft from the canyon. It was a buzzard, patiently waiting its time. Its business was with the dead— not the living. It was a scout. Before long, its mates would begin to gather, floating high overhead on motionless out-stretched wings until they deemed it safe enough to land. They would fly many miles for such a feast as that which lay below them. Dave had never figured out *how* they knew, but they *always* knew.

CHAPTER 4

SHE WAS BREATHING EASY. NOW AND THEN SHE OPENED her eyes, only to close them again and drift off for a time. Her wounds were only superficial. The welt on the side of her head had hardly broken the skin and the arm had only been cut through the soft flesh. Dave studied her. The bandage around her head gave her the look of a sleeping nun, but Dave was willing to bet she had never seen the inside of a nunnery.

Her hair was thick and dark with faint reddish highlights. Her skin was fair, with a deep, creamy quality to it and touched with some redness by the sun. The nose was fine, perhaps a mite too large. Dave had always admired big-nosed women. His mother had had such a nose, but she had been more handsome than beautiful or even pretty. He liked his women that way. The woman's full lips were dry and somewhat sun-cracked. Her teeth were white and even. This was no frontier frump dried out long before her time.

Her clothing was of good quality. She wore a split skirt of corduroy, a fine linen shirt that was open at the throat, a silk bandanna, and a short leather riding jacket of vaquero style. The boots were of good quality, likely Mexican made, but more for dress than utility, especially in this country. They were scuffed and scraped, and the left sole had split away from the upper.

Dave had brought in her cantle and pommel packs and saddlebags. He poked through them. A canvas traveling bag in the pommel pack emitted the faint scent of lilac

38

when he opened it. It contained lacy underthings, fine hose, a Mexican-style skirt, and a white linen camisa embroidered in a silk, floral pattern. There were small Mexican huaraches and other articles that were hardly suitable for wear in Hell's Forty Acres.

"Have you found that for which you are looking?" she asked in English. Her throaty voice was well modulated.

"Jesus," Dave murmured guiltily. He stuffed the clothing back into the bag and turned to look at her. Her eyes were gray, calm, and big enough for any damned fool of a man to fall into and *never,* by God, be able to get out of them. There were too many contrasts in her features to make her beautiful, but with eyes like hers any man would have all he could do to handle them.

She kept her right hand inside her shirt. She tapped the head bandage and glanced down at the arm bandage, instantly lifting her eyes to watch him. *"Gracias,"* she said.

Dave shrugged. *"Por nada."* He stood up. "You're Mexican?"

She shook her head. "No, but I have lived there."

He filled his cup with water and held it to her lips. "Slow and easy," he advised. "Not too much for starters."

She sipped greedily but took her time, then lay back with a soft sigh. Her right hand was still concealed inside her shirt.

"How do you feel?" he asked.

"As well as can be expected. I'll have a fierce headache. I'm tougher than I appear, though. Thanks to you for saving my life. Where are the Paiutes?"

"They won't bother you again. They crossed three rivers today."

She narrowed her eyes. "What does that mean?" She studied this big man with the hawklike visage and the startling light blue eyes. She noticed at once that they hardened when she mentioned the Paiutes.

Dave shrugged. "Bad medicine, for them. No Paiute will cross three rivers in one day's travel if he can possibly avoid it." He grinned. "Not that there's much chance of doing that in this country. Running rivers, at any rate. Maybe dry ones count. There are plenty of those. At least in this damned country."

She smiled. "I understand."

"Were you alone?"

"Why do you ask?" she queried quickly, a little *too* quickly.

"I thought they might be out there somewhere and need help."

She shook her head. "I was alone."

He started a blaze in the fireplace. "A long way from nowhere," he suggested. He glanced back at her. "It's a helluva country for a *man* to be alone."

"Like you?"

He nodded. "Like me. I'm Dave Hunter."

"Lila Duryea," she responded.

He opened one of his cans of beans and dumped it into a pot. "Just what *were* you doing out there alone?" he asked over his shoulder.

"Isn't that *my* business, *Mister* Hunter?"

He stirred the beans, then looked at her with those ice-chip eyes of his. "Not anymore, Miss—or is it Mrs. Duryea?"

She ignored his query. "Why is it your business?"

"Because this is *my* canyon. What goes on around here is my business. *Comprende?*"

She shrugged. She didn't have any choice at the moment, and perhaps not for quite some time to come. The recent memory of her ride into that suburb of Hell and the Paiute attack reminded her of that crucial fact.

She studied his broad back. "Just how far does your personal jurisdiction extend?" she asked tartly.

He glanced at his Sharps. "Half a mile to a mile," he replied quietly. "The accurate range of 'Old Reliable' there."

Dave unfolded the tripod legs of his spider and placed

the frying pan over the thick bed of glowing embers. He put the last of his rancid bacon in the pan. Most of the fat had already melted from the heat into his tin can. He poured the fat into the frying pan. When the bacon was crisp, he removed it. He placed two of his dwindling stock of hard biscuits into the fat to soak.

Dave stood up. "We'll mess as soon as the beans are hot."

She looked at his faded Yankee Hardee hat with its faded and almost colorless blue hat cord. "You've been a soldier?" she asked.

Dave nodded. "Among other things."

"Such as?"

"College student. Buffalo hunter. Civilian scout for the army. Drove a freight team for a time and rode shotgun on stagecoaches."

"Haven't you left out something?"

He looked at her. "So?"

"Prospector?"

"I thought that was fairly obvious."

"It is. Silver?"

Dave turned the biscuits over. He removed the spider from the fire. He stirred the beans. He put his battered kettle on to boil. When it steamed, he used some of the last of his Arbuckle coffee beans. He placed the food on a flat rock. He eyed her. "Do you want to say grace?" he asked dryly. There was no expression on his face.

She studied him. "Do you?"

They grinned at each other.

Dave put the beans and bacon on two battered tin plates. "You'll have to let go of that stingy gun you've been holding inside your shirt," he suggested. He paused. "You can put it beside your plate, ready for a killing shot across the table at a man placidly eating his simple meal. But, consider this, Señora Duryea: I'm your only hope of staying alive and eventually getting out of this country."

She withdrew her hand and place a pearl-handled double-barreled Remington derringer on the rock beside her plate. "One never knows," she said quietly.

Some men called those deadly, little, extremely short-range pistols "whores' guns." They were hardly accurate beyond ten feet, but at close range they could blow a hole in a man's belly big enough to stick a fist into.

They ate silently. When they had finished, he took the hot bacon-fat-soaked biscuits from the spider and sprinkled a teaspoon of brown sugar on each of them.

Lila bit into the concoction. Her eyes widened. "French pastry!" she cried in delight. "You're full of surprises, Mister Hunter."

Dave grinned. "We called it skillygalee in the army. The New Englanders learned it from sailors and whalers and passed it on to us. One develops the niceties while soldiering and prospecting."

He got out his pipe and filled it with Lone Jack.

When she had removed her hand from inside her shirt, some of the buttons had come undone, revealing flashes of her deeply clefted, full breasts.

"Seen enough?" she asked.

Dave waggled a hand. "Sorry. I've been out here alone too long."

She made no effort to button up the shirt. "I've got the makings in one of the saddlebags," she offered.

"This tobacco *is* dry," he admitted. "Like everything else in this damned country."

He shaped two cigarettes from the powerful Mexican Lobo Negro tobacco she carried in a rawhide tobacco canteen with a silver top. He placed one between her lips and lit it with a splinter from the fire.

She poked a slim finger through a smoke ring, then eyed Dave. "You've found something, haven't you?" she asked quietly. She looked meaningfully at the float specimen resting on the crude rock mantel over the fireplace.

"A little float," he admitted.

"Where there is float, there should be silver," she said.

So she knew what float was.

Dave shrugged. "You can find float anywhere. Sometimes miles from its source. Gold and silver are where you find *them*."

"Why would you be holed up in this Dutch oven of a canyon unless you had good reason to do so? You're not a hermit, I hope?"

He blew a smoke ring and, imitating her, poked a finger through it. "You ask too many questions, Mrs. Duryea." He studied her. "It is Mrs. Duryea, isn't it?"

She nodded. "A long time ago. Now it is you who are asking too many questions." She settled back on the bed. "There's a legend about a fabulous silver mine in this area. Do you know of it?"

He shrugged. "I might," he admitted.

She studied him. "You do."

Dave nodded.

She smiled. "Now, if we have to stay here together, that is, until you're ready and willing to take me away from here, you might as well tell me the truth."

"All I have found is that float specimen."

"In here?"

He shook his head.

"Come on!" she challenged. "You know a helluva lot more than that! My woman's intuition tells me so! Besides, who built this hut in this godforsaken place? It's old, isn't it? There's obviously water here. So, you see, you'll have to admit it now!"

Dave flipped the cigarette butt into the fireplace. He leaned toward her a little and fixed her with those cold eyes of his. "I don't have to admit a goddamned thing to you or anyone else. What makes you think I have to let you in on anything at all?"

"It's either that or take me out of here."

"I'm not ready to leave here yet."

She smiled. "So, you see, I *win*!"

He shook his head. "I'll tolerate you, lady. That's the

limit—toleration. I don't know who you really are. I don't even know where you were going in this damned hellhole and how you happened to be here all by yourself in a place where the toughest and hardest of men can barely survive. Where *were* you heading, anyway?''

She looked him straight in the eye. "Stone's Ferry on the Colorado River."

"Then where?"

"California, hopefully."

Dave studied her. "Alone?"

She nodded.

"You're either not too bright or you're mad."

"I have my reasons."

It wasn't a country where people inquired too much about other people's business. Live and let live was the unwritten law, or suffer the consequences of a bullet or a knife thrust.

She smiled sweetly. "Anything else you'd like to know? My age? Weight? Height? Birthplace? Political affiliation, if any?"

He shook his head. "Just one thing . . ."

"Yes?"

"If you were heading for Stone's Ferry, you were a helluva long way from the trail and were heading almost directly away from it. How can you explain that?"

She showed no emotion. "I had a guide and escort. He lost the way or couldn't remember it. I paid him off and went on alone."

"And ended up in a lost canyon riding into a Paiute ambush."

She nodded. "That was a complete surprise."

"Not to them it wasn't. They must have spotted you long before you saw them. Most Indians are seen only when they want to be. The moment you headed into this country, wherever you started from, they knew of you."

"How is that?"

He shrugged. "Trail dust. Campfire smoke. Your tracks. Horse droppings. Things few, if any, white men would notice." Something crept into his mind. That illusive, mysterious spark of light he had seen at night to the west and south. Probably she or her guide had lit up. "When did you know you were lost?" he asked.

"Just this morning."

He had seen the light far off the river trail that led north to the ferry. She didn't know the country, but she had been heading away from the trail probably a day or so before she claimed she'd known she was lost.

"Will you let me stay?" she asked quietly.

"Until I can get you out of here."

"I want more than that."

He shook his head. "No!" he snapped. She was getting to him.

"I can help you. I'm strong. I can cook and do your laundry. I'll work for a small percentage of your take. If you find nothing, I get nothing."

"I play a lone game."

"You'll need supplies. Tools! Blasting powder, most likely. From the looks of you, you don't seem to have a grubstake. How do you plan to get it?"

He looked away. "I'll manage," he said.

She laughed. "By digging in your mine for enough silver to stake you? You could starve to death in here before you find it."

She's right, Dave thought. Damn her, anyway!

"Look here!" she cried. She stood up and heedlessly ripped open the front of her shirt. Several of the buttons pattered onto the floor. She exposed her full breasts. He could see their dark nipples. She hastily unbuckled a canvas belt and pulled it free. She flung it at him. "Open it!" she said.

It was a money belt, heavy in weight and damp with her sweat. He opened it and suppressed a soft whistle. It was packed with greenbacks of high denominations and gold coins. There was a small fortune in the belt. He looked at her. "So that's why you were running," he said slowly.

"Away from the frying pan, into the fire. Whose money is this?"

Her face hardened, losing its beauty. "Damn you! It's mine! I earned it! Take it! Cache it somewhere if you'd like. You can use as much as you need. But it will be the collateral of my part in your venture. Agreed?"

She was right—he had planned to grubstake himself with what he might find in the mine, *if* there was anything in there. If not, it would be back to work in someone else's mine or to work as a teamster. Meanwhile, what could he do with her? If he took her back, to civilization, what would prevent her from shooting off her mouth about his canyon of silver?

"Well?" she queried.

"You need rest," he replied. "We'll talk about it later." He left the hut.

She lay down. "You'll do it, *Mister* Hunter," she murmured. "You'll damn well *have* to do it. Keep me and my money, or kill me and have done with it. I have nothing to go back to, anyway."

CHAPTER 5

IT WAS GETTING DARK IN THE TUNNEL. SWEAT DRIPPED from Dave's face and torso. It soaked his drawers and trousers. His hands were raw. His backed ached intolerably. His breath burned in his lungs. At last he stepped back and studied the implacable wall of fill material that still blocked his way. He would have quit hours ago if it hadn't been for that damned irritating mystery of a woman. He knew he was punishing himself because of her. He walked to the entrance and felt the warm night wind dry his sweat. The breeze brought the odor of cooking food to him. His belly tightened. He hadn't eaten since he'd made the meal for the woman and himself the night before.

The eastern sky was faintly pewter and touched with the suggestion of light from the rising moon. It was a damned lonely place and deadly dangerous to boot. It was no place for a man and certainly not for a woman. But she was there, sure enough! *She* was no mirage. Wherever Lila Duryea was, people damned well were aware of her, as Dave knew quite well by now.

He picked up his Sharps and gunbelt with holstered Colt and sheathed knife. He walked down toward the *tinaja*. Earlier that day, he had gathered up the bones of Captain Don Pedro Melgosa and buried them in a cleft. He had said the Twenty-third Psalm and then placed the crude cross he had made at he head of the grave. It was quite a distance up the canyon from the mine entrance.

"You wanted a partner, Dave," his mind's voice seemed to say.

He was surprised to see that the *tinaja* water was much clearer and that the debris and growth had been cleaned out of the pool. He could even see the bottom. He tasted the water. There was still a touch of gaminess in it, but it was much better than it had been before.

Her clear voice came from the hut. She was singing the tragic ballad of the Confederates, "Lorena." He had heard it many a time at night emanating from the Rebel encampments while he was on picket duty.

He allowed himself the unaccustomed pleasure of washing his body at the outlet trough. Then he dressed and walked to the hut.

She was stirring a pot at the fireplace. The coffee pot bubbled in the embers. Her braided dark hair had been wound about her head over the bandage. She wore the wide Mexican skirt and the camisa he had found in her pack. The leather huaraches were on her small feet. As she moved, he could see her shapely bare calves. The blouse bared her shoulders. The fire and lamp light glinted from an exquisite necklace of chrysoberyl, an extremely hard crystal cut in such a way that parallel and needlelike inclusions of microscopic size reflected a streak of light. This quality had given it the common name of cat's-eyes. The crystal was relatively rare and extremely expensive.

She turned as though sensing his presence. "Well, *Mister* Hunter?" she said challengingly. She tilted her head to one side and held his steady gaze with her lovely eyes.

Dave slowly shook his head. "A mirage," he said slowly.

She whirled in a dancer's pirouette. The wide, flaring skirt rose and undulated, revealing her legs to midthigh. She winced as her bandaged arm touched the mantel. She came close to Dave. The fragrance of lilac came with her. She placed her smooth hands on each side of his face. "Was *that* a mirage, Mister Hunter?" she asked softly.

An almost overpowering urge to sweep her off her feet and carry her to the bed seized him, but there was always that canny streak in Dave that he had inherited from his Scottish ancestors. He had damned it many times in favor of sudden impulse and powerful emotion, but the check rein was *always* there. Lila Duryea was no mirage. She had begun to change his little isolated world and lonely life in the short time she had been there. Somewhere, behind the vast backdrop of the canyons and mountains, the Paiute and Mohave gods were laughing derisively at Dave—Dave Hunter, *the loner* . . .

She prattled brightly like a schoolgirl while they ate. She had changed abruptly from the cool, posed woman he had first known, and again from the tough frontier-town hellcat who had flung her money belt at him and challenged him for the right to be in on his strike. Then, again she changed, a swift metamorphosis from the slightly wanton creature who had been waiting for him in the hut when he had returned from the mine into the facsimile of a bright, little girl child telling an adult of all the clever things she had done with her hands: cleaning the hut and the *tinaja*, washing his filthy extra clothing, and making the meal they were eating. She told of seeing the distant buzzards wheeling high in the brassy sky over the outer canyon, as though they were watching and waiting, always waiting. Perhaps she had wondered about why they were there, perhaps not. Dave thought she must know. She had been around, so to speak.

She filled his coffee cup and pipe. She lighted the pipe in her mouth and placed it between his lips. "A man thinks better with his pipe, is that not so, David Hunter?" she asked with a slight smile.

He puffed on his pipe. "Where did you learn that?"

She shaped a cigarette. "From my father. Why do you ask?"

Dave shrugged. "He was a wise man. What was his name?"

"Charles Armitage," she replied.

"An American?"

She studied him. "English, but his mother was Welsh."

"And your mother?"

"Look at me," she invited.

"Mexican, perhaps?" he suggested.

She threw back her head and laughed. "Louisiana Cajun. I was born in New Orleans. You never give up, do you?"

He nodded. "It still puzzles me why a lovely woman, obviously intelligent and well educated, with fine clothing and a small fortune in her money belt, of mingled English, Welsh, and Cajun French origin, should be riding alone in this hellhole of a country, claiming she was heading to Stone's Ferry and yet many miles from the trail that leads there and in a much different direction."

"I said I was lost," she murmured.

He shook his head. "You must have known Stone's Ferry was north. You had the sun to guide you by day, the stars and moon by night. Yet you rode almost due east from the trail to the ferry."

A sudden veil seemed to drop over her eyes. "You're a strange man, Dave, but I don't find it displeasing." She reached out and placed her right hand on his. "Am I to stay?" she added quietly.

He shook his head.

"But I thought . . ." Her voice trailed off.

He leaned toward her. "It's not the money. You can't buy your way into this life-style of mine. This is no place for you. I'm not too sure it's the place for me. Those three Paiutes I killed will soon be missed. I buried them as best I could, but by now the coyotes will have dug them up and the buzzards will clean up what is left. The bleaching bones will be scattered far and wide. Some of their people may come looking for them. There's very little going on in this country they don't know about. In time they're sure to learn we're in here. I'm not sure they'll come into this canyon, because I suspect they believe it's haunted, but that's no assurance.''

"But we'll be safe in here for a time, won't we?'' she asked. "If the worst comes to the worst, we could leave. We have the money belt. I'll share it with you outside.''

Dave shook his head. "I *have* to stay.''

"Why? What forces you to stay?'' she asked curiously.

He held her eyes with his. "Myself. This is *my* canyon, *my* strike. No one will drive me from it! No one! Do you understand?''

She looked away from his piercing gaze and shivered a little inside.

Dave leaned toward her. "Listen! I'm almost thirty-five years old. I enlisted from college at the age of eighteen and fought throughout the war in just about every major battle with the Army of the Potomac. I returned to college after the war and lasted two years before the restlessness overpowered me. Since then I've drifted from place to place, always farther west, making only enough money to grubstake myself. Right now, all I really own are the clothes on my back, my prospecting gear, my guns, and my burro Amiga. There's nothing but failure, as I see it, beyond this canyon. So here I stay, come hell or high water, and take my chances against this country, the Paiutes, and whatever else fate throws at me.''

"And in the end, Dave?'' she asked quietly.

"A fortune, perhaps, or death,'' he said, albeit some-what dramatically.

She hesitated. "There's always me, Dave, whether or not you make a strike.''

He stood up. "Isn't that a somewhat hasty offer for the few hours we've know each other?'' he asked dryly. He turned and left the hut.

Later, as he checked the sorrel, he saw her come from the hut and walk to the *tinaja*. She scoured the utensils with sand, then washed them in the overflow.

He watched her. She had been on the trail before. She

was a horsewoman, seemingly an expert rifle shot, and trail-wise as far as he could tell. She was a puzzler, an enigma even. He sketched a mental map of the country in his mind. To the north was the gorge of the Colorado and Stone's Ferry, the end of "The Death Trail," so-called because it was on the far side of the desolate and deadly country that had to be crossed by those in quest of California gold back in the Fifties and Sixties. It was also beyond the head of navigation for the Colorado River stern-wheelers. There were a few isolated and remote mining camps along the river and desolate Fort Mohave as well. They were hardly places where a woman like her might be found. Miles to the south and on the west side of the Cerbat Mountains was Chloride, a silver mining center settled in 1864. It was a place as rough as a sun-dried cob. Still, it could conceivably be where she had come from.

She called down to him, "How are we fixed for food?"

He shrugged. "Some beans, a little four, hard bread, coffee, salt, and tobacco for my part. I figured I could last two weeks before you came. I thought of rolling over a deer if I could find one."

"I have a dozen cans of embalmed beef, some coffee essence, some canned vegetables, and five cans of peaches."

He nodded. "It will have to do before we leave for Chloride."

She was startled. "Chloride? Is there no other place to get supplies?"

"Some of the Mormon settlements in Utah, but we'd have to cross the river to get to them. No, it would have to be Chloride."

"But it will take you away from your work."

"Where I'll starve to death." He grinned. "Ain't hardly worth it, ma'am."

"I'd rather not leave with you, Dave."

He shook his head. "You have no choice. My mind is made up."

Later, as he lay trying to sleep in the rude blacksmith-and-tool hut, he stared at the dark ceiling above him. Finally he rose and padded on bare feet to stand just outside the window over Lila's bed. A faint wash of dying moonlight came through another window, just enough to limn the full shape of her lush body beneath the thin blanket. He turned on his heel and walked back to his hut. The old haunting loneliness came over him. It was much worse than it had been before, because now his fantasies had become a real flesh-and-blood woman, no longer a figment of his imagination engendered by moonlight, and she was just within a few paces to satisfy his intense and always repressed woman hunger.

CHAPTER 6

DAVE DROVE HIS PICKAX INTO THE TIGHTLY PACKED cliff face and worked the fill loose. It cascaded down over his boots. He stopped for a breather and wiped the sweat from his face. He heard the pattering of hoofs on the hard floor of the tunnel floor. Lila led the burro toward Dave in the dim and guttering light of the lantern. She halted Amiga and opened the tops of the crude *aparejos* Dave had fashioned from the tarpaulin he had used to cover the loaded packsaddle.

Dave mechanically filled the sacks. For three days it had been so, digging away at the fill, loading the sacks that Lila took outside to dump down the slope. She had worked as hard as he. She would leave at about noon to prepare a light lunch. It had to be light, for their food supplies were running low. Several times he had hunted for a deer with no success. No animals had come to the *tinaja* at night for water, evidently scared away by the presence of humans in the area. After lunch Lila and Dave would work until dusk, when she would leave to prepare the evening meal. When he came to the hut, she would be washed and dressed in her maddening ensemble of the white low-cut blouse, wide skirt, and tiny sandals.

"It's late," Lila said, as he filled the last sack. "I'll give you another hour in here."

They looked at each other in the dimness. They had hardly spoken during the hot and stifling days of toil in the tunnel. In the evening he would also be silent most of the time, drugged by the manual work he had been doing.

"Are you all right?" she asked.

He nodded.

"You still plan to keep on?"

"Until we have to leave for supplies."

"That will be soon enough."

"Yes."

She seemed to be expecting something. She was close to him and he could smell her fragrance. Despite her hard work, she always seemed fresh. She had learned to wash her hair without soap. Dave had taught her to dig up the roots of some of the sparse growths of yucca up the canyon. The roots were saponaceous and could be mashed for use as soap. Dave had learned it from the Apaches, a people with thick, lustrous hair of which they were inordinately proud.

He turned away from her and attacked the fill.

She waited a moment and then led the burro out of the tunnel.

He glanced after her, paused for a moment, and then drove the pickax into the face with redoubled vigor despite his weariness. He was a good forty feet inside the tunnel. There was no sign of drifting or crosscutting. God alone knew how deep the mining operations had been. The tunnel was not straight. It was crooked and uneven. He stepped back and eyed the fill. "Goddamned stuff might go on clear through to the other side of the mountain," he grumbled. "Damned fools put more time into filling it than they did digging it."

He raised the pickax for one more blow before he quit. The point went clear through and he fell forward because of the lack of resistance. Stones and dirt fell about him, and then the face crumbled inward with him on top of it shielding his head from the hard rain of dirt, stones, and rock fragments pattering down from above. For a moment the horrible fear of a collapse filled him and then the pattering stopped. He looked into a dark void. A cool draft of astringent-smelling air played about his face, drying the sweat.

Dave crawled back for the lantern. Then he came back to the face and thrust the lantern forward. There seemed to be no more fill. The tunnel was somewhat larger and made a turn to the right just ahead of him. He crawled over the mound of fill and poked around in front of himself with his pickax, feeling for a deep hole, possibly a vertical shaft. The floor was firm. The irregular trend of the tunnel was typical of the early Spanish and Mexican miners. While the Americans followed the British and other Europeans' method of driving in a tunnel then drifting and crosscutting to pick up the vein, the Spaniards and Mexicans usually followed the vein, tortuous though the tunnel might be.

By rights the air should have been dead, but it seemed comparatively fresh, perhaps because of an opening somewhere up ahead or possibly a shaft had been driven up to find air. Dave walked forward, probing with his pickax for a shaft or hole. The tunnel wound on, with crooked side tunnels opening into it. The whole mountain might be honeycombed in that manner.

He was deep inside when he reached a wider area, like a chamber, from which three tunnels led. He tried the tunnel to the right. Twenty feet within it, the tunnel widened. Dave held the lantern up. There, directly in front of him, was grayish rock thickly marbled with black splotches intermingled with others of reddish hue. He placed the lantern on the floor and drew out his sheath knife. He tested the rock wall with the point. It crumbled rather easily. He kneaded a fragment. It was malleable. He took out a silver dollar, his last, in fact, and held it against the rock, then hammered hard on it with the heavy stud of his knife handle. The coin remained stuck on the wall. He pried it loose and looked at the wall closely with the light of the lantern.

There before him was the faint but definite impression of the coin face.

Dave stepped back in awe. "Jesus God," he said softly.

He worked his way along the vein. He probed at it. It was soft. He struck it with his pickax and pried out a chunk as big as a large walnut. *It was pure, solid silver. . . .* If he could trace the vein, he would know if he had made a strike worthy of all the time he had spent in Hell looking for one.

He explored farther. The vein was about four feet long, but it wasn't very deep and, oddly enough, it seemed to vanish into the solid rock. He dug out the point where it seemed to enter the rock but found only solid rock. He went back and dug out the other end with the same result. He was puzzled. What had he run into? He had worked veins in other men's mines, but none of them had been as thick as this short piece, yet they had gone on and on for many feet while the miners drifted in and crosscut to pick it up again. But this vein seemed to be intact in itself. Solid silver, it was true, but hardly enough to warrant dreams of a vast fortune or even a small one.

Dave probed farther into the labyrinth of tunnels, twisting and turning, dipping low and rising again, but nowhere could he find a trace of silver such as he had discovered earlier. The air within the maze of tunnels was comparatively fresh and in certain areas he could feel a faint draft from an outer source. There were more tunnels to explore, but in some of them the roofs had fallen partially or even fully, blocking entry. The lantern was guttering low. There would be plenty of time to explore later. There must be more silver in quantity somewhere in the darkness beyond the wavering pool of dim lantern light.

Before the lantern went out, he grubbed out samples of ore here and there along the tunnels and especially around where he had found the short vein. Then he returned to the mine entrance. It seemed a much longer way back than it really was. He took his Sharps rifle from the hiding place near the mine entrance where he kept it.

The canyon was dark. He could see the faint light of the hut far below him. What part would she play in his life from now on? She would know intuitively that he had found some silver and had high hopes of finding more.

She was mending one of his shirts when he entered the hut. Beans and chunks of embalmed beef bubbled in a pot. She looked up at him with a smile, then her eyes narrowed as she studied him.

He'd have to tell her. "I've made a small strike, Lila," he said.

"Just a *small* one?"

"There will be more. There's every indication of it."

He dumped the samples out on the floor but kept the chunk in his pocket. "I'll have these assayed. They look good. Maybe thousands of dollars to the ton."

"Then why did the Spaniards leave it?" she asked.

"*¿Quién sabe?* Heat, loneliness, fear of Indians, a dwindling water supply. Any one of them, perhaps all of them. They might have taken out all they could and planned to return for more. Evidently, none of them came back." He wouldn't tell her about the remains of Captain Don Pedro Melgosa.

She served the food. "What happens now?"

"I'll have to go to Chloride and get these samples assayed and file a claim. I doubt if one was ever filed on it, but one never knows. If the samples assay out well, I'll come back and work the mine until I'm sure it's worthwhile."

"And after that?"

He shrugged. "I'll have to hire an engineer to come in and make a survey. Beyond that, I'll need miners and modern machinery."

"And?"

He grinned. "Trust in God that the vein holds out to make it all worthwhile."

"There's no chance we can work it alone?"

He shook his head. "You know that's impossible. We could scratch out some of it, but it would hardly be worthwhile. No, if it *is* a lode, it will have to be a major project."

She studied him. "Is that what you really want?"

His eyes widened in surprise. "Certainly!"

"I wonder," she said quietly. "Once you go to Chloride to show those samples and file a claim, you'll have every footloose claim jumper in the Arizona Territory swarming in here."

He fixed her with hardening, cold eyes. "No one takes my claim away from me," he stated flatly.

"There are ways, you know," she hinted.

"They'll have to kill me first!"

She nodded. "That, too."

"We'll leave as soon as we can," he said, to change the subject.

"We have only one horse."

"I can walk," he said stubbornly.

She filled his coffee cup. "Is it that you don't want me to stay here? What can I do? I can't steal your mine and take it away from here. Besides, you'll have a better chance alone. You said yourself the Paiutes might not come in here because of superstitious fear. I have guns. You know I can shoot. Dave, we'll just have to risk it. Besides, you'll need a grubstake. I can give it to you."

"No deals," he said harshly.

She shrugged. "As you say, Dave."

He walked outside and filled his pipe with the last of the Lone Jack. He walked partway down toward the big canyon. She was right. Once he showed up in Chloride with those samples and filed a claim, he'd be watched day and night until he left town and then he'd be tailed. There were men who'd follow him through the gates of Hell itself if they knew he had made a strike.

She had the shapeliest hips and well-rounded breasts he

had ever seen, and her long, slim dancer's legs were a delight.

He couldn't take her with him and he didn't want to leave her here alone, and yet there was no alternative. He *had* to go.

Her hair was thick and lustrous. Her eyes, well, a man could drown in them and maybe lose his soul, so deep and unfathomable were they.

She moved softly through the darkness behind him. He sensed her fragrance and warmth. "You'd better leave now while it is still dark. You can make many miles unseen before daylight." She placed the money belt across his broad shoulders.

"I won't need all of it," he said, without turning.

"Take that which you need. I'll make up some food for you and fill your canteens." She was gone into the shadows as he turned.

"What the hell am I to do?" he asked aloud.

There wasn't any answer.

The moon was just a faint suggestion in the eastern sky when he saddled the sorrel mare and slung his Sharps from her saddle. "You've got your Winchester and pistol, Lila," he said. "Cache food and water in the mine in case you have to hole up in there. Don't let any smoke show from your fire, at least during daylight. Amiga is better than any watchdog. I'll be back as soon as I can. If I'm followed, I'll have to throw them off my trail, which might take me in a roundabout way and use up more time. If you run out of food and I'm not back, don't stay here waiting. Amiga can maybe lead you to the river. Remember, the river is closer to the north than to the west. Do not, under any circumstances, travel east. It's about as waterless as the moon." He looked closely down at her. "If you're not sure of your directions, then travel due south and you'll likely run into the Chloride Road. There are mines in that area. It might be your best bet at that."

She shook her head firmly. "I'll try for the river," she said.

Dave hesitated. "Do not allow yourself to be taken alive by the Paiutes. Do you understand?" He felt intensely dramatic, but he wanted to impress it upon her.

"I understand," she replied. She came close to him, slid her arms about his neck, pulled his head down, and sought his lips with hers, then twisted away and ran swiftly to the hut.

Dave stood there for a few minutes. "Hellsfire," he said softly. He led the sorrel down the slope. Amiga brayed a farewell. It was the first time in three years she had not gone with him.

Dave reached the passageway. He looked back. He stood there for long tortured moments, wanting to leave, yet yearning to stay.

He turned and led the sorrel back to the branch canyon. Amiga brayed again. Dave went up the slope. The hut was dark. He tethered the sorrel and walked to the hut. Lila must have heard Amiga and the hoofs of the mare striking the hard ground, but there was no sound or sign of her.

Dave stood in the doorway. There was a faint red and secretive eye of fire peeping through the thick bed of ashes in the fireplace. When Dave's eyes grew accustomed to the dimness, he saw that she lay on the bed covered by the thin blanket. Her clothing was piled on the flat rock that they used as a table. She did not move or speak. She must know he was there. He could see the mass of her long hair about the pale oval of her face. Dave stripped himself to the buff.

"Lila?" he said softly as he approached her bed.

She stretched out her arms toward him. He knelt beside the bed and buried his face in her fragrant hair. She pulled him to her. He threw aside the blanket. Their lips met. His hard hands passed down her smooth, warm softness.

"I wanted you to go," she whispered huskily, "but I prayed you would come back."

"I'm here, Lila," he whispered.

The night wind whispered through the canyons.

Más allá . . . On beyond . . .

CHAPTER 7

DAVE LED THE WORN-OUT SORREL THE LAST TEN MILES into Chloride at about dusk. She had nearly given out earlier that day. All that was keeping her going now was heart. It had been four days of hell for man and beast. Dave's throat was brassy dry like a long, disused plumbing pipe. His eyes felt as though red-hot needles had been poked into them. The soles of his feet felt like he had been dancing a juba atop a hot stove.

The livery stable was the first building to the south of Chloride and about five hundred yards from the town proper. A bewhiskered old coot was leaning against the side of the wide-open double doors watching Dave approach.

Dave halted and passed a hand down the sweat-lathered neck of the mare. She shivered convulsively. A long thread of yellowish saliva dripped from her dry mouth.

Old Whiskers straightened. "She's about done, ain't she, friend?" he said. He shook his head.

"Can I leave her here?" Dave asked. "She might recover."

"You're Dave Hunter! Didn't recognize yuh with all that fur on your face. Sure, you can leave her here. I'll see what I can do, but don't hope for too much." He studied Dave. "The name is Wassell. Amos Wassell. I own this shebang—that is, I'm partners in it with Ash Mawson. You know him? He's the marshal around here."

Dave shook his head. He took his bag of samples and his Sharps. "I'll be back later," he said.

"You need a room for the night?"

"I'll need one."

Amos jerked his thumb over his shoulder. "Got a bunk up in the loft. Two bits a night."

Dave nodded. "Fair enough."

Amos eyed the sample bag. "Specimens?" he asked.

Dave shook his head. The old bastard would know soon enough. He limped toward the town.

Amos watched him, then looked at the brand on the mare's dusty flank although he already knew what it was. He led the mare into the stable. "Come on, little lady," he said. "I never expected to see you again. Now, I wonder how in hell *he* got hold of you? Have to tell ol' Ash about this."

Dave was heading for the Miner's Repose with but one thought on his tired mind—*cold beer!* He pushed the bat-wings aside and walked in. He leaned his rifle against the wall at the near end of the long bar and dropped the bag of samples at his feet. There was only one other customer in the place, a well-dressed man standing at the far end of the bar talking to the bartender.

The bald bartender ambled to Dave's end of the bar. "Your pleasure, mister?" he asked. He was new to Dave.

Dave shoved back his hat. Collected sweat ran down his face, cutting furrows through the dust and into his whiskers. "Any cold beer?" he asked hoarsely and *hopefully*.

Baldy grinned. "Mister, this is Chloride!"

Dave shrugged. "I know that! One can only hope. Warm will have to do."

Baldy laughed. "I meant we have got cold beer. New ownership here. They brought in the only ice machine south of the Colorado and north of Wickenburg."

"Thank God from who all blessings flow," murmured Dave.

The bartender pulled out several beers and put them on

the bar, then placed a plump bottle, dewed with sweat, in front of Dave. He was about to pull away the wire holding the cap on but was a fraction too late. Dave's dirty paw shot out, ripped off the wire, pulled off the cap, and raised the bottle, upending it to let the blessed liquid pour into his dry mouth and down the corroded brass of his arid throat to put out the twenty-four-hour embers still glowing there. Some of the beer ran out of the sides of his mouth, through his whiskers, down his neck, and then soaked into his sweat-black shirt. Dave's throat worked convulsively until the bottle was drained. He slammed the dead soldier down on the bar. His eyelids fluttered as he drew in a deep breath.

"Remarkable time," the man at the end of the bar observed. "Possibly a world's record—territorial, anyway, for sure."

Baldy nodded. "I like a man with a thirst."

Dave eyed him. "You've got a dandy on your hands right now," he said hoarsely." He opened his right hand to clamp it onto another bottle. Half of that went down before Dave came up for air. "Jesus God," he said with a gasped. "What a goddamned country!"

"Best seen through the bottom of a whiskey glass, or, in your case, a beer bottle," the other customer agreed.

"Amen to that," Dave murmured.

"You're from down south?"

Dave shook his head and drained his beer bottle.

"From across the Colorado?"

Dave waggled his head. He slammed the empty on the bar and reached for the next full one.

"Then you must be from up north," the bartender said triumphantly.

Dave looked affectionately at the third bottle. "Wait a spell, little friend," he said dreamily. "Your turn will come soon—almost instantly, in fact."

The man at the end of the bar came down close to Dave. "Is that right?" he asked. "You came from up north?"

Dave spat into the spittoon at his feet. He could have sworn there was dirty cotton in the saliva. "Hell, no, mister! I'm a big bullfrog just come paddlin' down the *río* from Stone's Ferry. I smelled the cold beer here in Chloride and hippity-hopped all the way up from Pyramid Canyon to put out the fire in me."

The man smiled and waved a hand. "Sorry, mister. I've no call to ask a man where he's from. Not in Arizona Territory, anyway. The name is Denton, Matt Denton." He extended his right hand.

Dave gripped the hand. It was soft. The grip was fairly strong, but it wasn't the hand of a working stiff, a miner, teamster, or whatever. Maybe mining engineer, promoter, even a political lawman, or most likely a Knight of the Green Cloth—a gambler. The eyes were a cold gray, hard and calculating. The mustache was light brown blending in with gray. His sideburns were more gray than brown.

"Can I buy you one?" Denton asked.

Dave shrugged. "Why not?" He emptied the third bottle.

"I'm planning a trip north in a few days. How are the roads?" Denton asked.

"I came from the river. Remember?" Dave replied.

Denton smiled, but there was a chill in his eyes. "I remember. The bullfrog from Stone's Ferry. I thought maybe you had been up around the Big Bend country. Hell's Forty Acres. Isn't that what it's called?"

Dave nodded. "There ain't any roads in that area and very few trails. Most of the trails lead to nowhere."

"So, you *have* been in there?"

Dave drank his beer. "*Around* there, not *in* there, Denton."

The batwings swung open. A powerfully built man limped in. He stared at Dave. There seemed to be a vacancy behind his gray-green eyes, as though one was peering into the dusty windows of an empty room. "You the one brought in that foundered sorrel to Wassell's livery?'' he asked.

Dave nodded. "I am."

"Amos told me to tell you she ain't going to make it. You musta rode hell outa her in this heat," the big man said, almost accusingly.

"I walked her the last ten miles trying to save her," Dave said. He raised his left foot behind himself. The dust coating the big hole in the sole of the boot was dark reddish. "It didn't help *me* any," he added. He tried not to affront the big man by wrinkling his nose at the sour and acrid smell of his body and clothing. It was much worse than Dave's own, and Dave at least had a damned good reason for his aroma.

"Small hoss for a man your build, stranger."

Dave eyed the man up and down. The cold beer was having a remarkable effect on him. "I said I *walked* her, stranger," he said quietly.

Mat Denton held up a plump hand. "Take it easy, men. I didn't get your name," he said to Dave.

"I didn't give it."

"You're Dave Hunter, ain't you?" the bar critter asked. "I heard about you. You was up north somewhere prospecting."

"Hunter, this is Cos Leach," Denton said, indicating the big man with a nod of his head. "He works for me. He means well. He just happens to love horses." He looked directly at Cos. "Don't you, Cos?"

Cos was startled. "Who? *Me?* Yeah! Yeah!"

"He didn't mean to rile you, Hunter," Denton continued. "Did you, Cos?"

Cos shook his head violently. "Hell, no!"

Dave emptied his bottle. He eyed Denton. "Can't he talk for himself?" He picked up his sample bag and rifle. "Thanks for the beer. I'll buy you one next time."

Denton shook his head. "I own the place. Bought it a couple of weeks ago."

Dave walked to the door.

"Mister Denton ain't through talkin' to you!" Cos called out.

Dave turned. Cold blue eyes held vacant gray ones. "I'm through talking to him," he said. He pushed through the batwings.

"Well, I'll be goddamned, boss," Baldy said.

"You want me to follow him and bust him up a bit?" Cos said, looking at his big, balled-up fists.

Denton shook his head. "Watch yourself with that one, Cos," he warned. "He's hardcase or I miss my guess."

"But the mare!" Cos blurted. "It's *hers,* I tell yuh!"

Denton looked quickly about himself as if someone other than Baldy might be listening. "Shut up about that! I don't want the whole goddamned town to know about it!" He looked at Baldy. "Rye," he ordered. "Tell me all you know about Hunter."

Baldy placed the bottle and two glasses on the bar in front of Denton and Cos. "He's been in and around this area for a couple of years. Before that he was down south somewhere for quite a spell. He's a prospector. When he's broke and wants a grubstake, he works in the mines. As soon as he gets it, he takes off again. Been up north somewhere. Some say he's been in Nevada and others say in California. I don't think so."

"Why?" asked Denton.

Baldly leaned close. "There's a rumor he's been looking for that lost silver mine the Spaniards were supposed to have found about one hundred fifty years ago."

Cos laughed. "Bullshit! There's ain't no such mine! That's a fairy tale if I ever heard one. Why, I . . ."

"Shut up, Cos," Denton ordered. "Go on, Baldy."

Baldy looked toward the batwings as though someone might be listening. "Back about nine or ten years ago a prospector by the name of Shorty Hebdon came to a mine in the Cerbats. He was almost dead from exposure and thirst. He was delirious and raved about finding a lost

Spanish mine up in the Hell's Forty Acres country. When they asked him where it was, all he could say was that it was in a canyon with two rock pillars hiding the entrance so that it could only be seen at a certain time of day from a certain place. Then he died.''

"See!" Cos bellowed. "I said it was bullshit!"

Baldy shook his head. "They found ore samples in a bag he was carrying, weak as he was. They assayed from six hundred to two thousand to the ton. . . .''

It was very quiet in the saloon except for the ticking of the big Regulator clock on the wall and the buzzing of flies.

"You say this is true?" Denton asked softly.

Baldy nodded. "As I'm standing here before God."

"How do you know?"

"I was *there*, boss. Joe Bob Manion, the assayer here in Chloride, did the assay on the samples."

"Did you hear any more about it?"

Baldy grinned. "Hell, no!"

"You mean nobody went up north to look for it?" Cos asked.

"Did I say that?" Baldy demanded. "Quite a few left town, all saying they were going to Wickenburg, or Tucson, maybe even Sonora, anyplace but Hell's Forty Acres."

"You see any of 'em come back?" Cos asked.

Baldy nodded. "Yeah, *some* of them."

"What happened to the others?" asked Denton.

"Who knows? Might have gone on to Nevada or California. Maybe the heat and thirst got them, or Paiutes. You know how them desert rats are—they live alone and they die alone, and God alone knows how they died or where they lie.''

"Go find Vic," Denton ordered Cos.

Baldy wiped the bar. "You think he ambushed your wife and took your money and that sorrel mare she was riding when she left here?"

Denton looked quickly about himself again. "Keep your

mouth shut. Do I have to do all the thinking around here? Yes, I'm sure of it.''

"Why didn't you call him on it, then?''

Denton poured himself another rye. "Until I know what happened to her, I'll have to play it cosy with Hunter. Besides, you see that bag he had? There's wasn't horse shit in that. He's found something up north, or I miss my guess. You've got to use your head, Baldy. If we call him on maybe getting rid of Lila and taking her horse and my money belt, we might be missing out on something ten times or maybe a thousand times better—a helluva silver strike, maybe even a mother lode of it.''

Baldy nodded. "By God,'' he said. "You sure use your head, boss.''

Denton downed his drink and wiped his mustache on both sides. He nodded. "Now, what we'll do is wait until those samples are assayed. We can't lose either way. If the samples are no good, we've still got our hands on him. If they are good, then we've likely got the money belt, maybe Lila, and a silver strike to boot.''

CHAPTER 8

AMOS WASSELL WAS STANDING NOT FAR FROM THE ASsay office when Dave limped toward it, rifle in one hand, sample bag in the other. "Your sorrel died, Hunter," he said. "I done the best with her I could. Wasn't no use. I'll have her hauled away for four bits."

Dave nodded.

"You still want to bunk in the stable?"

Dave looked down at his tattered, dusty clothing and almost soleless boots. "You know of any hotel that would take me in like this? Smell and all?"

Amos shook his head. "Not even in Chloride."

"I'll need a pair of horses and another of burros," Dave said.

"Can do. Buy 'em from me and you can stay in the stable for nothing, Hunter. You can even have your breakfast on me."

Dave grinned. "You're all heart, Amos."

Amos waved a veined hand. "I know. It'll be my downfall one of these days. How long will you be staying?"

"I didn't say."

Amos nodded. "Yup, you didn't." He studied Dave. "Saw you down at Tucson once some years ago. You was headin' south to Sonora."

"You know a helluva lot about me, don't you?" Dave asked coolly.

That didn't bother Amos. "You was lookin' for Scalphunter's Ledge that time."

Dave turned away from the garrulous old bastard.

Amos shifted his chew. "Friend of mine knew you in New Mexico Territory once. He said you was lookin' for the Lost Adams Diggins that time."

Dave turned slowly. "Who *was* this friend?"

Amos scratched inside his tobacco-stained beard. "Charley Wasco. They useta call him Loco Charley because he was always talkin' about the Lost Adams Diggins. He said he had been with Adams in 'Sixty-four when they found a canyon where they picked up nuggets as big as acorns and the sand along the stream sparkled with flakes of gold."

Dave nodded. "He was loco, all right." He turned to walk away.

"Yep," said Amos quietly. "Loco enough to follow *you*."

Dave halted in midstride. He turned back again. He narrowed his eyes. "So?" he said quietly.

Amos shrugged. "Took a one-way walk into the country around the west fork of the Gila. He never come back. . . ."

They eyed each other closely in the dark street.

"You saying I had anything to do with that?" Dave asked slowly, *very* slowly and carefully.

Amos figured he had gone too far at last. "I got a big mouth. I talk too much." He looked up and down the deserted street. He looked into those cold, unblinking eyes. He felt a warm dribbling down his left leg; he was a right-handed man.

"If you've got more to say, you say it, loud and clear, mister, or I'll kick your skinny ass all the way back to your stinking stable."

"Wait a bit! I told you Marshal Ash Mawson was my friend and partner in the livery stable. You'd better watch your step around him."

Dave nodded. "I sure will. Where *is* he by the way?"

He thoughtfully watched Amos speed away down the street. He was damned fast for an old goat.

There was a light on in the assay office. Dave entered and placed his bag on the scratched and battered counter. "I'd like you to run an assay on these," he said to the man behind the counter.

The assayer nodded. "But not until tomorrow. I'm closing soon." He untied the bag and dumped the samples onto the counter. His eyes widened a little. He looked up. "You from around here? Seems as though I've seen you before."

"Not exactly, mister." Dave's tone didn't invite further questioning.

Joe Bob Manion was used to close-mouthed prospectors. The only time these single-blanket, one jackass desert rats got gabby was when they were full of tanglefoot and even then they could lie like Ananias, maybe better . . . "This isn't local stuff," he suggested thoughtfully. He looked up at Dave.

"You're doing the guessing."

Joe Bob looked away from those cold, penetrating eyes. "So I am," he admitted. "I'll have your report tomorrow afternoon, Mister . . . ."

"Dave Hunter," Dave replied. He turned and left the office. He crossed the street and looked back in through the dusty window. The assayer was studying the samples through a large magnifying glass.

Dave ate in a lunchroom, bought a quartet of long nines, lit one, and strolled toward the livery stable. Chloride was on the slopes descending west from the Cerbat Mountains toward the distant Colorado. Here and there, above and behind the town, were twinkling lights from mining installations, sharp and bright in the clear atmosphere. To the north was the hot and empty darkness, and somewhere out there was Lila Duryea. Dave neared the livery stable and glanced casually back over his shoulder. The street was lighted by the elongated rectangles of yellow lamplight streaming from windows. He thought he saw a quick movement about fifty yards behind him. Someone was following him.

The stable was unlighted. He glanced back as he walked through the wide entrance. Again he sensed rather than actually saw a furtive movement. He shook his head. Maybe he *had* been out in the deserts and mountains far too long.

Dave found the lantern hanging on a post nail. He reached for it and suddenly noticed a slightly different odor than the usual stable miasma of fouled straw, sweat-soaked leather, manure, and the ammonia smell of horse piss. It was a faintly acrid and sour smell, which he had noticed earlier that evening. He whirled, dropping his right hand to the butt of his Colt as he did so. Something slapped him hard alongside his head just over the left ear. For a split second, the sour odor was more noticeable and then Dave hit the floor and went into a deep sleep.

Water splashed against Dave's face. He sat up, spluttering.

Amos Wassell stood in the lamplight grinning down at Dave. "Jesus, but you can sure get likkered up, Dave. Yuh musta hit the hard stuff after I left yuh. Ain't no good for a man like yourself who's been out in the canyons too long by himself. The ol' tanglefoot can sneak up on yuh and lay you down quick and hard."

Dave explored the left side of his head above the ear. He held out his fingers. There was no stain of blood. the blow had struck the down-turned brim of his thick Hardee hat. He might have had a cracked skull otherwise. "I got buffaloed," Dave said sourly. He looked up into the grinning face of the old man. "If you . . ."

Amos quickly shook his head. He gave Dave a hand to his feet. "I was asleep in my office," he said.

The old man was fragile, with hardly the strength to swing a heavy six-shooter or club hard enough to knock out a man as tough as Dave.

Amos went into his office and came out with a bottle.

He handed it to Dave. "Robber?" Amos asked. He grinned again. "I wonder what he figgered *you* might have he'd want." He studied Dave intently.

Dave could feel the heft and weight of the money belt about his waist. "How fast did you get out here?" he asked.

"As soon as I heard you hit the floor."

"You see anyone?"

Amos shook his head. "I heard him pounding the street getting away."

'You have no idea who it was?"

Amos hesitated. "Wal, it was a sorta step and a half run. You know what I mean? Like a man who maybe had a gimp leg."

Dave drank from the bottle. The memory of the sour and acrid odor came back to him, as well as where he had noticed it before—in the Miner's Repose when Cos Leach had come in surrounded by that miasma like a cloud of hovering flies.

"Where are my saddle and saddlebags?"

Amos pointed to where they lay atop a hay bale. Dave examined them. The straps had been cut with a razorsharp knife. The contents had been dumped out.

"Looks like whoever buffaloed you might have been surprised in the act," Amos observed. He eyed Dave speculatively. "Anything in there of value?"

Dave shook his head.

"Somethin' maybe like a map or *derrotero*?" persisted Amos.

Dave eyed him. "You never give up, do you?"

Derrotero was Spanish for a treasure chart or set of directions to find a mine or treasure.

Amos yawned. "Best get back to sleep." The sour smell of rotgut whiskey came from his gaping mouth.

"You *sure* you didn't see who buffaloed me? Whoever he was, he was in here while I was gone. But someone *else* was tailing me along the street. I think there were two of the bastards in on the deal.''

Amos shrugged. "Wal, we'll never know, will we?"

Dave reached out a big hand and carefully grabbed a fistful of shirt right under Amos's Adam's apple. He hated to bully the old drunk, but he had to know who it had been. Dave drew Amos so close that his beak nose and Amos's rum blossom of a smeller were inches apart. He peered into Amos's red eyes with his cold orbs. "You certain sure?" he asked quietly.

Amos nodded stiffly.

Dave's grip twisted and tightened the shirt about the old man's skinny throat. Amos could hardly breathe. The grip grew tighter and Amos felt himself being lifted until only his toes touched the ground.

"I'll talk," he said huskily. "Gawddammit, let me down! I oughta get Ash Mawson after yuh!"

Dave grinned evilly. "Ain't that too bad? Ol' Ash is missing again just when you need him the most. Talk, damn you!"

"The man in the stable was Cos Leach. A stupid numb-skull who could break your back over his knee."

Dave nodded. "I thought so. Works for Matt Denton, doesn't he?"

Amos paled. "I wasn't goin' to say that."

"You didn't have to. Who was the other one?"

Amos hesitated. "Le' me go fer a minnit," he said. He scurried to the door and peered up and down the street, then scurried back. He came close to Dave. "A man named Vic.''

"What about him?"

Amos rolled his eyes upward. "Texan. Confedrit vet-eran. Never took the oath of allegiance after the war. You know, one of them unreconstricted rebels."

"Unreconstructed. What else about him? He work for Denton, too?"

Amos nodded. "He's downright mean, Dave. Gunfighter and killer. They say John Wesley Hardin ain't got nothin' on him. They say he don't notch his Colt butt because it would ruin the shape of it.''

Dave smiled a little; it was a cold smile. "Sounds like a right nice fella.''

"He's fast as greased lightnin' and eleven claps of thunder with a six-gun and a helluva shot with a Winchester. They say there's wanted posters and warrants by the dozen all over the Southwest for him. They say there ain't any lawman would dare to face him down.''

"What about your *compañero* you're always threatening me with? Ash Mawson, isn't he?''

Amos reached for the bottle. "They ain't never had to try each other." He drank deeply, wiped the mouth of the bottle, and handed it to Dave.

Dave drank, then said, "In case of a showdown, who'd you bet on, Amos? Sounds like Vic might have the edge from what you say.''

Amos thought for a few seconds. "I've known Ash for years. We were in the Army of the Tennessee for four years together. Thirty-first Illinois. Forts Henry and Donelson, Shiloh, the Vicksburg campaign, the Atlanta campaign, and the March to the Sea. The man is a fightin' fool. After the war, we drifted west, ended up prospectin' in Arizony Territory. Ash, he took later to being a lawman, and a damned good one—one of the best . . . Ain't no better *compañero*. Dave, I ain't never seen any man back *him* down. Still, Vic is a hardcase, as tough a nut as I've ever seen. Ash, he kills because he's forced into it. Vic, I'll swear to God he kills for sport. Christ's sakes, don't never take your eyes off'n him or turn your back on him.''

"What about Cos?''

"Does whatever Denton tells him to, like a trained dog. Never questions orders. Him and Vic make a good team.''

"Under orders from Denton?''

"That's about the size of it."

They sat down on bales, passing the bottle back and forth.

"You want some good advice?" Amos asked after a time.

"I can always use it."

"I know you for sure by now. Things have come back to me."

"Go on," Dave said dryly.

"Hunter by name and hunter by nature. That's you. They say you got a fix-something or the other for lost mines and buried treasure."

"Fixation, old-timer."

"Yup. Now, you been up around these parts for a couple of years. Up north around Hell's Forty Acres, I'd say. Then, all of a sudden, you're in the garden spot of America—Chloride . . ."

Dave drank. "Panther piss," he said.

Amos eyed him like a wise old owl, a boiled one at that. "The rye or what I'm tellin' yuh?"

Dave shrugged. "Both."

Amos picked thoughtfully at his nose. "Then, all of a sudden, you show up here in Chloride with a dying sorrel mare, a hoss no *man* would ever ride. The saddle is Mex made—Durango from the style of it. A *woman's* saddle! You got a mysterious bag with yuh, samples of ore. You take it to Joe Bob Manion for assay. You're mebbe plannin' to file a claim tomorrow?"

Dave shrugged.

Amos grinned triumphantly. "There, by damn! Then yuh *have* found somethin'!"

"Such as?"

Amos looked back over both shoulders, then leaned closer to Dave. "The lost Melgosa mine. Some call it the silver canyon."

"You don't say!" exclaimed Dave. He took another

drink. The tanglefoot was dulling the throbbing headache
the buffaloing had given him.

"What else could it be? By God, Dave, me and Ash
looked all over this gawddamned hellhole of a country for
it. There ain't hardly a square acre up there we ain't prospected!"

"And found nothing. Don't you get the idea? If experts
like you and ol' Ash looked for it and never found it, has
it ever occurred to you that it just *might* be a legend?"

Amos ruminated about that. He scratched in his beard.
He hiccupped. "By damn," he said thoughtfully, "I never
thought of that." He eyed Dave. "But, if there ain't such
a mine, how come you're lookin' for it?"

"Who says I was looking for it?"

"You got a reputation down south. Mebbe it ain't followed you up here yet, but you can't fool me. Come in
here dead beat, with a dying hoss and you with a thirst like
the desert during a two-year drought. You had a bag of ore
samples and a tight-shut mouth. Mebbe you didn't find
anything and mebbe you did. Now, it seems to me if yuh
did make a strike out there somewheres, it don't mean a
gawddamned thing if yuh can't work it. Right?"

"You talk like your head is loose."

Amos ignored him. He was off on a freshet of gab, almost as though he was alone in the stable, talking to himself for his own benefit. "You look and act like a loner. I
heard about you down south like I told yuh. I'm no fool.
Well, yuh can search alone and live alone and, by damn,
yuh can drink alone, but if yuh have made a strike up north
somewhere, it don't mean a damned thing if yuh can't
work it, like I said already. That takes more luck and sense
than findin' a strike. You got to have one partner at least
to watch your back in case of claim jumpers or Paiutes
creeping up on yuh to put a bullet through the back of you
skull. You got to have a partner who'll sit and smoke with
yuh at night and talk about good things like all the likker

you're goin' to swill and all the fillies you aim to sleep with once you're rich. I *know*!''

''Why, you dirty old man,'' Dave said with mock surprise. ''Helluva lot you know about sleeping with the fillies, even *a* filly.''

''By damn! I useta!'' Amos snapped proudly.

Dave grinned. ''Regular old stud, ain't you?''

Amos leaned forward. ''Listen to me, Davie boy. I like you. You get you a partner and split fifty-fifty with him— hunger and thirst, heat and Paiutes, and when your bonanza comes in, you split that fifty-fifty, too!''

Dave studied him. ''Now, just who do you have in mind for my partner? You?''

Amos slowly and reluctantly shook his head. ''Not me. I'm too old to go prospectin' anymore, 'specially in that hell of a country up there. Ain't many, if anyone, outside of you would do that, *unless* he knows somethin' no one else does. You got an acid burnin' inside of you, my thickheaded friend. One of these days you'll go over the edge. You won't know when, but the loneliness, heat, and hardships will get to you like a Paiute sneakin' up behind you and you won't never know when your time comes. That's when yuh might have a split second, or maybe you won't, to realize I was right when I said you should have a partner.''

Dave yawned. ''Maybe I have one.''

There was a long moment or two of silence.

Amos finally spoke. ''Yeah . . . Mebbe . . . But I don't think so. I know your stamp. Born loner. An outrider. You'll end up someday in some lost canyon or out in the middle of the desert. A heap of whitened bones scattered by the coyotes and buzzards. Your grinning skull will be lying just this side of Hell where your blasted soul left it. But *you* won't know what you're grinning about!'' Amos stood up and stamped angrily toward the rear of the stable. He turned just as he reached the rear door and looked back. ''By damn,'' he said slowly, ''yuh ain't got a *woman* hid-

den somewhere's up in that damned hellhole, have yuh?''
He leered slyly.

Dave reached for the bottle to hide the expression on his
face. The old bastard knew or suspected something. Amos
was no fool. Booze and all, he could still put two and two
together. Dave should have gotten rid of the sorrel and
cached her saddle before he came into town. He softly
cursed himself for not doing so, then slowly realized he
could not have done it anyway. He had felt sure the mare
was bound to die, but he hadn't had the heart to turn her
loose to die or to kill her himself.

"Well?" Amos demanded.

Dave studied him. "You think I'm that big a fool? Why
did you ask? You must have had a reason for it.''

Amos turned on a heel and stamped out into the darkness.

Dave carried his Sharps and the saddlebags up into the
loft. There was a sort of fenced-off space in the front
corner. He piled straw in it and threw an old tarp over
the top of it. He drew up the ladder as a safety measure.
He pulled off his boots and lay down, laced his fingers
at the nape of his neck, and idly watched the dust motes
floating in the faint rays of moonlight coming through
the holes in the roof. He raised his head and looked across
the loft to an opening through which he could see the
distant mountains to the north. He had a partner, all right,
and the sight of her would likely make old Amos's
knobby Adam's apple bob up and down like a tin monkey
on a string.

There was a lot in what the old bastard had said. Maybe
the heat and thirst coupled with the alcohol he had absorbed
since being in Chloride had worked on Dave more than he
realized. Maybe he had lost some of that razor-sharp sixth
sense that had kept him alive through the four years of war
and the years since in the Southwest. A good partner might
make all the difference in whether Dave lived or died, or
was ever to enjoy the wealth the silver mine might yield.

There was one major problem, and probably an insolvable one at that—having a woman like Lila Duryea in that lonely, isolated canyon camp with two virile men would lead to more than just arguments and bitterness. It could damned well lead to outright murder.

CHAPTER 9

IT WAS ALMOST NOON WHEN DAVE FINISHED BUYING
new clothing and boots and ordering his supplies and mining tools, including half a dozen big cans of Kepauno Giant
blasting powder.

George Ward, the storekeeper, totted up the bill. Dave
paid him with greenbacks from the money belt. He had
removed them from the belt in the security of the stable
loft. He didn't feel like exhibiting the gold pieces as long
as he didn't have the need to use them.

Ward handed Dave his change. "You want me to have
these delivered, Mister Hunter?" he asked.

"I can pick them up myself," Dave replied.

Ward nodded. "Any time. We open at six A.M. and
close at eight P.M. I'll keep your order in the storeroom
until you're ready for it."

Dave hesitated. "I don't know exactly when I'll leave.
Might decide to leave when you're closed."

"At night or in darkness, then?" Ward said quietly.
There was no one else in the store. "Mister Hunter, you're
a man being watched, but I suspect you know that by
now."

Dave studied him. "Why?"

Ward shrugged. His eyes held Dave's. "Look," he said
in a low voice, "it's none of my business. Word around
town is that you've likely made a strike up north somewhere. You know what that means as well as I do. You're

certain to be followed when you leave. It won't be easy to slip out of town unobserved."

"Go on," Dave suggested.

"God forbid you should be followed. But it's almost certain. There are men in this town who'll ambush and kill for far less than a silver strike. I'd like you to allow me to take your order and store it behind my house, which is just east of here, half a mile up the slope, on the edge of that big arroyo. I have a shack out in the rear with a padlock on the door. I'd like to store your order in there and lock the door. I'll let you have an extra key so that you may leave whenever you like."

"And I can trust you?" Dave asked.

Ward smiled a little. "You'll have to, won't you? Who else do you have in this town to trust?"

Dave grinned. "You have me there." He nodded. "It's a deal." He peeled a twenty off the wad of greenbacks and held it out to the storekeeper. "This is for your trouble."

Ward shook his head. "Just promise me, if you do make a fabulous strike, that you'll do all your future business with me."

Dave held out his hand. They shook hands. "I promise," he agreed.

Then Dave walked to the assay office. A GONE TO LUNCH, sign hung on the locked door. Dave turned back toward the town center, avoided going into the Miner's Repose, and instead chose the Arizona Star right across the wide street from Denton's saloon. The place was empty except for the bartender who had one glass eye. He served Dave silently and then returned to reading his copy of *The Chlorider.*

Dave idled over his second beer. His head still ached some from the buffaloing and he had a bit of a hangover from the potent rye he had absorbed with Amos. The world outside was bright with sunlight, but Dave's world was a little on the drab and gloomy side.

Someone coughed behind him. He turned to look into a

lean, mahogany-hued visage that was dominated by a beak of a nose. A pair of gimlet-sharp green eyes adorned a face that looked as though it had been left out in the desert sun too long like a dried-out boot. A thick salt-and-pepper, tobacco-stained mustache hung down raggedly from under the nose, covering the upper lip.

"Howdy," Beaknose greeted affably.

Here it comes again, thought Dave.

"Hot, ain't it?"

Dave writhed a little inside. "Yeah," he agreed.

"I've seen it hotter hereabouts."

Dave shook his head in despair. "Look, friend, I'll buy. But, for Christ's sake, don't mention two things to me: how hot it is and where do I come from."

Beaknose nodded. "Fair enough. Beer, Glasseye!" he roared.

Glasseye jumped as though stung by a scorpion. He rushed to get a bottle for Beaknose. The beer came sliding along the bar to smack into a big, callused palm. Then it was raised upward in a fluid motion, the cap ripped off, and the bottle top thrust into the mustached mouth. Half of the contents were gone when the bottle was lowered. Beaknose wiped his thick mustache both ways, heedless of the beer spray that touched Dave's face, a small pleasure on such a hot day.

Beaknose peered at Dave like a predatory chaparral cock eyeing a plump eight-lined, whiptailed lizard. "Mother's milk," he said. He hiccupped. "Name of Ash Mawson. You're Dave Hunter."

"Right on both counts, Mawson. Six feet tall, or thereabouts. One hundred and eighty-five pounds of pure grit and muscle. I've got a minié ball scar along my left ribs, or is the right ribs? I forget sometimes. Born in Michigan. Left after the war. I used to vote Republican until I wandered too far from a voting place. Raised a Protestant, but decided I wasn't protesting against anything, least of all the Catholics, so I wandered far from the church. I'm single, never married, no children that I know of, but it's possible. I—"

"Ain't you the born comedian, though," Ash interrupted. He spat into the spittoon with ringing force. "Amos Wassell told me all about you. He likes you, sonny. Ol' Amos knows men. We used to ride together until he got too old and fragile-like and the tanglefoot got a crotch hold on him and he never shook it loose, so his brains got pickled somewhat."

Dave nodded. "Somewhat," he agreed dryly.

"A good man was Amos. None better. We was in the war together."

"Thirty-first Illinois . . . Forts Henry and Donelson clear through to the March to the Sea with Sherman. Get to the point, Mawson."

Ash eyed Dave. "Amos was tellin' me you needed a partner."

"You already said his brains were pickled and addled. It's all in his head like when a gelding sees a mare in heat." Dave threw change on the bar and walked toward the batwings.

"You'll make a fine-lookin' corpse up there in Hell's Forty Acres!" Ash called out.

Dave stopped in midstride. He turned slowly and fixed Ash with his cold blue eyes.

Ash Mawson wasn't afraid of man born of woman, anything with fur, fins, feathers, claws, and fangs, or the Devil himself, the odds being fair enough. Flinty blue eyes held hard green ones. For a moment, no more, they stood there facing each other, two hardcase fighting men, and then Ash turned away first. The son of a bitch Hunter wasn't yet ready for a partner and maybe never would be.

Dave turned to the batwings.

"Watch your back, Hunter!" Ash called out.

Glasseye looked up from his paper. "Lay off, Ash. Matt Denton and his boys have got some kind of interest in him from what I hear."

"I'm worried," Ash said dryly.

Dave lit a long nine in the shade of the saloon porch. He'd have one hell of a time shaking the dust of Chloride off his feet. Every able-bodied man in town was likely keeping a covert eye on the loner who had drifted in from the north with a bag of ore samples. Well, Dave Hunter could move faster and last longer than most men; and if he was caught up with, there was always a 500-grain chunk of hot lead propelled by ninety grains of gunpowder to remind a follower or followers to mind their own affairs and keep out of his.

Cos Leach lumbered across the street toward Dave. "Matt Denton wants to see you, Hunter, in the Miner's Repose."

"If he wants to see me, you can tell him where I am."

Cos spit casually. "I'd go if I was you."

"And if I don't?"

Cos smiled mechanically. There was no mirth in his flat, vacant-looking eyes. "I'd hate to have to *make* you go."

"I'll bet you would."

"You comin'?"

Dave shrugged. He went more out of curiosity than of fear.

He heard Cos's curious step-and-a-half walk behind him, so close behind him that Dave wrinkled his nose at the sour-and-acrid body smell of the big man.

Matt Denton was seated at a rear table. The place was empty except for Baldy the bartender. "Nice to see you, Hunter," Denton said with a smile. "Cos, get a bottle of good rye and some glasses. Sit down, Hunter."

Dave sat down. Cos delivered three glasses and a bottle of rye. He pulled out a chair for himself. Denton shook his head. He pointed at the glass Cos had placed where he planned to sit down and then at the bar. Cos obediently picked up the glass and limped to the bar, trailing his aura behind him. Baldy was industriously polishing the big, brass, harp-type Rochester hanging lamp he had lowered from the center of the ceiling. He was put well out of earshot, probably by Denton's orders. Cos took up a position just out of Dave's sight.

Denton filled the glasses. "I've got some mining interests in the Big Bend country up north. I hear you know that country."

Dave shrugged. "Some. Not as well as others. It's not an easy country to know."

Denton nodded. "I've never been up there. I recently bought some claims. I'm a promoter, interested in that area. It's said to have remarkable prospects. I need a guide and someone who knows prospecting. A man such as yourself."

"I wouldn't go up there at this time of the year unless you're used to it. That country kills more than it allows life. Few can survive up there except the Paiutes and Mohaves, and they don't stay around there much during the summers. They also don't like strangers."

Denton sipped his rye. "Still," he said thoughtfully, "I have business up there and it can't wait for cooler weather or less hostile Paiutes and Mohaves." He smiled a little. "That is, if they're ever less hostile."

"You've a point there, Denton. I can't work for you in any case. I've got business of my own to take care of."

Denton studied him. "Ore samples. Assay reports. Supplies for a couple of months. Maybe registering a claim or two unless you're too smart to reveal where you've made a possible strike. I think you are. If you return there, as I'm sure you will, it might be for a long stay in an area plagued with heat, waterless to a great extent, and haunted by hostile Indians and maybe a Spanish ghost or two—that is, if you believe in such phantoms."

It was very quiet except for the soft sound of the polishing cloth against the harp lamp and the steady, measured ticking of the big Regulator clock.

Dave cleared his throat. "I mind my own business," he said slowly. His meaning was clear.

Denton nodded. "I can make it worth your while. Say, a percentage of the strike, if any. In any case, I'll pay you well, win or lose."

"I have my own business to attend to," repeated Dave.

Denton waved a hand. A diamond ring on his left forefinger flashed infinitesimal shards of reflected light. "You refuse to work with me?" he asked quietly. He was a man who wasn't used to being refused.

Dave nodded. He drained his glass and stood up.

Denton glanced quickly at Cos. The big man sidled closer along the bar. The bartender put down his polishing cloth and placed his hands below the bar where the hideout shotgun was usually kept.

Denton drained his glass. "Then we have other business."

"Such as?" Dave asked.

"Where did you get that sorrel mare you brought here yesterday?" Denton glanced toward the front door. The batwings' hinges creaked as they swung back and forth after someone's entry.

Dave turned. A tall, broad-shouldered, slim-hipped man stood there. He moved a little, accompanied by the soft chiming of roweled spurs. Dave found himself looking into a pair of the coldest, deadliest-looking gray eyes he had ever seen outside of those of an aroused diamondback rattler. From the flat top of his narrow-brimmed muley hat to the tips of his low-cut Mexican boots, and then back up to the low-slung, tied-down, cut-out, Mexican-carved leather holster carrying a Colt with staghorn buttplates, the newcomer gave but one impression: gunfighter and killer. This one would never give an honest warning like the swiftly vibrating rattles of a diamondback but would strike with the deadly speed and silence of a sidewinder.

"Have a drink on me at the bar, Vic," Denton invited him.

Vic nodded. He walked to the bar, reached for the rye bottle in front of Cos, then moved upwind quite a few feet from the big man. He tapped the bar with the bottle and held up one finger to Baldy. Baldy kept his right hand under the bar and slid a shot glass down the bar with his left hand.

An uneasy feeling crept through Dave. His gut became cold. In short, he was *afraid,* particularly of Vic. Amos's words about Vic came back to him in a rush: "I'll swear to God he kills for sport. Christ's sakes, don't never take your eyes off'n him or turn your back on him."

Vic poured his rye. He eyed Dave. "Seen enough?" he asked.

Dave looked down at Denton. "Thanks for the drink," he said. He could almost feel Vic's eyes boring a hole into the back of his skull.

"Sit down, Hunter," Denton said quietly.

Dave sat down. A man has to realize when the deck is stacked against him. Vic's arrival had been the clincher.

Denton leaned forward and refilled Dave's glass. "Now, about that sorrel?"

"I bought it from a Paiute up near Black Canyon," Dave lied. He knew they'd never buy that whopper, but it was worth a try.

"Hear, hear," Cos said.

"Shut up, Cos!" snapped Denton.

"You can go look for the Paiute and ask him," Dave suggested. He couldn't resist that.

"I'll try again," Denton said patiently. "Where did you get that sorrel?"

Vic moved a little. His spurs chimed softly. Could be some silver in them, thought Dave.

"*Mister* Hunter?" Denton asked.

Dave glanced out the corner of his right eye. Baldy, Cos, and Vic were all there, looking directly at him.

"Mister Denton is talking to you, Hunter," Vic said in his flat voice.

Dave half smiled. "I said, I got it from a Paiute."

"Not good enough," Denton said.

"There *was* a Paiute with her, boss," Baldy said tentatively.

Denton shot a hard glance at the bartender. "You mean the mare, don't you?" he demanded.

"Yeah, yeah, I meant *she* was the mare," Baldy said quickly and somewhat nervously.

Dave had cached the money belt in the livery stable. It had been Lila's mare. What was it she had said? "I had a guide and escort. He lost the way or couldn't remember it. I paid him off and went on alone." Dave had asked her who the guide had been, and she'd replied the he was a half-breed Indian of some kind who had said his name was Ahvote.

"There was a woman riding that mare, Hunter, or was until *you* found her. What happened to the woman?" continued Denton.

And the money belt, Dave thought. Damn him for a sentimental fool for trying to save the mare. He should have shot her.

"You didn't answer me, Hunter," Denton said.

Dave looked him in the eye. "The mare was a stray," he said.

"You didn't see the woman?"

Dave shook his head.

Denton looked up at Vic.

"Hunter," Vic said quietly in his soft Texan accent. "Mister Denton asked you a question. When are you going to reply like a gentleman and tell the truth?"

Dave looked back at Vic's cold, masklike face. He was just behind Dave. "What's that got to do with you?" he asked, rather foolishly.

Vic's backhander struck across Dave's mouth. The speedy reaction surprised even him.

Dave rose while gripping the edge of the table. He upended it against Denton. Denton's chair went over backward. His head struck the floor, momentarily stunning him. Dave crouched, whirled, thrust down his left hand to clamp it over Vic's Colt, then drove in a foot-long right jab just above his big belt buckle. The wind went out of the Texan. He doubled over involuntarily to meet an upcoming knee that hit him alongside the jaw. Dave clasped his hands together and brought them down full force against the nape of the gunfighter's neck, driving him flat onto the floor. A bootheel caught him alongside the head and put him into instant sleep.

Cos charged, fists outthrust. Dave leaped to one side, stuck out his left hand, and reached down to grip Cos's right wrist and pull him forward, aided by the impetus of the big man's charge, across his leg. Dave let go of the wrist as Cos sprawled across the prone Vic.

Baldy was raising a sawed-off, double-barreled, Greener ten-gauge shotgun loaded with split-wadded Blue Whistlers. Dave snatched up the rye bottle off the bar, gripped it by the neck, and threw it in a direct line toward Baldy's jaw. Baldy had just swept back the hammers of the Greener with his left hand.

"Don't kill him!" Denton shouted.

Baldy looked at him just as the solid bottom of the rye bottle hit him on the point of the jaw. He rolled backward, raising the shotgun, and in a reflex action, fingered back one of the triggers. The Greener blasted smoke and fire. The charge blew a big hole in the embossed tin ceiling as Baldy went down behind the bar for the long count.

Dave was about to vault the bar to get the Greener when Cos, roaring like an enraged grizzly and moving with surprising speed for one of his bulk, reached out, grabbed Dave by the slack of his shirt, dragged him back full force, and hurled him halfway across the room. The shirt ripped. Dave broke free. He snatched up a chair. Cos came on under full steam, head and shoulders lowered. Dave swung the chair high and brought it down full force on Cos's bulletlike head and thick, muscle-padded shoulders. He stared in disbelief as Cos shook his head and came on. Dave turned and ran for the rear entrance. Denton reached out, grabbed Dave's left leg, and hung on to be dragged a little way until Dave fell sideways against the wall. Dave kicked himself free just in time to face Vic.

Blood leaked from the gunfighter's mouth. His eyes were wide and unblinking as he closed in. He could have dropped Dave with one shot in the back, but he no doubt wanted the feeling of hard fists smashing into flesh and bone, to hurt, maim, and possibly kill. His left sank into Dave's lean gut while his right bounced off Dave's left shoulder and hit his jaw. Dave's head turned right to meet Vic's left rising in an uppercut. It caught Dave under the chin, snapping his jaw up. He felt some of his teeth powder together as he went down. He still had enough sense to roll over and over to escape Vic's boots and their cruel, roweled spurs.

Dave rolled up onto his knees. He clawed for his Colt. He raised it partway, but Cos kicked it, spinning, from his hand. It slid across the floor behind the upended table. Dave came to his feet like a jack-in-the-box. He rushed Cos in a mad frenzy, avoided the bearlike arms, and butted him in the thick pad of solid flesh beneath his rib cage. Cos went backward and fell over the broken chair Dave had previously hit him with.

Vic came in, dancing right and left, stabbing out rights and lefts, feinting and waving, bobbing and weaving like a real Fancy Dan. Dave liked that, despite the odds of three to one against him. He knew he was eventually going to lose the uneven battle against the four men. Dave was an infighter; take two to get in one. He took two on his face to get in one, a sledgehammer blow to the gut. It hurt Vic. He shook his head and then returned to his prize-ring performance. Dave changed his tactics and feinted with a left and then with a right, and lopped a left over Vic's close-in guard to bounce a hard one off Vic's head. It was a pile-driver blow like the previous one to the gut, powered by muscles developed by many months wielding a single jack in the mines. Vic closed in, forgetting his science in his anger and frustration. *That* was a mistake. Dave maneuvered so that the upturned table was behind Vic. A slamming one-two caught Vic in the belly while he tapped Dave with a left to the face. Vic bent over and was immediately straightened with a vicious uppercut that seemed to come clean off the floor. His head snapped back, and he hit the table behind him and crashed to the ground.

Cos had his turn. A chair sailed over Dave's bent-down head and hit the bar front. Baldy rose from behind the bar and raised the Greener, looking for a clear shot at Dave.

By this time, Denton had regained his feet. He forgot his usual caution and made the mistake of thinking he could take the man waiting for him with a lopsided grin on his bloody face. A smashing left hit Denton and set him up. A whistling right cross did the rest, knocking him ass-over-teakettle on top of Vic.

Dave plunged for his Colt. He hardly felt the blows he had taken. There was no fear in him now. It had been burned out by hate and replaced by an insensate killing rage.

Denton got up and ripped out a double-barreled derringer from inside his left sleeve cuff. He thrust it toward Dave as he cocked both hammers. Baldy raised the Greener for a killing shot from behind the bar. Cos picked up a bottle, smashed it against the bar front, and charged, thrusting the jagged bottle toward Dave. Vic got up slowly with his Colt cocked and ready in his right hand.

"That's it, gentlemen! *Time!*" The commanding voice came from just within the batwings. Ash Mawson cat-footed forward. A heavy, balanced knife lay flat in his right hand point-forward for a powerful overhand cast. A cocked Colt was in his left hand. "First man that moves gets this Missouri toothpick in his back or guts! The choice is yours!"

Baldy moved the Greener. The knife instantly flicked through the air and pinned the bartender through the flesh of his left bicep to the back bar. He dropped the Greener onto the bar. The hair trigger slipped. The Greener blasted, shattering the brightly polished brass Rochester lamp and driving it off the end of the bar in a shower of kerosene from the reservoir.

Ash grinned. "Who's next? I shoot damned near as good as I throw a knife!"

Denton carefully let down the derringer hammers. Vic placed his cocked Colt on a chair. His face was set and fixed and taut white. Blood leaking from his nose and mouth showed in direct contrast against his skin. Cos stared stupidly at Ash, then at Denton. Denton slowly shook his head.

"You're a brave man with the drop on someone," Vic said in a low voice.

Ash grinned. "Only way to be, sonny."

"You want to step outside man to man?" Vic asked.

Ash shook his head. "I'm brave, but I ain't stupid. Some other time, maybe."

Dave wiped the blood from his mouth. His knuckles were scraped and bloody. "Howdy, Ash," he murmured weakly.

"For Christ's sake," blubbered Baldy. "Someone get this knife outa my arm."

Ash walked behind the bar, never taking his eyes off the quartet of men on the other side of the mahogany. He jerked the knife free. Baldy promptly fainted. Ash wiped the blood from the blade on Baldy's apron. He sheathed the knife. He placed the cocked Colt on the bar and pointed it toward Vic. He reached under the bar and brought up two Blue Whistlers. He broke the Greener and ejected the brass cartridge cases. He reloaded it, snapped it shut, cocked both hammers, and placed it on the bar, again pointing it toward the four men silently watching him.

Ash grinned. "Now I feel somewhat better, gentlemen." He looked at Dave. "I figgered I owed you a drink. Came over to buy. Don't like this sewer but heard you was in here with your friends. I didn't mean to spoil your fun, Hunter."

Dave shrugged. "I was going to let them get away before I got real serious. No fun in licking all four of them at the same time."

"You son of a bitch," Vic grated.

Dave looked slowly at him. "Well," he said quietly. "Neither one of us has a gun. We've got a first-class referee with Greener's Rules of Order in his hands. You ready to try again, you son of a bitch?"

Ash shook his head. "The performance is over."

Dave slowly picked up his Colt. He carefully put it in his holster. "I'll take that drink, Ash," he said. "Across the street, with my back to the wall. Besides, Cos stinks up this place too much."

Ash nodded. "Of course. I wouldn't have it any other way around here. Our local society ain't exactly cultural."

"I damned near gotcha, you bastard!" roared Cos."

Dave walked past him, looking sideways. "You shit, Leach," he said coldly. "By God, mister, you come at me again and I'll fill your fat belly with half a dozen slugs."

Denton straightened his clothing. He put away his hideout gun in the wrist spring clip under his left cuff. "Shut up, Cos. Let him go, Vic. Our time will come."

Ash cat-footed out from behind the bar with the Greener in one hand and his Colt in the other. "Come on, partner," he said to Dave. "These boys are downright mean. They play a little too rough for *one* man."

They pushed through the batwings. Ash handed the Greener to Dave. "Be my guest," he suggested.

Dave took the heavy shotgun. In one fluid motion, he let one barrel go at the right front window of the Miner's Repose and the other barrel at the left front window. The twin reports thundered along the street. The glass crashed into the interior. Dave broke the Greener, ejected the hot brass cartridges, snapped the barrels up to lock them, and hurled the still-smoking weapon back in through the batwings.

Ash and Dave walked across the street to the Arizona

Star. The marshal looked sideways at Dave. "You're a man after my own heart, partner," he said.

Glasseye asked no questions as he placed two bottles of beer on the bar. Such conduct was not polite in Chloride society. He vanished into the storeroom at the back in case the play went into a second act.

Ash and Dave sat down at a rear table, backs to the wall, with a clear view of both front and rear doors.

Dave wiped the blood from his face. He sipped the cold beer gratefully. "Ash, old friend," he asked thoughtfully, "just how long were you standing outside watching what was going on over there?"

Ash shrugged. "You were doing all right. I figgered if they got too rough, I'd have to step in."

Dave felt a loose tooth. "You damned near didn't make it."

Ash nodded. "Yeah, I was a mite off in my timing."

"I ought to kick your skinny ass up around those big hairy ears of yours."

"Maybe yuh can see now why Amos recommended me for a partner."

"That I can," agreed Dave. He emptied his beer bottle. He stood up and hitched up his belt. "But that doesn't mean I'm going to take you on."

"Why, you bastard! After what I done for you!" exclaimed Ash.

Cold blue eyes studied Ash. "That's your job, isn't it, town marshal?" Dave asked. He turned on his heel and walked to the door. The batwings swung back and forth behind him.

Glasseye had been listening through the keyhole. He came out of the storeroom.

"What the hell!" cried Ash. "I'll be dipped in fresh manure!"

Glasseye walked behind the bar. "You ain't too bright at times, Ash. That Hunter, he's a loner if I ever seen one. Whatever he's got up north he aims to keep for hisself."

Ash drank his beer. "Maybe, Glasseye. We'll see. . . ."

Glasseye brought Ash another beer. "Won't matter much. He's got to be more than just lucky to get out of Chloride alive."

Ash shook his head. "Oh, he'll make it out of here, all right. But when he reaches where he's goin' and shows the way to whatever he's got up there, that'll be the end of him."

"Amen," echoed Glasseye.

CHAPTER 10

THE ASSAYER LOOKED UP AS DAVE ENTERED HIS OFFICE. "Jesus," he murmured as he saw the bruised face.

Dave nodded. "I spent some time in rough company."

"It's all over town. By God, Hunter, you've got more luck than brains. Those four bastards would do well haunting a graveyard."

"They won't kill me yet. They did get carried away a little, but they didn't want to silence me permanently."

"Thank God, Ash Mawson walked in on it."

"Praise be," Dave said dryly. "You've got the assay done?"

Joe Bob Manion nodded. He handed Dave a yellow sheet of paper. "One sample ran three thousand to the ton; another six hundred; the third was a poor relative—only sixty. You can't really estimate the value of a strike by such a small number of samples, but you've got some mighty good prospects there or I miss my guess."

Dave folded the paper and put it in his shirt pocket. He paid the fee and turned toward the door.

"You're going to file, aren't you?" the assayer asked.

"Pretty soon," Dave replied. He couldn't file now. Not with those sidewinders at the Miner's Repose interested in his business, and now, by word of mouth, everyone else in Chloride as well. He'd have to keep doubly alert and file a Sharps rifle claim until such time as he could, God willing, make it legal.

"I saw you with Ash Mawson, Hunter. It's none of my

business, but that damned green-eyed Gila monster can smell a good strike fifty miles off and upwind at that. Never made a big one, or even a relatively good one, himself. Anyway, he's always broke. He and old Amos Wassel were supposed to be a pair of the best, or worst, to be more correct, claim jumpers in Arizona Territory, although it was never proven and I doubt it myself. You take my advice. If you have a claim worth working, you get the hell out of Chloride as fast as you can and stand not on the order of your going, like it says in the Bible.''

Dave nodded. "I suppose the assay report is all over town by now?''

Joe Bob Manion nodded. "Can't hardly keep one like that under wraps.''

"How much have you charged for anyone to look at it?''

The assayer couldn't look into Dave's eyes. "Well," he growled. "There isn't that much money in the assay business.''

Dave walked out into the glaring sunlight. There was no reason to stay any longer in Chloride. His supplies were ready to be picked up. All he needed were the horses and burros, plenty of water, and a two-hour start after the moon rose. The question of Lila Duryea was eating in his mind like a canker. What was her relationship to Matt Denton? Denton knew whose sorrel the mare had been. He wanted to go up into that country. He could kill two birds with one stone that way, by having Dave guide him: find the woman and locate the silver strike as well. It was the woman who had brought all this onto Dave's shoulders. Damn her! That was why she had not wanted to come with him. She should have warned him about going to Chloride riding her sorrel mare, which had put immediate suspicion on Dave. Now, not only was his strike in jeopardy but his life was as well. He had no illusions about his fate once Denton located the woman and the silver strike. Damn them all to Hell! It was Dave Hunter's lode and he meant to keep it that way.

Dave bought three bottles of rye and went to the livery stable. Amos lay asleep on a straw bale under a cloud of flies hovering about his gaping mouth. Dave wondered why they hadn't been stricken by the alcohol fumes. Well, perhaps they were getting a secondhand jag-on.

Dave roused Amos. He opened one of the rye bottles and handed it to him. "Now listen, you gabby old parrot. I'm pulling out of here tonight. I want that blocky bayo coyote dun and the little claybank, plus a good pair of burros. I'll give you a twenty-dollar bonus if you'll take the claybank out on the west road after dark. There's a big wash three miles out from town. Go out on the west road, then cut across country to the wash. You know where it is?"

Amos hiccupped. "I dug the damned thing myself one Saturday afternoon." He grinned.

"Don't let anyone see you. *Comprende?*"

"*Yo comprendo.* You think I'm that stupid?"

"You make me answer that and you'll spoil a beautiful growing friendship."

"You saw Ash?"

Dave nodded. "You know damned well I did. I told you I didn't need a partner."

"That's not what Ash told me. He said you didn't know how to take care of yourself. He told me about the Miner's Repose tea party. You ain't too bright, Hunter. You got more luck than brains. Why didn't they kill you?"

"Ash gave me a little hand," Dave admitted dryly.

Amos shook his head. "There was more to it than that." He scratched inside his noisome shirt. He drank from the bottle, then looked sideways at Dave. "Did you kill Denton's woman?" he asked slyly.

Dave shook his head. "No," he replied quietly.

"You were stupid enough to bring her sorrel into town."

"So? I didn't know anything about Denton at the time."

Amos nodded. "That was what I figured."

"What's your interest in all this? How did you know it was her sorrel?"

Amos grinned weakly. "I sold it to her. It was after midnight. She wanted to go north to Stone's Ferry, and right away at that. I warned her about that damned hellhole of a country up there, but she said she had a good guide. He was waiting for her just out of town, she said. When she left, I followed her a ways in the dark and saw her guide."

"Who was it?"

Amos drank again. "An animal in human form. A triple breed if there is such a thing—Paiute on his mother's side. His father was a mulatto, half white and half black, a trooper stationed at Fort Mohave. Someone with an education said Ahvote had inherited all the vices of the three races and none of the virtues. Even his own people kicked him out. Somethin' about raping a twelve-year-old Paiute girl and then murderin' her. Her relatives, and maybe his, too, would kill him on sight. He hangs around Chloride because the Paiutes don't come in here, at least not very often. I guess he thinks he's safe here and, besides, he can drink all the tanglefoot he can beg, borrow, buy, or steal. Man, Davie, he's got a thirst bigger than mine and yours combined."

"Yours will do," Dave said dryly.

Amos waved a hand. "Howsomever. Anyway, Ahvote gen'rally graces Chloride like a stinking saddle blanket hung over a corral fence to dry out. Best not to get downwind from him on a hot day, or any other day, for that matter."

Dave nodded. "Like Cos Leach."

"You got it, Davie! He's got one good quality, although I ain't sure that's quite the right word for it—he knows that Big Bend country better'n any man alive—white, Paiute, Mohave, and Hualpai. You probably know most Indians, and whites, too, if they got any sense at all, keep outa that country, in partic'lar that Hell's Forty Acres country. Then again, there's damned fools who go in there now and again. Most of them never come out." He closed one bleary red eye and studied Dave with the other.

"Like me, maybe?" Dave asked.

Amos nodded.

"And you and your partner Ash?"

Amos nodded again.

"Knowing all this about Ahvote, why didn't you stop her from going with him?"

Amos drank. "I couldn't catch up with them."

"You're lying!"

"Wal, mebbe. I didn't want to get mixed up with Denton's woman and I didn't want to face down Ahvote. You never know what he's goin' to do, Davie. He's a dark-minded animal, but an animal kills mostly for food. Ahvote, when he can, kills just for the hell of it. And, Davie lad, he ain't never been caught at it. Just that once by his own people." He closed his eyes and passed a hand over them, then opened them and looked up at Dave. "The pretty lady? She's alive?"

"Why should I tell you?"

"I won't tell anyone, Davie. I just have to know. If she's dead, I don't want to know what happened. You didn't do it. I know you better'n that. But if he did . . ."

"She's alive, Amos," Dave said. "But, by God, if you let it out, I'll come back, dead or alive, and hunt you down. You understand?"

Amos looked into those cold, set eyes. He dribbled a little in his drawers. He nodded. "No fear," he blurted out weakly.

"Now, listen to me!" Dave said. "Before you take the claybank out on the west road after dark, I want you to take the pair of burros out of here. You know where George Ward lives?"

Ash nodded. "I useta work for him until one time I got drunk and accidently set fire to his storeroom."

"*Bueno!* Take the burros and picket them in the big

arroyo just below his house. I want packsaddles on both of them.''

"I gotcha, Davie lad," Amos said.

"And, for Christ's sake, keep your big mouth shut!"

"I will! I will!"

Dave left the stable. He couldn't make his move until after dark. Meanwhile, he'd have to try to make it obvious he wasn't in a great hurry to leave town.

Amos watched Dave stride uptown. "Why shouldn't I help you, Davie lad?" he murmured. "I'd be stupid not to. One way or another, you got to take Ash as your partner, for our good as well as yours, you thickheaded, stubborn jackass!"

CHAPTER 11

GLASSEYE MOPPED THE BAR. "ASH MAWSON WAS IN here lookin' for you, Hunter." He eyed Dave's bruised face. "You're living on borrowed time after that fracas in the Miner's Repose. What I can't figure out is why they haven't come after yuh and gunned yuh down."

"Beer," Dave ordered.

Glasseye placed the bottle in front of Dave. He leaned across the bar. "Maybe they think you know somethin' they want to know?" he asked in a low voice.

"Such as?"

"That strike you made up north."

"It's possible," Dave agreed.

"Maybe it's about that woman who went up north."

"Hard to say, Glasseye," Dave said.

Glasseye studied him. "You ain't talkin', then?"

"You're quick at catching on. Now get the hell back to mopping the goddamned bar, or whatever the hell you do all day, like a good boy."

"I was only askin'," growled Glasseye. "Bastard," he murmured as he turned away.

"Wrong," Dave said. "I was the third of seven children, all legitimate."

"Funny man. You're a real comedian, Hunter."

"What did the missing woman look like, Glasseye?" Dave asked after a time.

"Thick dark hair with kinda highlights in it. Beautiful skin. Peaches and cream, my mother used to call such.

Fine eyes, big and gray. Looked like she might be Mex, but, you know, of good family without Indian blood. Beautiful voice. I heard her sing a few times. I think she might have been on the stage at one time. She could tear the heart outa yuh when she sang. We have quite a few ex-Rebels in and around Chloride. She knew that. I think she may have come from the Old South. Jesus, when she sang "Lorena," there wasn't a dry eye in the house—Jonny Reb *or* Billy Yank."

Dave emptied the beer bottle. "What was her name?"

"Lila Denton," Baldy replied. "You ready for another beer?"

Dave nodded. It figured. A coldness crept through his mind.

Baldy placed a fresh bottle on the bar. "Kinda strange about her. Beautiful woman mixed up with Denton and his *corrida* of shabby characters. Took off outa Chloride one dark night. Some say she was headin' for California by way of Stone's Ferry. Personally, I figgered the Paiutes got her except for one thing . . ."

Dave eyed him. "Such as?"

"You showed up here yesterday with the horse she bought from Amos Wassell." He looked directly into Dave's eyes. "I guess maybe you didn't know she was Matt Denton's wife."

"I didn't say I had met her, now, did I?"

Glasseye turned away from that icy, penetrating stare. "No, you didn't. Ain't none of my business, anyway."

Dave drank his beer. He lit a long nine. "But you've made it your business. Go on with your theory."

"What's a theory?" Glasseye asked, puzzled.

"You were just expounding it," Dave replied.

"What's expoundin'?"

Dave slapped a callused palm on the bar. The beer bottle jumped. Dave caught it and upended it. He put it down empty. "For Christ's sake! Go on with your suspicions, and don't, for God's sake, ask me what *they* are."

Glasseye was hurt. "You think I'm stupid?" he demanded.

Dave grinned a little. "Don't ask me to answer that."

Glasseye shrugged. "Rumor has it that she took off with Denton's bankroll. Rumor also has it that the last time you was here in Chloride you was dead broke, with nothing but your hoss, a burro, and a few supplies. Weeks later, you show up with Lila Denton's hoss, a sack of high assay ore samples, and a wad of greenbacks big enough to choke a hog. Ash Mawson should have arrested you on suspicion instead of savin' your ass from Denton and his *corrida.*"

"Maybe he's got his reasons. Maybe you've got a theory on that, too."

Glasseye nodded. "And I'll expound on it." He grinned. "Every soul in Chloride, and mebbe Arizona Territory as well, knows that if Ash ever gets a sniff of a possible strike, he'll be gone from here like the snow after a spring thaw. Hunter, if you ever needed a partner, you need one now, and Ash Mawson would be the best investment you'd ever make."

Dave paid for his beer. "Thanks for expounding your theories, Glasseye. By the way, what's your given name?"

Glasseye hesitated. "Zacharia," he admitted at last. "I don't much care for Glasseye, but it's better than Zacharia."

Dave nodded. "I see what you mean." He walked to the batwings, turned, grinned, and whispered loudly, *"Zacharia . . . "* He was gone before the beer bottle hit the wall next to the door.

Dave looked up and down the deserted wide street. Those who didn't have to brave the killer sun were inside their houses or places of business. The miners who lived in town had left before dawn for their shifts. The night-shift men were still asleep. There was no sign of Denton and his *corrida,* nor of Ash Mawson, for that matter. They would be waiting for him to make his move.

Dave lingered over a long, late lunch. He stalled quite

a spell in Sam Walker's gun shop, buying cartridge cases and a few spare firing pins for the Sharps. They had a tendency to break because of the weakness of their unusual shape. The block was much too short to use the same type of firing pin used in the .45/70 Army Springfield rifle and it had been necessary to design a peculiar U-shaped firing pin. As a result, the full force of the hammer was not transmitted to the cartridge primer, much of it being lost in the side thrust and twisting that at times caused the firing pin to break.

Twilight shadows lingered when Dave left the gun shop. He returned to Ward's merchantile to buy tobacco, matches, and other odds and ends. He thought of buying some feminine sort of gift, but it would be a dead giveaway of Lila's presence in the silver canyon. He felt that he could trust Ward but realized he was not in a position to trust anyone. He went back to the Arizona Star and had a few beers while the night came on. There were several men in the place playing poker, one of them being Joe Bob Manion.

"Ash Mawson been in?" Dave asked.

Glasseye nodded. "About an hour ago. I ain't seen him since."

It was dark when Dave left the saloon. He'd have to go to the stable. They knew he was staying there and that he'd need a mount at least. He walked to an open-topped public latrine, stalled long enough to fake his personal business there, then went up and over the back wall. He moved like a disembodied soul through the shadows. He scouted the vicinity of the stable but saw no one. The stable itself was deserted. The claybank and the two burros were gone. Amos had fulfilled his part of the bargain.

Dave worked swiftly in the darkness. He cut up an old hide to make boots for the dun. He got his Sharps and the money belt from their separate caches. He left the stable by the rear door and again checked the area for any possible observers. There were none. He led the dun out of the stable by the rear door, then to the arroyo near Ward's house. He saw no one and heard nothing. The two burros were picketed in the arroyo. Dave tethered the dun and cat-footed up to the storehouse.

"Don't shoot," Ward advised out of the darkness. "I'm here to give you a hand. Two of my sons are watching for anyone nosing around."

They worked swiftly, carrying the supplies down to the burros and packing the *aparejos* on the packsaddles. When they were done, the two men gripped hands.

"I wish I could do more for you, Dave," Ward said.

"You've done more than enough."

"Do you think you can make it now?"

Dave grinned faintly. "I'll bust my butt trying, George."

Ward nodded. "Take off, then. I'll walk toward town. My sons and I will make sure you're not being followed. Move fast!"

The moon was just below the east side of the Cerbats when Dave reached the wash where Amos was to leave the claybank. He looked back at the lights of Chloride twinkling in the clear atmosphere. The faint pewter glow of the rising moon was already limning the mountain rim.

A soft whistle came from the darkness of the wash just east of the road. Dave turned, half-cocking his Sharps. A horse snorted.

"That you, Hunter?" a man called.

"Amos?" Dave called back. It didn't sound like the cracked voice of the old man.

"Hell, no! He's half seas or more by now. On a real high lonesome. It's your good ol' *amigo*. You know, the *hombre* who saved your life back in the Miner's Repose. I—" His voice was cut off sharply as Dave fully cocked the rifle.

"Come out of there with your hands up," Dave called out. "Grab those big ears of yours!"

Ash Mawson came out of the shadows with his hands high. He knew what that big cannon could do at such short range, or even at *long* range, for that matter. "Whyn't you get a civilized Winchester?" he growled.

Dave grinned. "One shot outa this Sharps is as good as a full magazine load from a Winchester. They waste too much ammunition."

"Frugal, ain't you?" jeered Ash.

The claybank and the two burros trotted behind Ash. There was another horse there—a big chestnut loaded with full saddlebags, cantle and pommel packs, and a scabbarded Winchester. Three big, cloth-covered canteens hung from the saddle.

"You planning on taking a trip?" Dave asked.

Ash grinned. "Figgered I'd ride along with you a spell, Davie."

"That so?" Dave kept the Sharps on him. "You should have asked permission."

Ash sucked on a tooth. "I forgot. Got to go north, anyways. Been hunting for a lost silver mine for a decade or so. Figgered I had a right to go look for it again. It's a free country. Bound to find it this trip, with a little help from you, partner, that is."

Dave shook his head.

"You owe me one, Hunter!"

Dave shrugged. "True. Turnabout is fair play."

"Saved your life back there. Kept an eye on them most of the day so's they wouldn't buffalo you again, me being city marshal and all. Besides, Amos said you wasn't quite right in the head from being out in the boondocks too long by yourself and you wasn't too bright in the first place, but you'd make a good partner because you're a hard worker, a good shot, and had a warm heart. I bought the whole bowl of chili on that last one—the warm heart."

Dave nodded. "A wise decision."

"We'd best get the hell outa here. Never know when Denton and his playmates will be along. I'd like to lighten the load on my chestnut in case we'll have to ride fast. I'll put some of it on the burros.'' He turned to his horse and reached out to remove the cantle pack. That was a mistake.

The heavy barrel of the Sharps tapped Ash hard just above his right ear. He dropped in his tracks without a sound.

Dave worked fast. He emptied Ash's Colt and Winchester of their .44/40 cartridges, which would fit his own Colt, and withdrew others from Ash's cartridge-belt loops. He poured them into one of his saddlebags. He removed Ash's cantle and pommel packs and placed them on the packsaddles. He did the same with the marshal's saddlebags. He added the three canteens to his own collection.

Ash stirred and moaned a little. Dave tied the long lead ropes of the burros to the dun's saddle. He mounted the chestnut and took the reins of the dun and the claybank. He looked down at Ash. "Rest in peace, old friend," he murmured. "I've got a partner, and, besides, I've never been able to cotton to knife fighters." It would take Ash quite a while to recover, head back to Chloride, and either stay there and forget his idea of partnering Dave or to re-outfit himself and get another mount to set out on Dave's trail again, this time with a vengeance. . . . Even with Dave's short acquaintance of Ash, he knew well enough that it would be the latter course that Ash would take. Dave would be forced to take risks and drive himself and his animals to their utmost to make sure that Ash didn't catch up. He had a feeling that if Ash Mawson ever did catch up, it would end with a shootout that one of them, perhaps both, might not survive.

Dave headed north. For a time, the thudding of rapid hoofbeats could be heard on the hard road and then they died away. When the moon rose above the Cerbats, a thin veil of trail dust drifted in the quiet air.

CHAPTER 12

THE MOON WAS ON THE WANE. IT SHARPLY ETCHED the shadows of the tortured Joshua trees on the slopes below the Cerbats. A warm wind wandered through the brush now and again, only to die away as though too tired to keep on. There was no sound in the night except the soft rustling of the wind in the brush and the steady beating of hoofs as Dave Hunter rode on, ever northward. Now and again he'd rise in his stirrups to look back down the long slopes under the dying moonlight. There were still no telltale signs of rising dust on the road far behind him.

He stopped in the deceptive light of the false dawn to rest and water the horses and burros. The chestnut was badly winded, for Dave had pressed the pace as hard as he could to get a good lead. The mouth of a little-used pass showed to the northeast. Dave had no idea of what was beyond the pass, for he had never been in that area. He had been told there was nothing there but a great barren valley that led to the north and eventually to the Colorado. It was said to be rough and deceptive country with few, if any, waterholes. It did lead in time to the area east of the silver canyon.

Every fiber of his being wanted him to keep going due north, driving the animals to the limit of their endurance. He wanted to see Lila and make sure she was alive and safe. But he knew he had been dumb lucky to get out of

Chloride as easily as he had done. He could not jeopardize that lead now.

He half closed his eyes, trying to visualize the great natural chessboard upon which he must now make his moves. He was on the defensive, with black, as opposed to his opponents, both nature and the human element, white and Paiute. He grinned wryly. "Black is my color, against white *and* red. A new type of game . . ."

One wrong turn in the tangle of canyons, mountains, and desert, and he could go on and on into nothingness and death.

The wind began to shift with the coming of dawn. He led the animals into the mouth of the pass and returned to a vantage point where he could see the slopes far, far below him and the faint thread of the rough road that led south back to Chloride. He raised his field glasses and searched the road. Nothing . . . Then he looked again and saw the faintest trace of dust rising from the road far to the south. It could be Matt Denton and his two hardcases or possibly Ash Mawson with blood in his eye, a pounding head, and Hell's own fury in his heart. Dave wasn't quite sure who he'd rather face.

Dave looked about himself. He could lead the animals deep into the pass, then return with his Sharps to the mouth of it. He could hold off a platoon of infantry there, but what would he gain? He would need sleep in time.

Dave led the animals through the pass to the eastern side. He watered them and then picketed them near some sparse vegetation. He rode the claybank back to the western end of the pass. He picketed the horse, took a canteen and some food, his long rifle, and field glasses, and plodded back to his vantage point. The desert slopes were still semidark.

He lay down. He was tired. A few hours' sleep wouldn't hurt. He'd need all the strength he could get for the next day.

Dave was on a griddle cooking slowly but steadily. He

awoke with a start. Sweat dripped down his face. The
sun was high up, driving its fiery fury down into the pass.
He looked down the slopes. There was still no dust with
the exception of a dust devil that sprang up on the slopes
between the pass and the road on the lower ground,
whirling rapidly only to disappear as suddenly as it had
appeared. A little while later, it seemed to reappear
hundreds of yards away to go into its whirligig of a dance,
then vanish again.

He mounted the claybank and rode back to the eastern
end of the pass. He saddled the dun and led the other animals down the long eastern slope toward the great wide
valley already shimmering with the heat of the sun. The
sunlight glinted on the salt of a wide dry lake. The sky
was a burning, cloudless blue, and the rays of the sun
seemed to be focused on Dave Hunter as though through a
gigantic magnifying glass.

In the middle of the afternoon, in the most overpowering heat of that hellish day, he found dubious shelter
behind a huge monolith of reddish rock that stood out on
the flat ground like a warning finger. There, with the
solid, smashing heat of the sun pouring down, he forced
himself to rest, not for his own comfort but for the suf-
fering animals.

Ash Mawson plodded up the long, heat-shimmering
slope dragging on the reins of his bay horse. The narrow
mouth of the pass to the east was above him. His hat sat
high on his head because of the bandage bound about his
skull. He had been buffaloed by an expert and for that he
was grudgingly grateful, but that didn't alleviate the burning hatred he felt toward Dave Hunter. There were few
men who could outsmart Ash Mawson, and some of them
had eventually paid the ultimate penalty for doing so. Ash
neither forgave nor forgot in his lexicon—*ever*. There had
been no other recourse for him but to return to Chloride,
round up more supplies—canteens, cartridges, a horse and

burro—and bind his throbbing skull. On the other hand, Hunter could have brought him to a permanent halt by killing him. Still, Ash thought he knew his man—Hunter was not a killer.

Ash meant to go plumb to the Colorado and beyond, if necessary. He knew that country as well as any man. Only the week before Hunter's arrival in Chloride, Matt Denton had wanted to hire Ash to guide him north on what he had claimed was an investigation into the mineral possibilities of Hell's Forty Acres. Ash had been out of town when the woman had bought the sorrel mare from Amos and headed north as though being pursued by the Devil himself.

Ash wasn't sure which route Hunter had taken to return north, but he figured that if Hunter knew he was being followed he'd try to use every possible and devious means to throw pursuers off his trail. Hunter was desert-wise, else he would never have been able to survive in that country during the summer months. Ash figured Hunter was shrewd enough to travel east in an out-of-the-way fashion, gambling that he'd be able to outlast or elude any pursuers. It might work with other people; it wouldn't work with Ash Mawson.

Ash was within half a mile of the pass when a chilling warning crept into his mind. He stopped short and dismounted, then walked around behind the bay. He uncased his battered field glasses, rested his arms on the saddle, and studied the pass environs. He had suddenly recalled the big Sharps Hunter carried as though it was an extension of his arm, part of his very being. The man was obviously a rifleman, exhibiting a man's bond with his rifle. Ash could almost visualize Hunter lying concealed up there, peering through his accurate, vernier-tang sights and getting a bead on the bay horse or Ash himself. As long as Ash stayed on that sun-bright slope, devoid of all but the scantest of cover, he'd be a prime target for that bastard Hunter. There was nothing Ash could do but wait for dusk, then scout ahead on foot until he was positive, beyond any doubt, that the pass was safe.

Four men rode out of Chloride when the sun was up on a day of Hell's own heat. Matt Denton, Cos Leach, Vic, and the Paiute half-breed Ahvote. The Paiute's bloodshot eyes were brooding and half-closed. He liked the country north of Chloride; he hated Chloride with a passion. It was like living with a woman he hated but couldn't live without. So it was with Chloride. Whiskey was his great love and consuming passion. He lived for nothing else. Chloride was where he could beg, borrow, steal, or buy the quantities of whiskey he craved. This passion had given him the nickname by which white people knew him—Whiskey.

Ahvote had known for quite some time that he'd have to get out of Chloride, at least for a while. He'd had no money or job, and he'd long ago run out of credit. Therefore he needed to find money or something with which he could barter for whiskey. By some miracle, he had almost achieved that goal when a beautiful white woman had hired him to guide her north to Stone's Ferry. She had a fine sorrel mare and a good saddle, a Winchester rifle and a Colt revolver, and evidently money. It would have been a bonanza for Ahvote but for one thing—he had another burning passion beside that for alcohol. This passion was buried so deep in his dark soul that perhaps his own gods and even his personal medicine spirit could not know of it. For a long time, between almost perpetual drunks and horrible, soul-shaking hangovers, Ahvote had wanted a white woman all to himself. He wanted one to play with and indulge in all his most secret fantasies. When that was done, he wanted to torture her slowly, *very* slowly, to death, in an effort to see how long he would let her live. That was to be a necessary part of the ritual.

Ahvote had made a mistake with the white woman he

had been guiding that had almost become fatal. At their first's night camp, he had made his try for her. Her first bullet had parted his hair; the second had passed through the slack of his shirt as he ran for cover. The third had gone through the head of his horse. She had then fled herself. The last laugh, in a sense, had been on her. The camp had been nowhere near the trail to Stone's Ferry. The direction in which she had fled was into the heart of the area known by the Paiutes as Tamesha, or Ground Afire, and by the white-eyes as Hell's Forty Acres. Ahvote had trailed her on foot, had seen her attacked by some of his people and then rescued by the big man with a rifle that could kill at half a mile. It was the same man who had come into Chloride with the white woman's sorrel mare and the rich ore samples. So she must still be alive and in a hidden canyon that Ahvote and the rest of the Paiutes knew of and avoided as much as possible because of its evil reputation. There were vengeful ghosts of long-dead Spaniards there.

Ahvote eyed the sweat-stained backs of the three whites riding ahead of him, letting him eat their dust while he led a pair of their burros loaded with water, food, and *whiskey*. . . . They had fine horses, rifles, pistols, and plenty of cartridges. The thought wandered through his blurred mind that if he could lead these stupid white-eyes into a Paiute ambush, he would become a hero among his people, they who had cast him from the tribe. Even if they accepted his offering of the three white men and their horses and goods and forgave him, however, he'd have to share the store of booze, which would certainly be considered loot to be shared among all members of the band equally, for that was the Paiute way.

"Whiskey!" shouted Denton. "Ride ahead and cut for sign! Get moving, you drunken bastard! I'm not paying you only to lead burros!"

Ahvote rode on, passing the burro lead rope to Cos. He

pulled ahead and began to cast back and forth along the road and on each side of it like a hunting hound.

Cos spat to the side. "I don't trust that breed bastard," he growled.

"Neither do I," said Matt, "but he's our only bet to track down Hunter. If Hunter gets into those canyons, our chances of finding him are fairly hopeless. Whiskey was hired by Lila to guide her north. I got him drunk and talked him into telling me what happened to her. He claimed she had fired him and had even shot at him!"

Vic grinned. "I would have liked to have seen that! Too bad she missed."

Matt shook his head. "If she hadn't missed we'd have no one who could guide us into that hellhole up north."

"I still don't trust him," Cos insisted. "He could lead us into an ambush."

"Hell, no!" Matt snapped. "His people hate him worse than the whites do. He's a pariah. So, unless he tries to handle all three of us alone, it isn't likely we'll have any trouble with him. Besides, if he does give us trouble, he'll be banned from Chloride. That would be the end of him. As long as we give him enough liquor to keep him going, we haven't much to fear. He does know the country. We *need* him. So watch your step with him. When we're finished using him, that'll be another story."

"Let's hope he don't drink up all the likker before that," grunted Cos.

Ahvote was far ahead of them by now. They saw him dismount, then lead his horse slowly along the road. Now and again he'd fade off into the brush, then come trotting back to continue to the north. It was the middle of the afternoon when they saw him stand up in his stirrups and point to the northeast.

Matt put his glasses on the slopes in that direction. It was difficult to see because of the heat haze, but slowly he began to discern a thread of dust rising in the air. He handed the glasses to Vic.

Vic studied the slopes for a long time.

"Dust devil?" asked Matt.

Vic shrugged. "Hard to tell. I know one thing—there ain't any other dust, if that *is* dust, rising anywhere else."

"So?" asked Matt.

Vic handed him the glasses. "Looks like the opening of a canyon or a pass mouth up there."

Matt studied the slopes. He nodded.

They rode on slowly through the shimmering heat waves.

CHAPTER 13

THE DARKNESS WAS THICK AND WINDY BEFORE THE RIS-
ing of the moon. Dave slogged onward, finding his way
more by instinct than sight. He could not stop. The passage
he had made that hellish day was vague and unreal. He
knew he was heading in a northerly direction again after
his easterly deviation through the pass, but he wasn't sure
exactly where he was. One could be sure of nothing in that
country. Even a compass could not be relied upon.

Just before the first faint light of the rising moon tinted
the eastern sky he skirted what looked like a dense shadow
on the ground. His tired mind did not grasp the fact that
there wasn't enough light to cast a shadow. It wasn't until
the last burro fell over the edge of a deep declivity, snapping its lead rope and falling with a clattering, clashing din
of loose rock, that he realized what the shadow really was.
The burro woke the sleeping echoes with a frenzied braying. That wouldn't do.

Dave looped the lead rope around a rock and slid down
the slope to the burro. A quick hand inspection revealed a
broken leg. Its pitiful braying echoed and reechoed. A pistol shot would carry for over a mile. Dave pulled back the
burro's head, stretching the throat taut. His sheath knife
sliced cleanly through the jugular. He unloaded the burro
and carried the load up to the top of the declivity. He
planned to load the supplies onto the chestnut. The horse
was gone. Its lead rope had been attached to the fallen
burro. The rope had broken. Dave raised his head. He could

hear faint hoofbeats dying away in the distance. It was just as well. He hardly had enough water left for the others. If he didn't reach the canyon or the river by dawn, it would likely be the end for all of them, anyway, including himself. He didn't regret the loss of the chestnut except for one thing—if he had a pursuer or pursuers and they had used the pass behind him, they might find the chestnut and know he had come that way. Well, if they did come, they'd likely find the dead burro anyway, at least by daylight. The buzzards would lead them to the corpse. He loaded the supplies onto the dun and the claybank.

Dave plodded on in the growing moonlight. The wind had died away with the rising of the moon. One footstep after the other, head down, he swung along in the long, loose, mile-eating infantryman's stride he had developed during the war. It was quiet except for the thudding of hoofs, the rustle and creak of leather, and an occasional snort by horse or burro.

On and on, mile after mile, into a seeming infinity.

A faint murmuring came to Dave. It was so faint that he wasn't sure he heard anything at all. He raised his head. He saw something blurry and indistinct moving swiftly toward him. He narrowed his eyes. The murmur grew louder, an eerie, moaning sound. A chill crept through him despite the hot air. "Furnace wind," he whispered through cracked lips.

The area to the north and east became a moving, shifting, whirling veil of dust-laden wind many feet high, billowing toward him. He bound his bandanna about his mouth and nose, bent his head, and walked to meet the deadly storm. Within twenty minutes he and the animals were enveloped by the stinging dust. His eyes burned from it. His skin seemed to grow taut. He plodded on, bent forward, staggering now and again from the insensate buffeting of the wind. To go down might be to die and be buried by the wind-driven dust, perhaps to lie for months, even years, a mummified corpse.

His right foot struck ground and sank through a crusty surface. The heat of the subsurface came through the sole leather. He opened his eyes. "Jesus God," he murmured in sudden and intense fear. He looked about himself. Stinging clouds of grayish, gritty dust swept across the dim, creamy-colored surface of a lakebed that had probably been dry for a hundred years or longer—a real devil's dance floor. Perhaps now and again a cloudburst would fill the ancient lakebed for a day or so, perhaps only for a few hours, turning it sparkling blue and tempting under the blazing sun and bright metallic blue sky, and then it would vanish down into the thirsty ground almost as suddenly as it had appeared.

Dave kept on. He couldn't go back. He couldn't stop. Every hour would bring him and the animals that much closer to dying of thirst and exposure, increased tenfold by the dry wind and alkali-laden dust. Perhaps Death was waiting for him; a grinning skull hidden in the whirling dust, staring at him with empty eye sockets. There was no choice but to go and meet it.

His feet sank deeper as he plodded on. Now and again he'd stumble and almost go down, and lurking fear would force its way into his mind, breaking the way for panic. Panic, he knew, would lead to self-destruction.

Sometimes his feet would sink deeper, pace after pace, as though eventually he would sink too deep to extricate himself, but somehow the softer areas would firm and he'd have better footing, only to find another soft spot and then another. It was no use trying to look ahead to see how far the lakebed extended. The dust limited his view in all directions and even overhead. Dave had faced raw death many times during the war; he had witnessed it on the Great Plains, the haunt of the fierce Comanches and Kiowas, while buffalo hunting. Later, in New Mexico, Arizona, and Mexico, he had met it many times in his quest for treasure. He had withstood all that, fearsome as it was, but, in most cases, he had at least been able to fight back.

No man could fight and defeat the sinking, sucking death that just might be a few feet ahead of him at any time. Deeper and deeper, first to the knees, then the thighs, restricting farther progress, then to the waist and then the chest, constricting his breathing. Then his head would be just above the queasy surface. Slowly, inexorably, he would sink to his mouth and nose. Struggle would be futile. In a few more moments, there would be nothing to mark his passage but a circular area leveling itself off over Dave, the horses, and burro. They would die alone, unseen, neatly trapped, buried and killed by implacable nature itself.

Somehow, he struggled on. It was his way. Fight to the last and then give it a few more ounces. He was of that breed that takes a lot of killing.

Hour after hour, he struggled against the moaning furnace wind with its shroud of stinging dust. He constantly sank halfway to his calves—no more, no less—dragging on the lead rope, feeling the lead animal struggling, sinking to its knees, then back-jumping forward to rise above the soft mass of the surface. The animals' breathing was harsh, stertorous, and uneven. They lacked the strength and spirit to bray or to whinny. It was a silent struggle for both man and beast against a silent enemy.

The moon waned and began to die.

There seemed to be no limit to the dry lakebed. Dave had no idea if he was walking across its middle or moving along the length of it with the shoreline not far away, or perhaps he was doing that which was quite common in such a situation: *He might be walking in circles.*

The moon was gone, leaving an ebony-hued darkness in its wake. The wind became fitful, boxed the compass, and at last died away, leaving the air thick with settling dust.

The ground firmed somewhat beneath Dave's feet. It was still crusty and now and then he broke through but sank only a few inches. Dave halted. He took a folding canvas bucket and emptied one of the large canteens into it. He sipped a few mouthfuls, then spat it back into the bucket and watered the exhausted animals sparingly. Their heads hung low; their legs were splayed out. Dave shook his head. He was more sorry for them than he was for himself, but he had to go on.

Dawn came almost imperceptibly. The eastern sky became pewter-tinted. It lightened. Then, with a vast silent explosion, the sun rose. Almost immediately, its killing heat became apparent to the lone man and his animals. The dust had settled hours past. He stood in the bottom of a vast bowl to which there seemed to be no boundaries; no limits to the naked expanse of the dry lakebed that blended imperceptibly into the barren wastes on all sides. There was no sign of life as far as the eye could see. There was not a single weed or bush. There were no tracks of animal or man other than those marking Dave's trail and vanishing back into the distance. In a matter of a few days, they, too, might be smoothed over by nature's continuous tidying-up process after man. No bird winged its hasty way to escape the hideous nakedness of the land. The only relief to the eye were the dim, humped shapes of the mountains, and when it got hot enough, they would seem to dance in the heat waves until the thickening haze hid them from view altogether.

Dave headed to the north and west. Once he had heard that there was a seasonal waterhole somewhere along the flank of the mountain to the west, but he couldn't risk taking the time to try to find it. The Colorado was north; the silver canyon and Lila had to be northwest. He'd have to head for the river first. Water was paramount. His canteens would be empty when and if he made it to the river.

He was forced to rest the animals long before he reached the Colorado. He sat in the meager shadow of the dun. The lakebed was now a shimmering, white, mirage-haunted expanse. The distant mountains seemed suspended off the ground. Again he thought he saw delightful lakes and pools of sparkling blue water, but he knew they were only cruel tricks. When he sought them in the final desperation of agonizing thirst, he would not know they *were* mirages. For the first time since the Iron Brigade had charged the Rebel breastworks at Cold Harbor, Dave prayed.

It seemed an eternity until the sun went down. The coolness dusk brought was only relative. Dave watered the animals and himself, then started off again, due north, one foot ahead of the other like an automaton. He entered a low-walled canyon after moonrise. It twisted and turned, and fear of it being a box canyon with unscalable sides haunted him all during the hours of moonlight.

Darkness came again. The water was gone. The canyon was a hell of heat, thickets of thorned cat-claw brush, and loose-treacherous rock flooring. The sound of clattering hoofs and clashing rock seemed like a horrendous din to Dave, enough to wake the dead.

He stopped and searched the darkness ahead. The terrain rose a little. He had to be near the river. Perhaps he had wandered back into the maze of box canyons that held the silver canyon. He'd probably have to wait until daylight to verify his position.

The burro brayed suddenly, awakening the echoes.

Dave turned just as the burro trotted past him. The taut lead rope snapped and the burro plunged on into the darkness. Dave ran after him, slipping and sliding on the loose rock flooring, while the vicious cat-claw thorns ripped at his clothing and flesh. He could just make out the rump of the burro, then it was gone. A second or two later, there was a splash, a pitiful bray, and then silence.

Dave ran on and stepped into air. He plunged down, grabbed hold of a bush to check his fall, and the next instant he was chest-deep in swift-running water that dragged him from his footing. He went under, rose, struck out for the dim shoreline, then went under again. His feet struck bottom, and half swimming and half walking, he managed to get hold of a bush overhanging the water. It gave him just enough purchase to get up on a sandbank before the bush, too, broke loose and fell into the river.

There was no time to waste. If the horses sought the water, too, they'd go over the brink as well. He caught the dun within fifteen feet of the edge and fought to get it turned aside, then led it down to the sand bank with the claybank trailing behind on the lead rope. He had a hell of a time getting them away from the water before they drank too much and foundered. He picketed them back from the bank and then allowed himself several widely spaced mouthfuls of the silty water.

Dave sat down on a rock to rest and think. He had lost nearly half his supplies, but had enough for Lila and himself to subsist on for at least several weeks with some rationing. Maybe he could roll over a deer to supplement it. Two of the six cans of Kepauno Giant blasting powder were lost. The remaining four cans, two each on the dun and claybank, would suffice for quite some time. If he did not get good results in his mining within the time limit of his food and blasting powder supplies, it might be an indication that the lode had been mined out.

At dawn light, he led the horses along the riverbank until he found a narrow slot of a canyon leading back into what he thought might be Hell's Forty Acres. Whether it did or not was nothing for him to debate. Again, as during his journey north from Chloride when he'd had had to trend easterly to shake off pursuers, he had no choice. Hours later, he picketed the horse at some scant vegetation and allowed himself to sleep until about moonrise. He knew he had to be close to the silver canyon, but, like the rest of its illusive history, it would not be easy to find.

He awoke and waited patiently for moonrise. It was madness to attempt those interminable winding, twisting, heat-soaked slots of canyons in the darkness. He plodded on. The moon was well up when he picketed the horses, took his rifle and a canteen, and went ahead on foot.

Dave rounded a huge towering rock wall of intermingled salmon, rose, and yellow hues. Somehow it looked familiar. Then there before him were two enormous crumbling rock pillars like the gateposts of some medieval keep.

Dave walked between the pillars. Ahead of him was the shadowed entrance to the branch canyon. He went toward it. A sudden braying broke the brooding quiet. Hoofs clattered on rock. Then Amiga came, pounding her little hoofs as fast as she could go. Dave slid an arm around her neck. He closed his eyes for a moment of thankfulness.

The branch canyon was quiet. No one was in sight.

"Lila! Lila! Lila!" he called hoarsely.

"Lila! Lila! Lila!" the canyon echoed.

She rose from a clutter of broken rock near the mine entrance, a ready carbine in her hands. She ran down the slope, then stopped short as she came close to him. What she saw was a gaunt caricature of a man standing in torn and ragged clothing, staring at her with hollowed eyes. He held out a hand to her. She took it and guided him to the hut. He collapsed on the bed.

"Are you all right?" she asked quietly.

He looked at her. "I said I would come back," he replied hoarsely.

"Rest there. Are you hungry?"

He nodded and then sat up. "I've got to go back for the horses. They need water. They have what's left of our supplies."

"Can't that wait?"

He shook his head.

She came close to him and kissed him. "Hurry back as fast as you can." There was a wealth of promise in her tone.

CHAPTER 14

ASH MAWSON SQUATTED, RUMINATING, BESIDE HIS BIG bay horse. He looked out across the great dry lake. It was dawn, and he was low on water. He knew he wouldn't last the next day without it. It was too late for him to go back the way he had come. Dave Hunter was somewhere beyond the dry lake. Foot and hoof prints showed it in a wavering line off into infinity. Who else but Dave Hunter? Not even a Hualpai or Paiute would cross that damned floor of Hell in the summer. Few white men knew that country better than Ash, but Dave Hunter, blast his soul to everlasting Hell, had taken up its deadly challenge right enough. Ash looked to the north. Supposing Hunter had made it to the river? It would be another cutting blow to Ash Mawson's magnificent ego, added to that sneaky buffaloing Hunter had dealt him. He half closed his eyes and conjured up a mental image of that unmapped country. There was a seasonal waterhole somewhere near Table Mountain. It was closer. But if Hunter *had* made it to the river, odds were Ash would never catch up with him if he made a detour to the waterhole.

Ash stood up. He rubbed the bay horse's neck. "Come on, Dearly Beloved," he said quietly. "Ain't no use sitting here waiting to die of thirst. Let's go meet it like men."

He led the horse and burro partway out onto the lakebed, following Hunter's footprints, which deepened the farther Ash went. He stopped and looked ahead, following the trail until it was lost in the distance. That indicated the surface was comparatively firm, at least as far as he could see the footprints, but what lay beyond them? Who knew how firm the surface was even a few feet to either side of Hunter's trail? Ash had prospected in this area some years ago, but he had not ventured out on the lake. It had a deadly reputation. Hunter was either desperate or a fool to have gone that way. It was obvious he didn't know about the waterhole at Table Mountain.

Doubt and uncertainty crept into the back of his mind. Supposing he did follow Hunter and during the full heat of the day, under the killer sun, the trail stopped suddenly, leaving only a disturbed surface on the flat expanse of the lake, miles from its distant borders?

Ash turned back and plodded toward Table Mountain.

Ahvote quested back and forth like a beagle after a cottontail. He had found horse droppings in the pass that trended to the east down into the dry lake valley. He passed brown fingers through them, testing the dryness, the softness of the core, and the composition. There were oats in them, a sure indication of a white man's mount. He nodded. He walked swiftly back to where the three white men stood smoking, waiting for Ahvote's report.

"Well?" demanded Matt Denton.

Ahvote leered a little. "Ahvote tell for whiskey drink," he said.

Matt hit Ahvote so hard his legs came up into the air as he fell. Matt Denton was a great hitter when no one was fighting back. Matt booted the Paiute in the side. "Goddamn you, breed!" he shouted. "Don't you bargain with me! Now, what did you find out?"

Ahvote touched the trickle of blood at the side of his mouth. "One man, three horses, and two burros pass. Later one man with a horse and burro. White men."

Matt looked at Vic. "What do you think?"

Vic shrugged. "The breed seems to know, all right."

"Someone with Hunter?" Matt asked.

Vic shook his head. "Not likely. He's a loner, or I miss my guess. Maybe someone else is following him."

"What makes you think so? It could be a chance traveler."

Vic grinned. "Going over there? At this time of the year? Only damned fools like Hunter and us would attempt it, or someone who's trying to join Hunter, or *find* him. "Give the breed a drink. He's earned it."

Matt shook his head. "I don't want him drinking now."

Vic walked to his horse and withdrew a bottle of rye. He pulled out the cork with his teeth. "Hold out your hands, Whiskey," he said.

"I said no," Matt said coldly.

Vic glanced back with cold, hard eyes. "I heard you. If you don't humor this bastard once in a while, he's liable to sneak out on us some night and leave us lost in this suburb of Hell. You're not using your head, Matt." He poured rye into the Paiute's cupped hands. Ahvote slurped it up so fast that some of it ran out of his palms and soaked his filthy shirt. "More, more, more!" he cried greedily.

Vic corked the bottle. "That should keep you alive," he said.

Cos looked toward the V notch of the eastern end of the pass. "I hear tell that's a helluva country over there. They say the Devil himself would have a rough time surviving."

Matt picked up the reins of his horse. "We'll go on, get some sleep this afternoon, and ride all night. I have a feeling Mister Hunter is going to have some visitors before too long."

Ahvote looked up at the blazing blue sky. Three buzzards were slowly wheeling high overhead. He trotted on. He halted, then waited for the three white men to catch up with him. He pointed down into a deep declivity. Vic looked, cursed, turned aside, and clapped his hand over his mouth, pinching his nostrils together to cut off the stench emanating from the declivity. A burro lay down there on its back. Its belly was so swollen that its legs stuck out like the stick legs of a clay model. One of the legs was twisted awkwardly. The burro's throat had been cut. The coagulated blood lay thick on the ground beneath its head. A mass of crawling, buzzing flies swarmed over the head and the blood, with others hovering in a dense cloud above them. The body moved, emitting a foul gas from the greatly distended belly.

Matt turned away. "Jesus," he murmured. "How long, Whiskey?"

"Not too long. Yesterday, maybe. Sun and heat make it look longer, but blood too fresh for much longer," Ahvote replied.

"Hunter?" Cos asked.

Vic had run backward about twenty-five feet upwind. He quickly rolled a cigarette and lit it to get the stench out of his nostrils. "Who else?" he asked around the cigarette.

Cos lumbered down into the hollow. He shoved the dusty rump of the burro up and to one side, disturbing the flies that rose in a dense cloud buzzing angrily. Cos pointed to the brand on the burro's flank. "That's Amos Wassell's brand," he said. "I know it for sure. There were some burros in the stable the night I buffaloed Hunter. They had this brand."

Vic looked at the breed. "Any water around here?" he asked. He felt that it was a downright foolish question.

Ahvote shrugged. He pointed out toward the dry lakebed shining with a dazzling whiteness under the sun's rays. "Not there." He pointed north. "River. Two days to get there." He pointed to the northwest toward a flat-topped mountain or mesa. "Waterhole. Sometimes there. Sometimes not."

Vic grunted. "Great. Sometimes water. Sometimes not."

Matt touched his dry lips with his fingertips. "Seasonal," he said.

Cos nodded. "And this ain't the season."

"We've got to cross that lakebed to get to the river," Vic said.

Ahvote showed fear on his usually impassive face. "No! No! Devil lake! People go out there. Days later footprints end nowhere. Not go on. Sink down into lakebed." He shook his head violently.

Vic studied him. "We could send you ahead," he suggested slyly. "You know. To test it out."

Ahvote shook his head.

Vic drew his Colt, flipped open the loading gate, and spun the cylinder to check the loads. He grinned at Ahvote. "I can *make* you go, breed," he said.

Ahvote shook his head. "You kill me first."

Matt looked at Vic. "He means it. Let him alone. Without him, we might not find any water at all."

Vic grinned again. "Just joshin', Matt."

"Well, forget it! That's an order!" Matt turned away.

Vic eyed Matt's back thoughtfully. His thin lips lifted in a sneer. "That's an *order*," he mimicked sotto voce.

Ahvote led the way into a narrow open area, skirting the western rim of the dry lakebed. The faint wind had died away altogether. The powdery alkali dust rose up about the men and animals, giving them a gray, ghostlike appearance. No one spoke.

Ash Mawson squatted in the shade of his horse on a promontory overlooking the vast empty terrain to the east dominated by the glaring white of the dry lakebed. Dust was rising along the near edge of the lake, heading in Ash's direction. Who would be traveling in that hellhole during the heat of the day, and especially in his direction? His field glasses picked out four men, four horses, and two burros veiled in a shroud of dust. He couldn't discern for certain who they were, but he could make a hell of a guess.

Ash led the horse and burro down the western side of the promontory and up a narrow canyon. He was not a religious man, in the true sense of the word, but there were times, such as now, when a mite of prayer wouldn't hurt. He prayed. The bay whinnied and broke into a trot. When Ash caught up with it, it was lapping up the water in a *tinaja* close to the side of the canyon. The water was covered with algae, there was a water skater o two, and a few feathers drifted on its surface. Animal droppings showed beyond the upper rim. Ash pushed back the algae and drank a little. He raised his face from the water. "Coyote tea," he grunted. He looked up quickly out of the corner of his left eye. "But it's *soooo* good, Lord! No offense!"

He worked fast. He filled one canteen. He placed his sweat-stained bandanna over the wide mouth of another canteen and strained the water from the first canteen through it. He filled all his canteens and hung them from his saddle. He eyed the pool. It was only about two inches deep, and much of it was silt and sludge with some soaked animal droppings apparent in it. Just about enough left for a round of drinks or two among the four men far down on the edge of the dry lakebed, and maybe enough for their animals. He didn't give a shit for the men, but he had sympathy for the animals.

Ash cut a chew and stowed it in his mouth. He carefully wiped out his faint tacks with a branch from a bush. He surveyed his work and nodded in satisfaction.

He led the bay and burro up the canyon.

CHAPTER 15

DAVE DROVE HIS PICKAX INTO THE ROCK FACE BEYOND where the vein had petered out. It was late afternoon of the second day since he had returned to the silver canyon. He felt sure there was nothing behind the rock face, but he hoped he might be able to pick up traces of the vein again. After a few minutes, he stopped working. The sweat dripped down his body. He could feel it greasing the inside of his boots. It was no use. It would be easier to remove the fill from some of the many narrow and crooked tunnels that wandered from one side to the other, rose steeply, then slanted down again. The tunnels ran off in all directions like an immense rabbit burrow. The area where three tunnels converged into a roughly hewn chamber was far behind him. The tunnel to the right had been where he'd found that tantalizing, short, and shallow vein of almost pure silver. He had probed and poked throughout the immediate area with no success in finding a continuation of the vein or even any signs of color. He had no idea how far into the mountain and how intricate the maze of tunnels was ahead of him. Possibly the Spaniards had found a chimney or chimneys of the silver ore that had been forced through a fissure by immense internal pressures when the mountain had been formed in prehistoric times. Perhaps the lode had faded out and the Spaniards had left nothing but the empty husk. *Or had they?*

He shaped a cigarette and lit it. The match flame wavered in that persistent and faint draft; the draft was always present in the mine, although he had never bothered to trace it to its source.

He returned to the silver vein and studied it again. If the main vein had indeed run out, why had they left this particular tempting little stretch of it, so easy to pry out of the virgin rock like an oyster out of its shell? It just didn't make sense.

Dave scratched in his beard. "Or *does* it?" he murmured.

He returned to where he had been working. He raised his lantern and squirmed his way through a narrow gap he had dug out earlier. Not much of the tunneling had been done through solid rock, but a great deal of it had pierced through a sort of conglomerate that threaded its devious way through the mass of the mountain. It was possible that at some time many millennia past parts of the mountain had been split and widely fissured, then filled with loose rock and sediment in another cataclysmic upheaval and distortion when the Earth was young and still forming itself. The passage of many years had compacted the looser material under the vast weight above.

He widened narrow places as he progressed. Now and again a loose piece would fall from the roof of the tunnel. He pushed his way through another narrow opening into a wider area. The lantern light reflected from something on the floor of the tunnel. He picked it up. It was a cat's eye. He narrowed his eyes. He had never been this far into the tunnel system and in order to get here he'd had to widen the openings to get through. A slender woman could easily have made it through, however. He searched the floor. Here and there he found spots of dried candlewax. Only the day before she had told him, "I haven't been near the mine. I'm afraid of it, Dave. I won't go in there unless you are with me."

He pocketed the cat's-eye. He moved cautiously along the narrow tunnel until he found several branches going off into the unknown. One of them had been filled with debris fallen from the roof. One ended up in a solid rock face. The third was partially blocked. It was getting late. He had been at it all day. The mine and its secrets could wait. It had been waiting a long time. It wouldn't disappear over-night.

Dave returned to the outer entrance. He had been so pleased to see Lila that he had put Denton and his *corrida* out of his mind. He should have known better. Still, Denton was not here. The canyon was the small world of Dave and Lila. Dave knew it couldn't last. But for the time being it made for some semblance of happiness, temporary though it was. He had begun to think of her as *his* woman. He wanted to dig out enough silver to please her. Once free of the canyon, he meant to lavish his love and wealth on her. At the moment, nothing else seemed to matter. Still, there was the matter of the cat's-eye. She *had* been probing into the mine.

It was dusk. He could see the faint hut light down the long slope of the branch canyon. She was singing again. He placed his Sharps rifle in the cache he had made for it out of sight of anyone in the tunnel, where he also kept Ash Mawson's Colt. There was a full canteen in there as well. He kept his own Colt down at the hut along with Mawson's Winchester. As the last resort, if forced to hole up in a tunnel, he'd have his Sharps. With it, he felt some-what smugly, that he could hold off a company of infantry, more likely, perhaps, a platoon.

Dave and Lila would have to clarify the future. "What future?" a voice whispered in his mind. He had no an-swer.

He stopped in the doorway to gaze at her, as he always did, savoring the moment when she would turn and look at him with those unfathomable eyes of hers.

She turned slowly, seeming to feel his presence. "How does it go, Dave?" she asked.

He shrugged. "There's a great deal of work to be done. The vein has petered out. The tunnel continues on. It might be dangerous to continue. There's quite a bit of fall in there. The Spaniards might have continued trying to pick up the vein. They usually gopher, following the vein, instead of drifting in and crosscutting. They might have gone on a ways, then given up. It might have been why they plugged the mine."

She studied him. "But the legend? Doesn't it tell of a vast lode?"

He smiled faintly. "After all, it *is* a legend, perhaps a myth."

"Legends have a basis of fact," she said quietly.

"It will be a lot of digging for one man. Months and months of work, perhaps."

"I'll help," she offered.

He looked at her soft hands. "It's no place for you. Yesterday I scouted around on the slopes above the mine and the top of the canyon wall. There are traces of side drifts and old shafts up there. The whole canyon side may be honeycombed with them. Of course, you haven't been into the mine any farther than I have." He paused and eyed her closely. She was not wearing her string of cat's-eyes, nor had he seen it since he returned.

She nodded. "That's right. You know I don't like it in there, and positively not alone. I wouldn't go up there alone if the whole place was solid silver."

He shaped two cigarettes, placed one between her lips, and lit it, looking full into those damnable eyes of hers. She was lying. He lit his cigarette. "I have been followed since I left Chloride. I didn't tell you up until now because I didn't want to frighten you."

"By whom?" she asked.

He shrugged. "Various people who knew I had brought ore samples in for assay. They know I left with a load of supplies. Even if they didn't intend to jump my claim, they'd still be interested in *where* I made the strike."

"But you did file, didn't you?"

"Yes," Dave lied. "It's legally my claim. They'll have to kill me to take it over."

"Don't talk like that!" she cried.

He looked out the side window toward the mine entrance, now veiled in darkness. "Sometimes I wonder if it's all worthwhile," he said quietly. "But then I have you and that must make it right."

She came to him and kissed him. "Yes, you have me," she agreed.

She placed the meal on the rock table, then sat down opposite him. She filled his tin plate and coffee cup.

"There *was* a trio of hardcases interested in me, or rather my claim," he said. "Names of Matt Denton, Cos Leach, and someone known only as Vic."

There was no expression on her face, but her right hand trembled a little as she placed it flat on the table.

Dave felt that he was baiting her, although that had not been his intention. "I'm sorry, Lila. I should have told you about them when I returned."

"Why didn't you?" she asked quietly.

"I was foolish enough to think that if I put them out of my mind that might be the end of them." He shook his head a little. "As if anyone could forget those three."

He told her of what had happened back in Chloride and of how he had outwitted them in his escape from the town and of his dangerous return by way of the barrens east of the mountains.

"Do you know if they followed you?" she asked.

"I saw some trail dust for a time, but there was no way of telling who it was. Few people are foolish enough to come into this country during this season. I'm one of them."

"And I'm another," she said quietly.

He studied her. "But that was not intentional, was it? You were heading for Stone's Ferry and probably California from there, weren't you?"

She nodded. "Why don't you ask me about the rest of it?"

"The fact that you're Matt Denton's wife?"

"Yes. Go on."

"It's the money belt, isn't it?"

"Yes. Go on," she repeated.

"It's none of my business," he said.

She shook her head. "I think it is, Dave."

Amiga brayed sharply. The echo died away.

She studied him. "You've changed. I noticed it when you came back. Despite your talk of making a fortune here and taking me from this place to lavish your wealth on me, I somehow can't believe you. Were you blind and foolish enough to think of me as a fairy princess who suddenly appeared out of nowhere into this godforsaken country to touch you with a fairy wand of pure silver so that we could live happily ever after?"

"You're sure about the silver?" he asked.

"Why do you ask? You said yourself it was a bonanza."

He shook his head. "Not in so many words. I was guessing, hoping against hope, and banking on those few ore samples I took to Chloride."

"But what about that vein of almost pure silver you found?"

"It petered out. I've not been able to pick it up again. Perhaps the Spaniards gutted the mountain of its silver. Miners are as superstitious as Indians. They would not take every ounce of silver with them. Leave some for the mountain, they'd say, lest we be cursed forever for taking it all."

"Yet there is always the possibility you might just be on the verge of a strike," she insisted.

Dave laughed shortly. "Perhaps. It's that hope that has kept me going all these profitless years."

She searched his face with her fine eyes. "Or is it the search alone that intrigues you?"

He looked away from her. She knew him better than he

had ever suspected. Why was she so certain there was a lode still within the mountain? She had been in there alone. The cat's-eye gave evidence to that.

"Dave?" she asked.

He looked back at her. "What makes you so sure there's still a fortune in silver within that damned rat's nest of a mountain? Do you have some secret method? Perhaps you used what the Mexicans call a *cartucho*. A metal cartridge filled with opium, poison, finely powdered black rock, and various other items. The treasure seeker leans over and swings the *cartucho* from his forehead and then follows the direction in which it oscillates the strongest. When he is over the treasure, the *cartucho* ceases its oscillations."

"You're making fun of me," she accused.

He could not resist. "Or possibly you use the *horqueta*, a fork fashioned from an animal scapula. The upright branch fits into a glass knob on top of which is a hole with screw threads. An assortment of hollow screws can be fitted into the threads. One screw is filled with gold dust, another with powdered silver, one with lead, another with copper or whichever mineral is being sought. The *horqueta* is grasped by the two lower prongs in the two hands, thumbs out and palms tuned upward. Then one follows the 'pull,' if there is any. There generally is, from the tales I've heard of its use. The *horqueta* will twist and strain in the direction of whichever mineral is the same as that in the hollow screw. It's as if it is drawn by a gigantic magnet. When the mineral is reached, the *horqueta* points straight down."

She stood up slowly. Her face was taut and white. "Damn you," she said quietly. "Why are you teasing me like this?"

Suddenly she raised her head and looked beyond Dave. Her eyes widened in disbelief. She slowly raised one hand to her throat. There was a crisp double-clicking of a hammer sear as a gun was cocked just behind Dave. "Go on, Hunter, tell her," Matt Denton said.

Dave turned his head a little. One window framed the broad, stupid face of Cos Leach. Then the rear window revealed the lean, bruised face of Vic.

"Nice and cosy in here," Denton said.

"It's me you're after, Denton," Dave said. "Let her alone."

Matt moved around to one side. He smiled crookedly. "Let *her* alone, he says. You hear that, Vic? Cos? Let her alone. Here the son of a bitch is, holed up with *my* wife and *my* money and sitting on top of a possible mother lode of silver, and he wants me to let her alone." He grinned. He looked at Lila. "Where's the money?" he demanded.

Lila removed a flat rock from the fireplace and pulled out the money belt. Dave had used only a small part of its contents in buying supplies in Chloride. She glanced at Dave, then threw the heavy belt with all her strength toward Denton's face. He involuntarily tuned his head to one side. His pistol swung away from Dave, who leaned to one side, then chopped his left hand down on Denton's pistol hand and hit him on the jaw with a right hook. Denton fell sideways. His Colt fired into the floor. Vic shouted as he scrambled through the window with a drawn Colt in his hand. Dave snatched up the coffeepot from the table and hurled it at Vic. The gunman turned sideways and raised his right arm to protect his face. It gave Dave just enough time to snatch up Denton's Colt and plunge toward the door. Cos was struggling to get his big frame through the small window. He withdrew as Dave dashed outside the hut. Dave met the big man rounding the side of the hut. Dave kicked Cos hard in the privates. Cos grunted and bent forward. Dave chopped down on the bulletlike head with the Colt's barrel. Vic fired from the doorway. The slug whispered just over Dave's head. Dave headed upslope in a try for the mine and his Sharps rifle. He rounded a ledge and glanced backward to check the pursuit. A dark figure rose from behind the ledge and thrust out a leg. Dave dropped the pistol as he fell over the leg but had sense enough to hit the ground with his right shoulder in a rolling fall. He got up on his knees, ready to run again. He looked up into the dark, expressionless face of an Indian who held Denton's Colt cocked and pointed right between Dave's eyes.

Vic came running. He looked down at Dave. "Move, you bastard, and I'll pin you to the ground with slugs! *Jeeesusss!* You haven't got enough sense to quit, have you?"

Dave shook his head. "Never got the hang of it, you bastard!"

Vic kicked him hard in the side. "Come up fighting," he urged with a thin smile.

"Don't kill him!" Denton yelled from the hut. "We aren't through with him yet!" He tuned back into the hut.

Cos lumbered through the darkness. He opened his big hands and spat into the palms. "Get outa the way, Vic. This time I want no fancy stuff from this son of a bitch. Stand up, *Mister* Hunter!"

Dave shook his head. "Your trainer, Mister Denton, doesn't want you to hurt me, you ugly bastard."

Cos opened his eyes wide in surprise.

Vic nodded. "He's right, Cos. Don't worry. Our time will come after Matt's through with him. Me first, of course."

Lila screamed sharply.

Dave started to get up. Vic booted him again. "Easy, Hunter. It's only Matt teaching that stuck-up wife of his not to run off with his bankroll and hole up with a tramp like you."

"Can't I rough him up a bit while Matt is busy?" Cos pleaded.

"We may need him. For a time . . . After that, no holds barred."

Cos nodded. "I guess you're right. You're smart, Vic."

Dave snorted. "That ain't hard with you around as an example. My little burro could make you look stupid."

Cos opened and then closed his mouth like a gasping fish. "I'll wait, like Vic says. It'll be worth the wait, all right."

Matt Denton came out to them. His face was set and cold. His eyes seemed almost reptilian in their unblinking stare. There was something odd about his expression, almost as though his face had been cut in half and then put back together somewhat askew.

"Cos, you go and get the horses and burros. I want you to water them," Denton ordered.

Cos spat. "Let Vic go."

"I'm telling *you!*" Denton snapped.

"Then let the gawddamned Paiute go then! That's *his* job, ain't it?"

Trouble in the camp, thought Dave. It might come in useful later when and if he made his play, providing, of course, he was still alive.

Denton looked at the Indian. "You go, Whiskey," he said.

The Paiute nodded. He started down the slope.

"Give me the gun first," Denton said quietly.

The Paiute handed it to him without a word and walked down toward the hut.

"He would have kept it, too," Vic said.

"Bad enough he's got a knife," Denton said.

Lila was repairing her ripped shirt as best she could. Matt had ripped it down around her waist in his anger. There was a red welt on her cheek where he had backhanded her. She would not cry. She looked up suddenly. The dark face of the Paiute looked in through a window. She covered her breasts with the shirt. She reached for her rifle that was leaning in a corner. Ahvote vanished like some demon into the night.

"Tie him up, Vic," Denton ordered, still outside. "Put

him in one of the other huts and make damned sure he can't escape.''

Dave was taken to the open-faced tool-and-blacksmith's hut. Cos brought a lariat. They tied Dave's wrists together behind his back, then looped the rope about his ankles. They drew up on the lariat until his back was bent like a bow, then lashed his ankles tightly together. They looped the running end though a rusted hook on the wall and pulled Dave's feet up until he was resting on his chest with his face hard against the floor.

Cos chuckled. ''Let's see you get outa that one, Hunter.'' He spat on the back of Dave's head.

Later, Dave could smell cooking food and heard the subdued conversation of the three men in the other hut. A slow fungus of cold and implacable hatred had begun to grow in his mind.

CHAPTER 16

AHVOTE SQUATTED BETWEEN THE TWIN PILLARS guarding the entrance to the silver canyon. He drank deeply from the bottle of rye he had taken from one of the saddlebags. He was in no hurry to lead the horses and burros back into the inner canyon. He drank again and wiped his mouth with the cuff of his filthy shirt. The canyon below him suddenly went out of focus and then snapped right back into sight again. Ahvote grinned foolishly.

Deep maroon thoughts flooded through his disordered mind. It was Ahvote who had led them to the waterhole at Table Mountain. It was he who had guided them to this canyon. Now they were probably through with him. They might kill him to save water and food. He let his thoughts slide backward into the canyon behind him. He thought of the woman in the hut. *Aieee!* She was just such a white woman as he had always wanted. And she had shot at him before. He knew just what sort of sweet revenge he'd like to take on her. . . .

The three white-eyes were mixed up in some affair of their own with the big white man they had come to find. It was none of his affair. He eyed the horses and burros. Four good horses. Three of them had full cantle and pommel packs. Fine rifles hung in the saddle scabbards. There was much whiskey in the saddlebags and on the burros. There was a lot of food and other items. He suddenly realized he was *rich*! There was no need to go back to the hut. He could be long gone in the trackless canyons before the white-eyes thought of looking for him.

There was another, more compelling reason for him to leave. The canyon was haunted. It had been so for many years, or so the storytellers of his tribe related. Since the Paiutes had no written history, their heritage was passed on orally from one generation to another; parts of the history might vary in some detail, but one that never did was the story of the haunted canyon. Now Ahvote was *in* it. As long as he was with the three white men, he had felt somewhat secure, for he felt they might have better medicine than he for combating haunts. Now he wasn't so sure.

Ahvote finally led the horses and burros on into the silver canyon. In the darkness before the coming of the moon, it was an eerie place. The dusk wind was still working its way through the mazes on all sides. The scant brush moved suggestively, rustling and scraping, as though night demons were in dark consultation about their plans. Perhaps they chuckled a little, for was it not Ahvote, an outcast from his tribe, who had dared to enter the forbidden canyon?

Ahvote drank, and drank again, trying to gain whiskey courage. He led the burros and horses to the darkly shadowed *tinaja*. He was rooting through one of the saddlebags for a reserve bottle of rye when he thought he heard something. He turned slowly. The moon was a faint glow along the rimrock. The wind moaned softly. The shadows seemed to close in on Ahvote. He got the bottle of rye. He debated mentally about taking a rifle, but if the white men caught him with it . . . They had no further need for him. He had led them right to the canyon where the man who shot and killed, unseen, at half a mile and the *woman* were hidden. The *woman* . . .

He put his hand on the smooth walnut stock of one of the fine repeaters. With such a rifle that shot many times without reloading, he could be a king among his people.

A faint, ever-so-faint moaning sound came to Ahvote.

The hairs prickled on the back of his neck. He turned slowly. He looked up at the rimrock. There was a quick movement up there, so quick he wasn't sure if he had actually seen anything.

The moan came again.

Ahvote stepped back from the horse.

Then he saw it. A human figure poised right at the very edge of the canyon rim with its arms raised high above its head. A fearful moaning drifted on the night wind. Then, behind Ahvote, something splashed in the *tinaja*, sending up a shower of water, some of which struck his back and legs.

That was too much.

Ahvote took off down the slope at breakneck speed, with a half-empty rye bottle in one hand and a full one in the other. He gained speed so fast he was almost airborne, hurdling brush and rocks in championship form. he reached the bottom of the slope.

"Who the hell is that?" Cos Leach roared from near the hut.

There was no answer from Ahvote. He was gone through the clinging shadows racing for the exit of the canyon.

"What is it, Cos?" Matt Denton asked from the hut doorway.

"Damned if I know, boss!"

"Is that damned breed back with the horses yet? It wasn't my idea to send him, anyway. Go look! Pronto!"

"I ain't so sure I want to go down there alone," Cos blurted out.

"Get moving!" Denton snapped.

Vic came out, picking his teeth with a splinter. "I'll go with the big baby," he offered.

"Baby? Shit!" roared Cos.

Vic grinned. "Not bad. Baby shit! Hawww!"

They walked through the darkness toward the *tinaja*.

The horses and burros were still drinking. There was no sign of Ahvote.

"We ought to get rid of that drunken breed," Cos growled. "He ain't no use to us now anyways."

Vic shook his head. He shaped a cigarette and passed the makings to Cos. "All the same, we'll need him to guide us out of here when we're ready to go. None of us know the way."

"Hunter might, Vic."

Vic lit up. The flare of the match revealed his lean, dark face. "What makes you think we're going to let him ever get out of here?"

Cos nodded. "How are we goin' to work out this deal, Vic?"

"Meaning?"

"We'll have to get supplies in, dependin', of course, on what we find in here. We'll have to get supplies and round up labor. I ain't no miner and neither are you, and I'll be goddamned if I'll work in this hellhole with a pick and singlejack. I just want to see pay dirt and lots of it, with me standin' around tallying up the profits."

"You've got a good point there," Vic agreed.

A faint wailing cry drifted over the canyon. It sounded like a creature in torment, hopelessly trying to free itself from Hell.

Cos dropped his cigarette and whirled toward the sound, while lowering his hand to the butt of his holstered Colt. "What the hell was that?" he demanded.

"Shit! I ain't heard no coyote or mountain lion ever sound like that."

"All right, then! What do *you* think it was?"

Cos shook his head. "I ain't sure . . ."

Vic flipped away his cigarette and rolled another, shaking his head. Cos was as superstitious as a Paiute.

It was very quiet. Now and again one of the horses stamped a hoof.

Cos took the makings and rolled another cigarette. He put it between his lips. He scratched a match on his belt buckle and held the flame to the tip of his cigarette.

The haunting cry came again, drifting from across the canyon and dying away faintly.

Cos was poised, match to cigarette tip. His eyes widened. He stared across the main canyon.

Vic scanned the canyon rim. He wasn't so sure himself now.

"Goddamn!" Cos grunted. The match flame had seared his fingers. He dropped both match and cigarette.

Dave looked across the canyon from the hut where he was bound to the wall hook. The moonlight picked out each detail of the canyon rim in sharp detail—serrated and stippled with coarse growths of strange and exotic shapes, tortured always by the strong winds that blew down the canyon with the coming of dusk, then reversed at dawn. There was no sign of life or movement up there now. It was like an etching from the hand of a master.

Matt Denton came across to the *tinaja*. "Who's making that noise?" he demanded.

"Ain't us," Vic said.

Cos looked at Matt. "Ghost," he whispered.

"You damned fool! It's the wind," Matt said.

"There *ain't* no wind," ·Cos said in a low voice.

"Animal, then!" Matt snapped. "Right, Vic?"

Vic was still scanning the rim.

"Vic?" Matt repeated.

Vic looked at him. "I don't know."

The cry came again, rising and falling, an eerie ululation as though a corpse had come back to life and was crying from the grave. It died away far down the main canyon.

Silence came in again on little cat feet.

"It's that damned Whiskey," said Matt.

Vic shook his head. "How could he get up there? It would take half a day to climb there."

Matt walked to the hut where Dave was imprisoned. "You hear that?" he asked.

Dave nodded.

"What is it? Or who is it?"

Dave shrugged. "I haven't got any idea."

"Maybe you heard it before?"

Dave shook his head. "No."

"Maybe you know what it is?"

Dave couldn't help it. He saw Cos and Vic coming toward the hut. "The place is said to be haunted, Denton. The Paiutes, Mohaves, and Hualpais won't come into Hell's Forty Acres at all if they can help it."

Denton eyed him closely. "You believe it?"

Cos's mouth hung open; his eyes were fixed on Dave.

Dave yawned. "I've been in the remote parts of the Southwest and Sonora long enough to believe. There are a great many things for which there is no explanation. I know that the Spaniards always left a *patrón* somewhere around their mines when they hid them after they had worked them for a time."

"Bullshit!" Vic said dryly.

"What's a *patrón?*" demanded Cos. He came closer, glancing furtively over his shoulder as he did so.

"A ghostly guardian," Dave quietly replied, *very* quietly. "The Spaniards would kill someone, usually an Indian slave or a *péon* laborer, and leave the corpse in the mine so that its spirit would guard against intruders. The Jesuits always put a curse on their mines. No Indian or Mexican in his right mind would go anywhere near such a mine."

It was very still again.

Dave gave them a little time to think. "The mine here was founded by Spaniards about one hundred fifty years ago or so. They had a Jesuit priest with them. A Father José Francis Dominguez. He never came back." Dave looked up at the rim. "They might have left him here as a *patrón*. That would make it doubly haunted. A vengeful Jesuit ghost would be something to meet up with . . ." He paused meaningfully. *"Maybe that's him up there now . . ."*

"You're loco!" snapped Denton. He turned. "Let's get

some rest. We'll have to set a guard. We've got a big, tough day ahead of us. Who'll take first guard?''

''Me,'' replied Cos. He jerked a thumb toward the far side of the canyon. ''I can't sleep with *that* goin' on.''

''I'll sleep with Lila,'' Denton said. ''Vic, you can find a place in one of the other huts.'' He walked toward the hut.

Cos watched him. ''I ain't so sure I trust him no more.''

Vic yawned. ''I never have, and I trust him a helluva lot less now that we're practically sitting on a pile of silver.'' He walked to his gear piled near the *tinaja*, took a blanket, and placed it in a hollow over a mat of vegetation. He unbuckled his cartridge belt, laid his Winchester beside himself, and then pulled off his boots. He lay down, tilted his hat over his eyes, and lay still. In a little while, he was asleep.

Cos sat with his back against a boulder between the hut where Lila and her husband were and the open-faced shop where Dave was cruelly bound. Cos kept his Winchester across his lap. Now and then he chewed on his dirty fingernails.

''Nervous?'' Dave called out.

''Go to hell!'' Cos snapped. He waited a spell, then looked toward Dave. ''Are you sure about them *patróns*?'' he asked nervously.

Dave nodded. ''Positive.''

''You know all about them things, eh?''

''A lifetime study, Cos.''

Cos ruminated. He looked again at Dave. ''Mebbe I'd better cut you down from that hook.''

''It would be nice.''

''No tricks now!'' Cos warned.

Dave shook his head. ''What could I do? Besides, you keep me strung up like this and by morning I'd be crippled and I couldn't do any of your dirty work around here.''

Cos cut him down from the hook and loosened the bonds about his wrists and ankles a little. ''Sorta give me a hand,

eh, Hunter? You know, in case anything strange happens
tonight.''

''A pleasure,'' Dave said.

Dave watched the big man return to his boulder. Cos
was the wholly physical type; a man with bobcat bristles
on his belly, who as a rule could handle anything physical
or material. The unknown was simply too much for his
low mental capacity.

Hours later, as the moon waned, a faint wind began to
whisper down the canyon. The brush moved gently, almost
imperceptibly, as the breeze passed through it. It was almost as though someone or something was whispering in
an unintelligible voice and was soon joined by others, as
though a supernatural council was being held.

The eerie, haunting cry seemed to have been stilled.

When darkness came, Cos nodded.

Dave fell asleep. Once during the night he awoke and
looked toward the *tinaja*. The animals seemed nervous.
They stamped their hoofs and whinnied softly. A horse
snorted hard.

Dave narrowed his eyes. He couldn't see or hear anything at the waterhole, but still he felt as though something
or somebody was there. He dozed off again, only to raise
his head quickly as he heard the faint splashing of water.
Then it was quiet again. Perhaps it had been a coyote. . . .

CHAPTER 17

DAVE PLODDED UP THE LONG SLOPE TOWARD THE MINE entrance. The morning sun was already stoking up the canyon. His three captors followed him closely. Dave's wrists were still tied behind him. He stumbled. Cos poked him hard over the kidneys with the muzzle of his rifle.

Dave looked back into Cos's stupid face. "I know the way, you bastard," he growled.

Cos grinned. "Fussy, ain't you?"

"A real prima donna," agreed Vic.

"What the hell is that, Vic?" asked Cos.

"One of them fellas in the circus wearin' tights who walks on a wire without a net under him."

"Oh, I get it," Cos said.

"Cut him loose," Matt ordered as they reached the mine.

Dave lighted the lantern. His Sharps was right behind him, close to a pit prop and partially concealed by another prop leaning against the first prop.

"Lead the way," Matt ordered. "No tricks."

Dave led the way to where the vein had petered out. The almost solid silver still embedded in the wall shone softly in the lantern light. Vic whistled softly. "Whyn't you dig it out?" he asked.

"There isn't that much value in there," Dave replied.

"You could have grubstaked yourself with it," Cos said.

"He didn't have to," Vic said. "He had Matt's money belt for that." He grinned.

Denton ignored him. "How far in does it go?" he asked.

Dave shrugged. "I've not been able to pick it up again. It might be all there is. It might have been a chimney, but it's hard to tell without further exploration and a helluva lot of digging."

"What the hell is a chimney?" Cos asked.

"Silver forced by pressure into a fissure. It could go up or down for hundreds of feet, depending upon which direction the pressure came from," Dave said.

"I always thought you just chopped out the silver in chunks from the veins like this one," Vic said.

Matt looked sideways at Dave. "They've found silver like that down in Mexico, eh, Hunter?"

Dave nodded. "Some of those chunks were a full load for one burro. In some areas they dug out so much they shoed their burros and donkeys with it. Iron was harder to get than silver."

Vic dug at the vein with his sheath knife. "Helluva country for mining here. Little water. Too much heat. A long ways to go to a smelter if you haven't got one here, unless you can dig it out in chunks. Then we've probably got Paiutes hanging around out there, and once this strike is known, there'll be claim jumpers to boot."

"You can always leave," Denton suggested.

Vic examined the chunk of silver he had cut out. "I didn't say I was planning to leave. I just said it would be a tough job working this mine."

"How'd you figure on working this, Hunter?" Denton asked.

Dave felt he might as well tell them. He didn't want to antagonize them, not just yet, anyway. They all had short fuses, particularly Vic, and Dave knew he'd have to play it careful. The odds against him were immense. He couldn't make mistakes. "I've done only a little exploring beyond this point. The best way would be to drift and crosscut until the vein can be picked up again, that is, if there *is* a further vein."

"Helluva lot of diggin' for one man," Vic said.

Cos grinned. "He's good at it. Lookit all the diggin' he done to clear out that fill dumped outside. Regular ol' gopher, he is."

Denton raised the lantern. He looked up one of the branch tunnels. "Let's get on," he said. "Hunter, you go first."

Here and there along the way soil sifted down from the ceiling, shaken loose by the impact of their boots on the tunnel floor. They passed the place where Dave had found Lila's cat's-eye. They stopped where an almost complete collapse had blocked the tunnel except for a narrow slotlike opening close to the ceiling. Dave stopped. The others were closely scanning the walls for traces of ore. He knew they were looking for another vein sticking out from the sides, ready to be dug out in almost pure form.

"You won't find anything," Dave advised them.

"You've been a miner," Denton said. "Where would the vein start in again?"

Dave shrugged. "Who knows? There's a whole damned mountain sitting on top of us and stretching miles ahead of us, to each side and up and down."

"Great," Vic murmured.

"It's one of the joys of prospecting," Dave continued. "There's always the hope that somewhere, just a few feet ahead, perhaps even inches or an inch, lies the vein."

"And you never penetrated those feet or inches?" Vic asked.

Dave shook his head. "Do I look like it?"

"Yet you keep on. Why?" Vic asked curiously.

"Perhaps it's the quest and not the fulfillment that leads me on," Dave replied quietly.

Cos shook his bulletlike head. "You're plumb loco!"

Denton handed Dave the pickax and shovel that he had left there upon quitting work. Denton jerked a thumb toward the fill. "Start questing. Cos, you stand first guard.

Vic will relieve you in a few hours. Keep the son of a bitch at it, you hear?''

The footfalls of Denton and Vic died away in the tunnel.

Cos sat down on a broken pit pop. "Start diggin', Hunter,'' he ordered.

Dave attacked the fill. Long and hard hours passed. Outwardly, he was calm. Inwardly, he had begun to hate. Hatred was not a part of his being. He had not hated the Rebels against whom he had fought and whom he had killed for four years. He had not hated the hostile Indians who had been a constant danger during his time spent buffalo hunting or those who had endangered his life during his scouting and later his prospecting days. He didn't like them, of course, but he could not find it within himself to *hate* them. He did not share the bitter hatred of the Americans for the Mexicans. He felt the same way toward the Mexicans as he did his fellow Americans. Some he liked; others he did not. Hate had never entered his mind in their respect. But something akin to hatred had come into his mind regarding Lila. She could have told him more about herself before he left for Chloride and walked right into the hands of Denton and his bully boys. Forewarned is forearmed. That old saw rankled in his mind. She had gulled him to a fare-thee-well. She had accepted him back as though she were innocent of any wrongdoing, while Dave, the poor, damned fool who had possibly made the first big strike in his years of prospecting, had now lost that strike and her as well, not that it mattered anymore. Beyond that, Dave knew with certainty that when Denton was though with him it would be the end of his life.

They heard light footfalls in the tunnel and then saw the wavering yellowish light of a lantern. Lila appeared. She carried a coffeepot and a tin plate of beans and hard bead.

"That for me?" demanded Cos. "It ain't hardly a bite for a man my size."

She shook her head. "It's for him," she replied.

"What about me?" Cos demanded.

"Vic is coming soon to relieve you," she said.

Dave leaned against a pit prop. Sweat streamed down his torso and soaked into his drawers and trousers. His breathing was short and heavy in the thick air. He looked directly into those unfathomable eyes of hers. They told him nothing. She held out the food to him. He turned away from her and started working again.

"Damned fool," Cos said. "That's good food!"

"All food is good to you, you fat bastard. You eat it," Dave said over his shoulder.

"Why, you . . . !" Cos started toward Dave with balled fists.

Dave turned quickly with one of the pick points a foot away from Cos's sweating face. The big man dropped his hand to his Colt. Dave smiled thinly. "Let's see fast you are compared to Vic," he suggested.

"He's got you there, Cos," Vic said from behind them. "You put a hole in his belly with a .44 and he'll likely have that pick point stickin' out the back of your thick head."

Cos backed away slowly.

Vic scratched the side of his lean face. "Damned little progress for half a day's work," he suggested.

Dave turned a little toward him with the pick held steady in his big hands. "Maybe you'd like to try," he suggested.

Vic smiled a little. "It ain't for me. Get going." He did not take his eyes from Dave's, waiting for that expression he knew so well, telegraphing a sudden, perhaps deadly move.

Lila handed the food to Cos and vanished down the tunnel.

Cos wolfed down the beans and bread.

"Leave the coffee for me and the workin' man there, Cos," Vic suggested.

Cos turned to leave the area. He shot a murderous glance back at Dave. "Sonuvabitch," he growled.

Dave swung from the hips and slammed the pick point into the tunnel wall a few feet from Cos's startled face. Cos vanished down the tunnel.

Vic studied Dave. "Man," he said quietly, "you like to trifle with sudden death, don't you?"

Dave shrugged. "That's been the story of my life since 'sixty-one." He half grinned. "Besides, none of you are going to kill good ol' Dave yet, or you'll have to do the digging yourselves."

"And after that?" Vic asked.

The two hardcase men eyed each other for a moment, then Dave turned and attacked the fill. Both of them knew the answer without speaking.

Three days passed with monotonous regularity. It was all the same to Dave. He hardly ever saw daylight. Up at first sign of the false dawn and into the mine; out of the mine at dusk. Time was lost in digging into a pair of blind tunnels, one on each side of the main tunnel, ending against blank solid faces marked by Spanish picks. There had been ore in the tunnels, but the Spaniards had dug most of it out, leaving nothing but the shell, so to speak. There was still a little ore in various walls. Dave had to sack it and drag it to the mouth of the main tunnel. It was getting to be quite a sizable pile, but certainly nothing exceptional in quality. Dave was getting more convinced that the Spaniards had cleaned out the silver, but there was still that puzzling shot vein he had discovered his first time into the tunnel. The fever was on Denton and his two bully boys. Perhaps one more pickax stroke would reveal another vein.

Another thing that puzzled Dave was the presence of Captain Melgosa's remains. Why had the Spaniard returned to this remote and dangerous hellhole to meet his likely death at the hands of a Paiute?

"Take a breather, Hunter," Vic said one afternoon.

Dave dropped his pickax. He dashed the sweat from his eyes and sat down on the floor with his back against the wall.

Vic tossed Dave the makings. "You're holding out real well."

Dave shaped a quirly. "None of you will get rich this way." He tossed the makings back to Vic.

Vic rolled a cigarette. "You were planning to do it."

Dave lit up. "Yeah, but I'm a loner. Some men would call me a dreamer. Besides, I never had to worry about a partner or partners if I did make a strike."

"What does that mean?" Vic eyed Dave closely over the flare of the match as he lit the cigarette.

A faint wraith of smoke hung about Dave's sweating lean face. "You're a great group, Vic. I think you three trust each other about as much as I trust all three of you together."

Vic spat. "Cos is as stupid as they come."

"Matt isn't."

"I can take care of Matt when the time comes."

Dave couldn't help but grin. "All three of you have to stick together until you can figure out a way to screw each other. Then you've got to find your way out of Hell's Forty Aces."

"The Paiute is still out there. He won't leave as long as we give him whiskey."

Dave nodded. "Hating your guts. I don't think any of you know how a Paiute, or any other Indian for that matter, can *hate*. But you'll never know. The word for them is impassive. God alone knows what's going on inside his dark mind."

"What are you diving at?"

"You're the only one of the bunch that seems to have any real sense. Denton is too involved with himself and his 'me first' principle. You and Cos, and Lila, too, are only a means to his ends. Cos, as you said, is as stupid as they come.''

Vic studied him. "Are you working toward some kind of a deal between us?"

Dave studied Vic in turn. Vic was almost as impassive as an Indian. One never quite knew where he stood with Vic.

"Maybe me and you?" Vic asked quietly. "Is that it?"

"You're doing the talking."

Vic slowly lowered his right hand to his six-shooter. He withdrew the Colt, raised it, cocking it at the same time, and pointed it squarely at Dave's face. "You've had your break. Get back to work. I trust you a helluva lot less than I do either one of them, and that damned woman least of all. She screwed Matt out of his money. She screwed you into believing she was something other than she was. Why, you damned fool, I believe you thought she was in love with you. You're not the first. She's two-timed Matt many the time. I *know* . . ."

Dave stood up. "You?" he asked. He thought he knew the answer already.

Vic just grinned.

Hours later, just after dusk, Dave staggered out of the mine carrying a sack of ore on his back. He swung it down to the ground and nearly fell over it, so tired was he from the constant hard labor.

"There's plenty more where that came from," Vic said. "Get goin', Hunter."

"Hold it!" Matt called from downslope. "We're wasting our time that way, Vic. Lila has something to show us. She's come to her senses at last. We've made a deal." Lila and Cos followed him up the slope.

Dave looked at Lila. She would not meet his gaze. The memory of finding the cat's-eye in the mine came back, along with the spots of candle grease. She had made some sort of deal with her husband, probably to protect herself. In any case, Dave was sure it boded no good for him.

"Lead the way with the lantern, Hunter," Vic ordered.

Matt laughed. "Now she'll show you what a sucker she made out of you, Hunter."

They halted this side of the original fill. Lila pointed to a narrow side tunnel the entrance of which was partially concealed by a heap of fill and some pit props leaning against it. Dave cleared the way. He had been partway into the tunnel. There had been no trace of ore. It ended in a blank wall whose base was half-covered by a heap of earth and broken rock mingled with long rotted leather *aparejos* the miners had used to carry ore from the mine.

Lila pointed at the blank wall. "There," she said quietly.

"Dig, Hunter!" Matt ordered.

Dave looked closely at the wall. The natural-looking surface had been closed off by what looked like roughly squared-off rock. He scraped it with his spade. There was no doubt about it! The wall was man-made! Dave reached for his pickax.

"Wait," Lila said.

She came close to Dave and pointed to a rock in the center of the wall. "That's loose," she said. "It keys in several more."

Dave looked sideways at her. "And you weren't in here when I was gone?"

She tuned away without a word.

"Get it out!" Matt snapped.

Dave dug powerful fingers in around the rock and was quite surprised to find that it came out easily. Lila was right. Enough of the rocks came out as well so that a hole roughly two and a half feet square appeared. Dave looked back at Denton.

"Get out of the way!" Denton said. He took the lantern and walked to the opening.

"Be careful," Dave said dryly.

Matt looked at him. "What the hell do you mean?"

Dave shrugged. "The Spaniards had nasty ways of protecting their treasures."

Matt handed him the lantern. "Then you look."

Dave took the lantern. He rested his left hand on the bottom of the opening, then pushed his head and torso through with the lantern held outstretched. The air was dead. Dave coughed in the thin dust. Gradually his eyes focused. "Jesus," he murmured.

"What is it?" Matt demanded.

The yellowish light had fallen on a grinning skull lying on the floor, staring eyelessly at Dave. The skeleton was covered with what looked like a rumpled black blanket, in reality a robe, thickly furred with dust. A cord was knotted around the middle. Skeletal hands were at each side, and bony feet encased in worn leather sandals protruded from the bottom. A large silver cross had once been suspended about his neck.

"Well, what the hell is that matter?" demanded Denton.

Dave looked back over his shoulder. *"Patrón,"* he said quietly. "The Jesuit priest."

"Then there has to be silver in there!"

Dave looked at Lila. She nodded. She had evidently been in there already.

Denton poked Dave hard in the middle of the back with his thumb. "Go on! Go on!" he ordered.

Dave drew himself back from the hole. He held Denton with icy eyes. "You poke me like that again, you son of a bitch, and gun or no gun, I'll break your goddamned jaw!" he stated flatly. He turned away from the startled Denton and pushed himself farther into the opening. He placed the lantern on the floor and pulled himself through. Then he stood up and reached for the lantern.

"Be careful, Dave!" Lila said abruptly.

Something rattled dryly right at Dave's feet and then

he heard, seemingly far below, a pattering and splashing. He slowly held out the lantern. There was a pit only six inches from his feet. He kicked a rock over the edge. It seemed an interminably long time before he heard the faint splash.

"What's in there?" cried Denton.

Dave looked back at him through the opening. "Why don't you come on in and look for yourself?"

Vic drew his Colt and cocked it. "Get on with it," he ordered.

Dave skirted the open shaft and the skeleton. He held the lantern high. The light shone on a large pile of what looked like billets of wood, dull and covered with thick dust. He picked up one of them and hefted it. It weighed about twenty pounds. There was no doubt in his mind. He was in Melgosa's treasure vault!

They came carefully into the vault. Dave kicked at the pile of ingots. "There it is," he said quietly.

Matt Denton drew out his clasp knife. He opened out a blade and shaved off a spiraling strip. The cut showed brightly. His eyes widened. "Pure solid silver," he murmured. "A fortune!" He looked at Dave. "How is it you didn't know about this?"

Dave shrugged. "Ask you wife, Denton. She seems to know more about this mine than you or I do."

Lila turned on her heel, skirted the shaft and climbed back through the hole. They heard her heels tap-tapping off into the distance.

Vic grinned. "You lost everything, Hunter. The woman *and* the silver."

Matt shook his head. "He never had either one. She could have kept her mouth shut about the silver and no one would have been the wiser. But she *didn't*! She told *me*. She's still *my* woman."

Vic was counting the bars. "Christ," he said softly. "Even a three-way split will make us kings."

"Four-way split," Matt corrected. "Lila gets a share."

Vic stood up. "What the hell do you mean?"

"She found it. She told me. She's entitled to it."

"I'll be a son of a bitch! That means the two of you will have a full half share, while me and Cos get a quarter each."

Dave leaned wearily against the wall. "You can always shoot him in the back, Vic, then you'll have a full half all to yourself."

Vic looked at him coldly. "You talk too damned much."

Dave shrugged. "I know," he agreed. He scratched in his short beard. "But sometimes I'm *right.*"

Matt and Vic looked at each other. The same thought was in their minds—get rid of Cos first, then Matt could get rid of Vic, or Vic could get rid of Matt and Lila. It is that way with treasure. There is a curse on most lost treasures. There could be a horrendous curse on the treasure of the silver canyon, what with a priest for a *patrón.*

Vic shrugged. "All right, Matt. It's foolish to talk about it. By God, like I said before—a split will make us kings."

Dave wiped the sweat from his face. "And a *queen,*" he suggested quietly.

They said nothing.

No time was wasted. Dave was put to work. Props were crisscrossed over the shaft after the *patrón* was unceremoniously dumped into it. Dave surreptitiously saved the cross. He broke completely through the wall on Denton's orders.

Cos came into the vault. His eyes bugged out when he saw the pile of ingots. "We gotta get this stuff outa here. Can't get a burro in this far to haul it out, though."

Vic grinned. "We've got a real-live two-legged jackass right here in Hunter. He can haul it to where we get the burros in."

They rigged slings and bags for Dave's shoulders. The bags were loaded. Dave staggered through the rabbit warren of tunnels, scraping his shoulders against the rough sides, bumping his head on the low ceiling, at times forced to bend from the waist to get through the narrower places. They drove him on, hour after hour, so obsessed were they with the treasure fever for which there is no known cure.

When the last of the ingots were outside, the moon was long gone. Dave fell flat on the ground. His lungs burned. His heart thudded against his rib cage. His temples pounded.

"We can take it to Stone's Ferry," Denton said. "Then by steamer down to Yuma and get it into a California bank."

"By way of the gulf to San Francisco?" Vic asked.

"Too dangerous. We'd be passing through Mexican waters until we reached the Pacific. We can freight it from Yuma to the coast, then by ship to Frisco."

Cos scratched his crotch. "First we got to get to Stone's Ferry. Ain't none of us know the way there from here exceptin' maybe Hunter."

Vic shook his head. "We can't trust him."

"The Paiute is our best bet," Denton put in.

So it was. They found Ahvote outside the great pillars. He was in bad shape. "Ahvote hungry. Ahvote thirsty for whiskey. I help you. Head hurt. No feel good. Want whiskey."

"It's a wonder the son of a bitch is still alive," Cos said. "Livin' out there."

Vic shrugged. "You can't kill 'em. They can live off a country where a white man'd starve."

"Devil in head. Ahvote need whiskey," Ahvote pleaded.

Denton squatted beside him, wrinkling his nose at the stench. "You lead us to Stone's Ferry, you understand. You can have anything you want when we get there. You can have the horses and burros when we get on the steamer and maybe a gun or two. The rest of the whiskey. I want to pull out of here long before dawn. We can travel while it's cooler. We'll load the horses land the burros right away. You and Cos, Vic.''

Cos and Vic went for the animals.

''You'd think he owned all that silver,'' complained Cos. ''The way he orders us about.''

The Paiute dog-trailed after Denton as the white man returned to the pile of silver ingots. Dave lay asleep near the mine entrance. He awoke when he heard them coming and feigned sleep. He heard the two of them talking in low voices.

Ahvote's eyes widened. ''You mean all for *myself*?''

Denton nodded. ''I promise.''

Ahvote grinned. ''Ah! Yes! Okay, okay, okay. Ahvote make deal. We shake on that.'' He extended a dirty hand, gripped Denton's hand, and solemnly pumped it up and down as he had seen white men do when they made a deal.

CHAPTER 18

THE THREE BURROS, COUNTING AMIGA, AND TWO OF the horses were loaded with some supplies and the heavy ingots. The big canteens were filled. By the time the dawn was a pewter-colored suggestion in the eastern sky, they were ready to leave. There was one more problem to solve—the fate of Dave Hunter.

"Do you think we got it all?" Vic asked Matt.

Matt nodded. "There may be more in that mountain, but we're in no position to get it out. It isn't an area where successful mining can be carried out. Not at present, in any case. We've got plenty."

"Especially you and your wife," Vic said dryly.

Denton ignored him. "We can always come back someday when conditions might be better."

"I still think there's a helluva lot more silver in that damned mountain," said Cos. "We just gonna walk away from it and let Hunter or someone else get at it? It's ours now, ain't it?"

Denton nodded. "There's a way we can stop Hunter and anyone else working it. There's another angle, too. I don't like the idea of him trailing us. He's a fighter. A real bulldog of a man. Once he gets his teeth into something, that's it."

"I ain't worried about him," blustered Cos.

"Matt is right," Vic said.

Cos snorted. "You afraid of him?" he demanded.

Vic shook his head. "Not as long as I can face him.

Cos, you're not too bright. You don't ever underestimate a man like him.''

"So, what do we do about him?" Cos asked in puzzlement.

Matt looked toward the mine. "The Spaniards left a *patrón*, didn't they? Hunter brought in blasting powder. He lost some of it, but saved four cans. Enough to blow up that mine entrance and bring a good part of the mountain down to cover it." He smiled thinly. Hunter should make one hell of a *patrón*, boys, don't you think?''

Dave was taken from his prison hut and marched up the slope to the mine. His hands were lashed behind him. Vic marched him back into the tunnel. They reached a turn in the shaft. Vic drew his Colt. The two diamond-hard men stood facing each other eye-to-eye. There was no fear apparent in the eyes of one or pity in the eyes of the other.

"You got anything to say?" Vic asked.

Dave shrugged. "What's to say?" he asked.

They could hear the muffled voices of Matt and Cos. "Light it quick, Cos," Matt ordered clearly.

Vic's saturnine face showed suspicion. He whirled and ran full-tilt toward the entrance. "Damn you to hell, you dirty double-crossers!" he yelled furiously.

Dave ran awkwardly after Vic. He saw the mouth of the tunnel. Vic was almost out of sight. A bright spot of flaring fire raced along the ground toward the entrance. The light reflected from the shiny red-painted surfaces of two cans of Kepauno Giant blasting powder. Dave whirled. There was no time to make the entrance. He ran back into the tunnel. He fell forward, got back on his feet, and then turned to look back. The blast of the explosion thudded against his eardrums. He saw just for an instant an incandescent wall of intense light, and then a mass of hot air and gas struck him. He sank into Stygian blackness and knew nothing more.

* * *

The shattering roar of the explosion bounced back and forth in the canyons and then rumbled sullenly away as though some angry giant was slamming smaller and smaller doors in a vast, empty house. A column of dust and smoke rose high in the air. Rocks cascaded down the steep slopes from high above the mine entrance and buried it under hundreds of tons.

"Damn you, Cos! You used too much!" Matt shouted. "It'll take months to dig through that again!"

Cos shrugged. "How the hell did I know? I ain't no expert."

Vic came stalking down the slope with his Colt in his hand.

Cos withdrew his Winchester from its saddle scabbard and walked around to the other side of his horse. He levered a round into the chamber, rested the rifle on the saddle, and sighted it on Vic.

Vic was no fool. "Why didn't you warn me?" he asked coldly.

Matt shook his head. "The fuse burned faster than we expected."

Vic looked at Cos. He knew the big man would shoot him the instant he made a wrong move. He'd have to play their game until his chance came. He holstered his Colt.

"What about Hunter?" Cos asked. He did not move his rifle.

Vic jerked his head back toward the mine. "There's a new *patrón* in there."

"Alive or dead?" Matt asked.

Vic shrugged. "It doesn't make any difference now, does it?"

Lila came swiftly up the slope. "Where is Dave Hunter?" she asked.

"Lead out, Cos," Matt ordered.

"Matt!" Lila cried. *"Where is Dave Hunter?"*

"Get on your horse," Matt said.

She stared disbelievingly at him. "But we made a deal!

You said if I showed you the silver cache I had found while he was gone, you'd let him go."

Matt shook his head. "You think I'm fool enough to let that cold-eyed killer loose on our trail? He'd have hunted us down if he had to crawl across Hell on his bare belly."

"But you *promised*!"

He studied her. "You think he would have felt any differently toward you if we *had* turned him lose?"

"Then you never told him of the deal I made for his life?"

Matt shook his head. "Besides, you're still my wife. *Remember?*"

"How can I ever forget *that*?" she replied.

They rode to the canyon entrance.

"What do you think, Vic?" Matt asked as he looked back.

Vic looked up at the twin pillars. "No use in coming back here. We've got more than enough silver."

Matt and the others rode on. Vic buried a can of blasting powder at the bottom of each pillar. He laid two long fuses down the slope, lit a cigar, and held the glowing tip to the end of each one. He mounted his horse and rode swiftly down the long slope.

The twin blasts roared out, awakening the echoes for miles. The pillars crumbled inward toward each other, held together momentarily, then collapsed in a mutual pile that sealed and concealed the zigzag entrance forever. Dust and smoke towered high in the still, dawn air.

The last echo died. An eerie wailing cry rose from the heights above the sealed canyon. Everyone looked back. There was nothing to see but the now-silent heights and the dust and smoke against the gray light of the false dawn.

Dave opened his eyes to pitch darkness. His eyes burned as though they had been exposed to full sunlight without protection. He coughed as the fumes and dust bit into his throat. He had expected death first from Vic and then from the explosion. This was a sadistic jest of fate, perhaps the last chapter of what it had had in store for him ever since he saved Lila Denton from the Paiutes.

He began to work on the bonds that lashed his wrists together. He worked them against a sharp-edged rock, abrading his wrists as he did so. His skin, greased with sweat and blood, finally allowed him to slip out of the bonds. He crawled toward the entrance over heaps of rock and fill thrown back by the blast. He was finally stopped by a solidly packed plug of material forced back into the tunnel. He had no idea of how far the fill extended. It could be at least fifty or more yards.

Dave remembered his father telling him about the three grim Fates: Clotho, who spun the thread of life; Lachesis who twisted the thread and measured its length; and Atropos who stood by with her keen shears to cut the thread. Somewhere back in the darkness might be grim Atropos honing her shears.

He felt along the right-hand wall until he found the niche where he had secreted his Sharps and cartridges, a full canteen, and Ash Mawson's Colt. He sipped a little of the water, idly wondering if there would be enough in the canteen to last until he dug his way to freedom. He wasn't optimistic about it. He cursed his stupidity for not having cached some candles and matches. He'd have to dig in the darkness like a blind mole. Well, *they* do pretty well, he thought with a rueful grin.

There was no time to waste. *Attack!* That was always Dave Hunter's credo. He felt his way along until he fell over one of his spades. He began to dig. It was hard going. He worked until the sleep born of exhaustion overcame him.

He awoke to deathly stillness. It was like being buried at the bottom of a tar pit. He fought off a sudden wave of panic. He dug again until he could hardly use the spade.

Dave opened his eyes. He had dozed off again. All he could hear was his own breathing, but something seemed to have awakened him. He held his breath. Something sounded faintly from somewhere behind him. Then it became tomb-quiet again.

Dave reached for his spade. The sound came again, louder this time. *Something* was moving through the darkness of the interior tunnel. *Tommyknocker!* The name came into his mind as though driven in by a pick point. They were the little people who were supposed to haunt mines and play mischief with the miner and his tools. The Germans called them *kobolds;* the Mexicans *duendes;* the English tommyknockers. The old hard-rock miner's song came back to Dave.

> *I'm a hardrock miner an' I ain't afeared of ghosts,*
> *But my neck hair bristles like a porcupine's quills*
> *An' I knock my knuckles on the drift-set posts*
> *When the Tommyknockers hammer on the caps and sills*
> *An' raise hallelujah with my pick and drills.*

The tunnel was quiet again.

Minutes ticked past in slow progression.

The dragging, shuffling sound came again, closer this time.

Dave stared into the darkness. Cold sweat trickled down his sides.

The faint smell of something burning, pungent, and greasy came to him—a burning candle, yet he saw no light.

"Hunter!" a vaguely familiar voice came out of the darkness.

"Who is it? Show yourself!" Dave called out.

There was no answer. Something scraped like footsteps on the floor. The stink of candle grease became stronger. Still no light was to be seen. "Damn you!" Dave snapped. "Light that candle and show yourself!"

There was a moment's hesitation. The voice came from within five feet of Dave. "The candle *is* lit, Hunter." Dave felt the sudden heat of something being passed back and forth in front of his face. The truth came into Dave's mind and sickened him. *He had been blinded by the blast.*

"You ain't so gawddamned smart now, are you, Hunter?" the dry voice asked.

Dave reached out with his hands and fanned air.

"You're blinded," the voice said.

"Ash Mawson," Dave murmured. "How did *you* get in here?"

Mawson laughed softly. "Through the back door of Hell, sonny. I had a helluva time trailing you. Amos was right. You needed a partner you could trust. We could have laid back and ambushed Denton and his boys. But, no, you were greedy. Now look at you. They're gone with the silver and the woman, leaving you blinded in an empty mine. A gawddamned *patrón*!" He roared with laughter.

Dave figured it was the end. The vindictive bastard could leave him in there to die or kill him, and no one would ever know the difference. "I was told you could smell a good claim from fifty miles away."

"Not quite. I been searchin' in and around this area ever since 1866. This is the Melgosa lode, ain't it?"

Dave nodded. "What's *left* of it, you mean. You saw Denton and the others leave?"

"Pulled out lock, stock, and barrel. That loco Paiute halfbreed Whiskey is with them. He guided them here and now he's guiding them out of here, likely to Stone's Ferry. I gave 'em something to think about. A little ghost wailing from the heights. By God, Hunter, I think it helped to run them out of here."

Dave nodded. "I heard you. You make a helluva ghost, Ash. I knew it wasn't any animal I had ever heard, but then I didn't figure on you being that animal."

"I wish I knew how to take that," Ash said dryly.

"How did you get in here?"

"I was hiding up on the heights by day. Came down to the *tinaja* for water by night. I scouted the whole area. Found a deep gully about half a mile up the canyon. I saw bats come out of it at dusk. Found a cave. The cave led into a mine tunnel. The mine tunnel led to you. I heard you picking away at the fill here."

"I'll make you a deal, Ash," Dave offered. "Get me out of here. Lead me to that bunch out there and I'll split the silver fifty-fifty with you. And if I can ever get back here, I'll take you in as a full partner."

"Shit!" Ash snapped. "You talk big now that I've got the upper hand! You double-crossed me once! I don't trust you!"

Dave shook his head. "I had no deal with you. It was Amos Wassell's idea. If you had been in my position, what would *you* have done?"

Ash laughed shortly. "You've got me there. But what's to prevent me from leaving you here, chasin' after them, picking them off one by one, and keeping the silver all to myself? Besides, sonny, mebbe you forgot you're *blind*!"

Dave moved suddenly, catching Ash by surprise. He dug powerful fingers into Ash's shoulders. His powder-blackened face and staring, reddened eyes were thrust close to Ash's face. Ash could have sworn that Dave could actually see him through sheer force of will. "Listen!" Dave grated. "I don't give a goddamn about those ingots or this mine! You want them? You take them! I have one condition: *Lead me to those people!*"

"What the hell can you do? You're blind and helpless!" Ash shouted.

The taut face was terrible to see in the thin, wavering candlelight. "I want the woman who is with them," Dave said in a low voice.

The tables had turned. Ash had held the whip hand over a blinded, helpless man trapped in a sealed mine. Somehow, Dave, by sheer, steellike determination had made Ash his ally if not his friend.

"I'll admit I have a lot to gain," Ash mused. "I don't exactly cotton to leading a loco blind man all over Hell's Forty Acres trying to find three hardcases and a woman, though. Well, I'll get you out of here, take a look at your eyes, and we'll go on from there."

Dave, Sharps in hand, was led from the mine by Ash. Ash examined Dave's eyes. He bathed them with water. "Hard to tell," he said quietly. "Had the same thing happen to me at Vicksburg. We charged a rebel battery. They fired. I hit the ground. Was missed by the shot, but the gun flash got me. Surgeon bathed my eyes with warm water a few days and after a time I was all right. I ain't predictin' it'll be the same for you."

"How long did it take for you?" Dave asked.

"Two or three days."

Dave nodded. "Let's get after those bastards."

Ash shrugged. "Your mommy ever let you fall on your head when you was a baby?"

Dave nodded. "A couple of times. It was a brick sidewalk."

"I thought so!" cried Ash.

They grinned at each other.

Dave was mounted on the burro. Ash led his bay. Ash was glad Dave couldn't see the narrow natural trail he had found leading out of the canyon. It was rough enough on Ash's usually steady nerves.

They were a curious sight in the moonlight—the plodding older man leading the burro and the bay, his sharp bottle-green eyes darting back and forth, seeing everything and missing nothing. The tall, gaunt man astride the burro, with his feet almost touching the ground and with a long-barreled Sharps rifle across his thighs, looking straight ahead as though he, too, could see everything and miss nothing through the bandage bound about his eyes.

CHAPTER 19

FOREBODING SILENCE HUNG LIKE A PALL OVER THE SUN-ravaged land. The dead-looking peaks, devoid of vegetation, seemed to grin in anticipation down onto the tangled labyrinths of heat-soaked canyons. The land was like a burial place of the lost, both men and hopes.

Only the Paiute Ahvote seemed at home in this place of heat and silence. He led the white people through it. He knew he was their only hope and salvation. A great secret in his addled head kept him going—a deal he'd made with Matt Denton.

Vic shaded his eyes as he looked up at the sky. "Seems to me we're too far east, Cos?"

Cos shrugged. "The Paiute knows this country. It's about all he does know."

"Yeah, but *we* don't. He could lose us in this hellhole and then give us the slip. We'd run outa water before we got outa here."

"We could travel north or northwest and we'd hit the river somewheres. Then we could follow it up or downstream to Stone's Ferry, whichever way it was," Cos insisted with conviction.

Vic shook his head. "Yeah, but which way do we travel *now?* There ain't any straight lines around here. You've got to follow the canyons. Even a compass wouldn't do any good. I still think we're too far east."

Vic glanced back at the others. Cos led the three burros loaded with ingots. Matt and Lila rode their horses. Vic held the lead ropes of the two other laden horses. Lila should ride, of course. She was a woman. Matt pleaded an old leg wound he claimed he had gotten at Chickamauga. Vic had always doubted he had been at Chickamuga or in the Confederate army at all for that matter.

The silver had to be split four ways. Vic and Cos still argued that it should be a three-way split. Matt could share his third with Lila. Vic wondered idly how much of her share Lila would really get. He speculated as to what kind of a deal he could make with Cos. He had never quite trusted Cos and he was sure the feeling was reciprocal. Cos might still feel some loyalty to Matt. Vic had no loyalty to anyone but himself.

The sun was low in the west. Long shadows crept down the mountainsides and into the canyon depths. Ahvote led the way into a narrow box canyon. There was some scant grazing for the animals. The Paiute climbed a crumbling slope and stopped at a ledge beneath a curving rock dome. He looked back down the slope and beckoned. Matt climbed the slope and looked down into a *tinaja* a few inches deep, covered with algae and tiny pink bladders. It smelled.

Matt looked at Ahvote. "Is this all?" he asked.

Ahvote nodded. "Enough for horses and burros and to refill all canteens." He wasn't about to tell Matt there was another, better *tinaja* not a half a mile away where Ahvote had made his sole camp many times.

"Where's the next waterhole?" Matt asked. He tried to keep his feeling of panic out of his tone.

Ahvote waved vaguely toward the northeast.

"How far to the river?"

Ahvote grinned lopsidedly. "Like bird fly—mebbe ten mile. Through canyons, mebbe twenty-five miles."

"Can't you do better than that?" Matt demanded. He gripped his pistol butt.

The dark and moody bloodshot eyes studied Matt. "You

kill Ahvote you *never* find water or river. You die in here somewhere. . . .''

They squatted beside the *tinaja* as the light failed, straining the dubious-looking water into their canteens. When the canteens were filled, they watered the horses and burros. When they were done, there was nothing left but an expanse of smelly, evil-looking mud.

Ahvote wandered off into the darkness. The others sat in the canyon gnawing at biscuits and dried beef.

Vic finished eating and felt for the makings. "I think we're way too far east for Stone's Ferry," he said.

Matt shrugged. "We can hit the river and follow it downstream."

Vic shook his head. "I've heard that if you get too far east the river flows in a gorge with steep, high walls. You can't even get down to the water."

"Well, I don't know! We'll have to see what happens," Matt said.

Lila had found a place to sleep. She was exhausted from the long hot day and the struggle to get through the canyons.

Vic was silent for a time. He looked sideways at Matt. "What kind of a deal did you make with Whiskey, Matt? You didn't promise him any of that silver, did you?"

Matt shook his head. "Nothing like that. Don't worry. It'll be all right."

"Maybe he doesn't trust you. Remember, he's got us by the ass right now. You make a deal with him and you keep it. Understand?"

Matt nodded. "We'd better get some rest. I want to press on when the moon rises. The sooner we reach the Colorado the better. I don't want another day of Hell like today. I think we'd better dump anything excess we have. Your saddles, extra food, and so on. We'll have to ration water for the horses and burros to keep them alive."

Vic drew in on his cigarette. The sudden glow faintly lighted his saturnine features under the low-pulled hatbrim.

"We can always cache some of the silver here. Make a map. Come back and get it later on. After all, Matt, our lives have to come first."

Matt stared at him. "Are you loco? We might never find it again, or someone else could."

Vic grinned. "Like who? The Paiutes have no use for it. Hunter is dead. The only ones who'll know about it are us and Whiskey. Once we don't need him anymore we can eliminate him."

Cos nodded. "Makes good sense," he agreed.

Matt shook his head. "The silver goes with us," he insisted.

Vic was not to be deterred. "The animals drink too much. They've got to have water or they won't make it at all. I say we cache most of the silver. We can leave Lila here with one of us to guard her and the silver. The other two can make the breed guide them to the river. Once we get to Stone's Ferry, we can get fresh horses and burros and plenty of water, then return here for the woman and the silver."

Matt did not answer right away. Finally he spoke. "Who makes the choice of who stays here and who goes to the river?"

Vic shrugged. "You're the big gambler. We can toss for it." He studied Matt for a moment. "Or we can leave the woman here—she's holding us back too much, anyway—load the silver on the burros, then ride the horses to death getting to the river." He paused. "Maybe *that's* what you want, eh, Matt?"

They stood there eye-to-eye. It was Matt who looked away first. He turned on his heel and stalked away into the darkness.

"Jesus, Vic," Cos said in a low voice, "you got him riled for sure."

Vic looked sideways at Cos. "You think he hasn't figured that angle already? You don't know him very well."

"Maybe not. I know one thing for sure: I wouldn't turn my back on him too often, Vic," Cos warned.

Vic laughed. "Him? He hasn't got the guts. Here's a thought—we can get rid of Matt. One of us can head toward the river with him. He just won't get there. The other one can stay here with the silver and Lila. The one who goes with Matt can get to Stone's Ferry like I already said, then come back here with fresh horses and burros."

Cos stared stupidly at Vic. "You mean . . . ?" His voice trailed off.

Vic nodded. "We've got our own asses to look out for. Besides, we can gain *all* the silver that way, a fifty-fifty split for us."

Cos ruminated for a moment. "What about Lila? Wouldn't she be entitled to her share and Matt's as well?"

Vic passed a hand across his face to hide his expression. "Who's to say?" he asked patiently. "If we get her to safety, that should be enough for her."

"Well, I don't know, Vic," Cos said hesitatingly. "She oughta get something."

Vic smiled. "Oh, she'll get something, all right. Don't worry."

Vic took first guard while Cos unsaddled the horses and unloaded the two that carried some of the silver and supplies.

The moon touched the eastern sky with soft pale light. The canyon rim was outlined sharply against it.

Cos happened to look up. He stared. The vague shape of a tall man holding a long-barreled rifle was silhouetted by the moonlight high on the canyon rim. Cos narrowed his eyes. It was a rock formation, a trick of light and shadow, anything but what he did not even want to *think* it was.

Vic looked at Cos. "What's wrong?" he called out.

Matt awoke. He instinctively reached for his rifle.

Cos pointed silently up at the rim.

Vic narrowed his eyes. "If I didn't know better I'd say that was Dave Hunter up there," he murmured.

Lila awoke and heard his words. She looked up. "Yes," she agreed.

Matt shook his head. "Impossible."

"It's *him!* I know that long rifle of his," Lila insisted.

"It may be his rifle," Cos said slowly. "But who, or *what,* is holding it?"

Vic raised his Winchester. "There's one sure way of finding out," he muttered. He aimed and squeezed the trigger. The rifle cracked. The echo raced through the canyon. The smoke drifted off. The motionless figure was still there. Vic levered a fresh round into the chamber and sighed. The figure seemed to dissolve into nothingness.

Cos was badly shaken. "I never seen Vic miss. Oh, God! What was that we saw?"

As though in reply, an eerie wailing cry like that which they had heard in the silver canyon rose and then quickly died away.

Ahvote watched from his cover farther up the canyon. *He* knew what was doing that wailing. He knew the country. It was haunted. It had always been haunted in the memory of the Paiutes. Whatever it was they had seen on the rim was not of this world. It might have been the man named Hunter who had been buried in the sealed mine, but if it was, he was no longer a thing of flesh and blood.

Fear floated down into the canyon on spectral wings. It settled itself on the canyon floor in the guise of a rusty-black crow. It eyed the silent people at the *tinaja* with bright, unwinking eyes. They were low on water. They were tired. They had seen the unexplainable on the canyon rim. *Good!* Soon they would turn against each other in their greed and desire for self-preservation, two of the strongest instincts in life. First it would be for the silver; then it would be for the water. Their eventual panic would lead them to destroy one another.

Ash Mawson crawled back from the rim. "That was close," he whispered.

Dave nodded. "Damned near parted my hair. The son of a bitch is good. Shooting uphill in that light. Are all of them there?"

"All but the Paiute."

It hadn't been difficult to catch up with the party. The Paiute was leading them in arcs and semicircles away from the river. Dave and Ash had been low on water when Ash found the *tinaja* below them in the canyon by letting the burro loose to look for it. He hadn't been back in the rim for twenty minutes when Denton and the others had appeared. Dave had wondered if Ahvote had noticed any signs of Ash's presence. The burro and horse had been well watered. The canteens were full. It would hold them through tomorrow at least, depending on how much longer Ahvote played blindman's buff with the unsuspecting whites. Surely some of them must be suspicious by now.

"What now?" asked Ash.

"We wait."

"Maybe they'll slip away. Probably one at a time if they get the chance. When they do, we'll be waiting for them. There's no loyalty among them, one to the other. Slow poison is working among them. They see the silver and the water. A great deal of one but little of the other. In order to keep the silver they've got to have water. Right now they each want *all* the silver and *all* the water. That will start the destruction among them," Dave said.

Ash scouted the rim again. He came back. "The horses and burros are picketed farther up canyon where there's a little forage. Denton, the woman, and Cos are asleep, or seem to be. Vic is still standing guard."

Vic glanced up at the sky. It was much lighter, but the canyon was still in darkness. The others were asleep. The Paiute had vanished.

The night wind whispered through the canyon. *"Now, now, now . . ."* it seemed to say.

Vic picked up a full canteen. He eased downslope to the canyon floor. One burro load would do for starters. If he could make the river with it, he could cache most of the load, taking just enough to grubstake himself for a time. Then he could come back, find the others, and take the rest of it. He coiled the burro's picket line and led it up the canyon.

Ahvote watched from cover. The soft, muffled sound of hoofbeats had died away. The tall man-killer with the hard eyes was gone. It was good. Let him go. He was the most dangerous of the three men. Matt was soft; Cos was stupid. Vic *might* reach the river. The silver meant nothing to Ahvote. The two white men left had good guns and other things of value to him. Then there was the woman. . . . Perhaps, if the gods were kind to Ahvote . . .

Ash Mawson awoke. The moon was still rising. The canyons were still in shadow. The wind brought faint sounds to him. "Dave," he whispered, "someone's on the move."

The canyon seemed like a river of ink. Ash felt as though he could throw a rock into it, watch it splash, then ebony ripples would wash outward to lap at the canyon sides.

The canyon was like a vast acoustical chamber picking up the most minute of noises.

The sound of striking hoofbeats rose from the side of the canyon.

Ash put his mouth close to Dave's ear. "One man. One horse or burro. That's as close as I can tell. Making heavy going of it. There's evidently a natural trail slanting up from the canyon bottom. He's likely heading for the river. Figures on trying to make it across the heights instead of wandering around in the canyons." Ash paused. "I can easily bushwhack him with my knife. He'll never know what hit him. No one will hear a sound."

"He's *mine*," Dave said flatly.

"You loco? You'd have to get close enough to beat him to the draw. Even with your full sight you probably couldn't do that."

Dave removed his bandage. Objects close at hand were fairly distinct. At a distance some blurring occurred. The moon was illuminating the rim, but there were still areas of shadow.

Hoofs clattered on the trail. Rocks fell and struck far below.

There was a huge boulder behind Dave. To his left and away from the rim about fifteen to twenty feet was broken rock and thick thorn brush taller than a man. The rim itself was no more than five to six feet away with a sheer drop interrupted slightly by the natural trail, then another almost straight drop to a deep talus slope that extended almost to the middle of the canyon.

"Drive him toward me," Dave said.

Ash shook his head. "You haven't a chance."

"I learned to shoot by sound during the war."

"You ever miss?" Ash asked dryly.

Dave grinned crookedly. "Most of the time."

Ash nodded. "I thought so. Hellsfire, Dave! You could bushwhack him just before he reaches the top of the trail."

"I want him to *know* who's killed him."

"If he doesn't kill you first."

Dave drew out his Colt and opened the loading gate. He revolved the cylinder to check the loads. "That, too," he agreed. He closed the loading gate.

"It's your life," Ash said. He started toward the trail top. He looked back. "If he *does* get you, you got any objection to me getting *him*?"

Dave grinned. "Be my guest. I'll never know the difference unless he and I meet each other in Hell."

Ash shrugged. "Whatever," he murmured.

When Vic reached the trail top, he'd have to turn right or left to circumvent the natural *chevaux-de-frise* formed by the broken rock and thorn brush. Ash could make him retreat if he turned right. Dave would then be in his path and waiting for him.

A pale oyster-white light was creeping up in the east with the moonrise. Shadows began to form on the westerly side of rock formations and of thick clumps of brush. Ash was about fifty feet beyond Dave and about twenty feet past the top of the natural trail by which Vic and the burro were ascending. Ash looked back toward Dave. He had hawk-sight, but it was almost impossible to distinguish Dave standing stock-still with his back against the immense boulder.

The sound of hoofbeats clattering on the loose rock became louder. Vic's head and shoulders appeared, then his torso. He gained the rim and turned to haul on the lead rope of the struggling burro.

Ash flipped a rock back over his shoulder. It clattered on the rim perhaps twenty or thirty feet behind him. He hit the ground.

Vic whirled, dropping his right hand to his Colt butt. He saw nothing out of the ordinary.

Ash dropped a rock over the rim. It struck far below and clattered down to the bottom of the canyon. The quick echo died.

Vic peered into the moon shadows. Maybe it was that damned Paiute. Vic wanted no part of him. A fanged knife could come ripping up into his crotch or back. Best to turn right and try for a clear passage across the mesa to the river.

Vic dragged on the lead rope. The burro dug in its front hoofs. Vic whacked him alongside its shaggy head. "Goddamn you," he grunted hoarsely. "We ain't got all night."

Vic dug in his heels and hauled back on the rope. What sounded like a dry cough came from behind him. He turned and looked toward an immense boulder. His imagination seemed to make out a formation on the boulder shaped like a tall, hatless man facing him. It couldn't be that damned

Paiute. The figure, if it *was* human, was too tall for that. Vic dropped the lead rope. The figure was part of the rock; it was a figment of his imagination or perhaps a hallucination brought on by heat, thirst, and exhaustion.

Dave moved a little. "Vic," he said clearly.

"Who is it?" Vic asked hoarsely.

Dave moved closer, separating himself from the background of the boulder.

Vic's eyes widened. "You're dead, you bastard!" he shouted.

Dave grinned evilly. "Are you sure, you son of a bitch!"

Vic went for his Colt.

Dave drew and fired as his Colt came up to waist-level, looking above the line of the barrel directly at Vic. Vic grunted as his big belt buckle was smashed back against his belly with the force of a .44-caliber slug. The wind went out of him. He fired his pistol. The shot went wild. Dave's second shot shattered Vic's left forearm. The third smashed his left shoulder. He was driven sideways and back. A bullet struck his right shoulder and spun him about, teetering desperately on the very brink of the canyon. His smoothly worn boot soles scuffled for traction on the slick rock. Two more bullets hit him in the belly just above his belt buckle. He went backward into space. Reflex action made him fire his Colt into the sky. Vic screamed hoarsely just once. His body thudded heavily onto the talus slope far below. The loose detritus gave way in a rushing, rattling cascade, carrying him down toward the canyon floor where he was neatly covered by the decomposed rock. The echoes of the staccato pistol shots and Vic's death scream died away erratically in the canyon. Powder smoke and dust drifted in the still air.

The burro had stampeded away from the gunfire toward Ash. Ash tried to block its passage. The burro lowered its head and butted Ash in the belly, knocking him flat and running right over him with its hard little hoofs. Ash made a desperate stab for the lead rope, caught it, and used its tug to help him to his feet. The burro was running blindly in panic. It did not see the dark belt of shadow that was the edge of the canyon brink. The burro went right over the edge with its legs churning air, then turned over and pinwheeled down, down, into the canyon depths to land with a smash on the talus slope. Ingots scattered everywhere. The burro slid down the slope in a cloud of dust until it reached bottom. The rushing talus buried most of the silver and the burro as well. Then it was silent again.

Ash had let the lead rope run, burning, through his callused hands. Another yard, and he would have accompanied the burro to his own death.

"Well?" Dave asked.

Ash looked over the edge. "By Jesus, Dave, I was a rich man for about ten seconds more or less." He grinned crookedly.

"There's more where that came from."

Ash nodded. "When and if," he said dryly. He looked at Dave. "Well, you did it," he admitted. He shook his head. "You've got guts enough to hunt grizzlies with a willow switch, but you're not too bright."

They grinned at each other.

CHAPTER 20

THE GUNFIRE WOKE MATT. HE WAS ON HIS FEET, RIFLE
in hand, before he was fully awake. "Where's Vic, Cos?"
he called out.

"He was supposed to wake me up to relieve him on
guard. He didn't," replied Cos. "I went to look for him
when I woke up. One of the burros is gone, too."

"I wonder where?" Lila asked dryly.

"What do we do now?" asked Cos.

"Go scout up canyon," Matt ordered. "See about that
gunfire."

"Send the breed," retorted Cos. "That's what you pay
him for."

Matt sneered at him. "You afraid?" he demanded.

"I don't see you goin'!" Cos snapped.

There was no sign of the Paiute. Panic got a toehold in
Matt's imagination. They had to make the river the next
day. Maybe the shooting he had heard was Vic killing the
Paiute, or, worse still, the Paiute killing Vic, then laying
in ambush for the rest of the party.

"We'll head up canyon," Matt said.

"You think that's the right way?" Cos asked doubtfully.

"It's the way Ahvote was heading when we stopped
here. Vic may be up that way, too. The river may be up
the canyon. We'll have to chance it. We can't stay here.
We'll travel while there's moonlight."

The moon was fully up when they realized they were in
a box canyon. They backtrailed to a branch canyon not far

188

from where they had camped. All the damned canyons looked the same.

Matt stopped short. A talus slope lay ahead. An arm protruded vertically through the loose detritus. The palm of the hand was facing Matt. It was almost as though it was a warning to stop passage that way.

Cos brushed past Matt. He scooped away the loose rock about the arm. The bluish, blood-streaked face of Vic appeared. The eyes were wide open, fixed in horror, staring blindly up at Cos. He turned his head away, sickened at the sight.

"Let's get on," Matt said. "Do you see the burro, Cos?"

Cos stood up. He shook his head. "I see some silver, though. Scattered about here and there. Maybe a dozen ingots or so."

"Is that all? Where's the rest?" demanded Matt.

"How the hell should I know? I know one thing—I ain't goin' up there to look for it."

"We've *got* to go that way! Come on!"

Cos glanced at the warning hand. "Not me! Don't you see? Vic is warning us to go back!"

Matt drew his Colt and cocked it. "*Vamos!* Move out! Now!"

"It'll be on your head!" Cos cried fearfully.

Matt pushed past Cos, leading his horse. A gun cracked flatly from high on the rim above the talus slope. The bullet ricocheted off a rock within two feet of Matt. Some of the fragments struck his pants and boots. A puff of smoke hung in the air near the rim. The thunderous echo of a large-bore rifle bounced back and forth between the canyon walls and died muttering in the distance.

"Dammit!" Cos shouted. "I told you!" He sprinted back the way they had come.

Matt and Lila followed the big man into the shelter of a huge rock shoulder that jutted out into the canyon. The horses and burros trotted back after them.

"We can't go that way until after dark," Cos said. "I ain't so sure I want to go up there at all."

Matt shook his head. "We can't wait that long. We either go on and risk it or we backtrail and find another way to the river."

It was that simple. The same thought was in each of their tired minds. All around them was the unknown—a vast, intersecting labyrinth of sun-baked rock, unmapped as the moon, and nearly as waterless.

"You think maybe that was Hunter shooting?" Cos asked fearfully.

"He's dead!" Matt said. "Don't you understand?"

"Yeah," agreed Cos. "But it could *still* be him."

Matt looked at him incredulously. "You mean a ghost? You damned fool! That was a *real* rifle! No one could have lived through that mine explosion." His voice died away as he saw the look on Lila's face. She must know now that he had deliberately planned to entomb Dave in his own mine.

"Where to?" asked Cos.

"Back the way we came!" Matt snapped. "The river isn't going to come to us. We've got to go to it."

They led the horses and burros back toward the *tinaja* area.

Ash patted the octagonal barrel of the Sharps. "She puts 'em right where you want 'em! I coulda taken Denton's head right off at the neck!"

Dave shook his head. "He's mine. Did they turn back?"

Ash nodded. "I didn't see the Paiute."

"He must have pulled foot on them."

Ash shook his head. "I think he's up to some deviltry of his own."

He looked over the rim. "There's some ingots scattered around where that burro landed and buried hisself. The kyacks must have split open. It's ours for the taking."

"It won't buy us a cup of water," Dave said quietly.

"Or vengeance, either," Ash reminded him.

Dave looked about. His vision was improving. There was no indication as yet that there had been permanent damage to the eyes. He'd know for sure in time. Meanwhile, there was much unfinished business at hand.

They trudged back along the rim toward the canyon through which Matt, Lila, and Cos were traveling in their quest for the Colorado.

Matt shielded his eyes with his forearm while looking up at the brassy sky and blazing sun. "It's no use. We should be heading north or west, but all we can do is travel easterly."

They marched on—trending east, then northeast, and then back to southwest. There was never any assurance that they were anywhere near the river. The sun slanted west and then was gone.

Matt came to a halt. "We'll rest until moonlight," he said.

Cos shook his head. "I say we keep goin'. It's better than sitting here in the darkness waiting to die of thirst. We can leave the animals here. They drink too much water and slow us down, anyway."

"What about the silver?" demanded Matt.

Cos spat dryly. "You want to die a rich man with a thirst, is that it?"

Later, Cos sat there in the premoon darkness listening to the slow breathing of Matt and Lila as they slept the sleep of the exhausted. Cos didn't feel too well himself, but his powerful physique had kept him going. Trouble was, how long could he keep it up? He thought hard—for him, anyway—and made his decision. He limped to the horses and burros. Cos was going to look out for his own ass.

A stone clicked on the ground behind him.

Cos whirled with upraised rifle.

"It's Whiskey," Ahvote said out of the darkness.

"Where have you been, you breed bastard?"

Ahvote paused. "Waterhole I know of." He shook a canteen. It gurgled as though almost full.

Cos touched his dry lips with the tip of his tongue. "Give me some," he suggested.

"Not yet. Make deal first."

"I'll shoot the shit outa yuh if yuh don't!"

The water gurgled again. "You got to see me first. You shoot and you wake them up. You don't want that."

"All right. What's the deal?"

"Full canteen for one gun."

"I'll need more than that to get to the river tomorrow. You show me the way to the river and two canteens, and I'll give you my Winchester."

"No deal. One gun, one canteen. You need two canteen to reach river. One for you. One for burro."

Cos thought quickly—for him. "All right. Show yourself, and I'll give you my rifle first."

"First you empty rifle. Then you put on flat rock in front of animals. Then you come back here."

Cos nodded. "It's a deal." He walked to the flat rock, emptied the magazine, and placed the repeater on the rock along with the ejected cartridges. He rested his hand on his Colt butt as he turned.

"Two canteen! Two gun! Empty Colt, too. Put it and cartridge belt on rock with rifle."

There was no way out. Cos eased his knife from its belt sheath and surreptitiously slipped it into the top of his right boot. He walked back to the animals.

"Catch!" Ahvote called. He tossed two canteens to Cos.

Cos drank from one of the canteens. He poured some of the water into his hat and watered one of the burros. He loaded two of the silver-laden kyacks onto the burro. He led it up the canyon. He looked back. "Is this the right way to get to the river?" he called out softly.

The weapons were gone from the rock. There was no reply from Ahvote.

* * *

Dave sat up suddenly. He hadn't realized he had fallen asleep. The noise of rattling stones and clashing rock came from below the rim of the canyon to his right. Dave was on a mesa top. To the west was malpais land, sharp-edged ridges with deep, narrow clefts between them. Ash and Dave had stopped there earlier to wait for the rising of the moon. Ash had gone ahead to scout for water.

The noise was louder and nearer.

Dave peered over the rim. The moon was rising, but there were many shadows in the canyons and lower elevations. There was just enough light to see a big man laboring up a transverse fault while hauling on the lead rope of a burro loaded with kyacks that brushed the wall on one side, while on the other they overhung the drop to the canyon depths.

Dave had left his Sharps back where he had been dozing. There was no time to go for it now. He drew his Colt and backed quickly away from the head of the trail just as Cos's head and shoulders appeared above the rim. Dave hooked a heel on a rock and sprawled backward right at the very brink. He flung out his right arm to break his fall. His forearm struck a sharp-edged rock. Reflex action caused him to release his grip on the Colt. It clattered on the trail far below.

"What the hell!" Cos yelled in a startled voice. He saw Dave getting to his feet. Cos unslung the two canteens he was carrying and dropped them to free himself for action. He charged.

Dave flung a rock. It struck Cos on the top of his head. Cos was used to fighting half-stunned. He kept on charging, head bent and arms outstretched. Dave sidestepped and hooked a hard left against Cos's jaw as he passed. Cos swung his right arm back like a bludgeon. Dave was driven backward, stumbling over the loose rock.

Cos turned. The growing moonlight revealed Dave. Fear coursed through Cos. "Hunter!" he yelled.

Dave started to run for his Sharps.

Cos charged. That was no ghost who had slammed that pile-driver hook against his jaw. This was his meat—a rough-and-tumble, eye-gouging, and head-butting brawl. He had killed two men that way and maimed at least a half a dozen or more.

Dave leaped to one side and thrust out his left leg. Cos fell over it. Blood spurted from his smashed nose. A boot heel struck him behind his left ear. He rolled over and over on the ground and came up on his feet with surprising agility for one of his bulk. He lowered his head and charged. This time he made contact. Dave had half his breath knocked out of him. He fell and was booted in the left side. He staggered to his feet and instinctively fought back. He slammed blows in over Cos's arms. When Cos raised his arms to protect his face, Dave dropped his attack to the belly and groin. When the big man dropped his arms to protect his lower regions, Dave returned to hitting the jaw and pounding on the smashed nose. It was like hacking at a mighty oak tree with a blunt ax.

Dave retreated from the swaying hulk of the big man. Dave's Sharps was somewhere behind him, but he did not dare take his eyes off Cos. The moonlight shone on the battered, bloody face. Cos began an inexorable stalking of Dave. His thick, powerful arms were held out in a wrestler's stance. To get caught in that vise would mean the end for Dave. Dave leaped in, struck, and then retreated. It was like a flea biting an elephant.

They finally closed; two powerful men, almost face-to-face. Cos was the more powerful by far. He closed his arms about Dave's chest. The fierce compression would soon crack ribs. Dave pushed the heels of his palms up under Cos's chin, forcing his head farther and farther back. Cos set his bull-like neck. They stood there, almost motionless, like a statue of Greek wrestlers. Dave suddenly brought his knee up into Cos's crotch and then stamped down full-force on his instep. Cos relaxed his grip for a fraction of a second, just long enough for Dave to break loose. Dave jumped back and began a retreat.

Cos drew a knife from his boot top. He charged. Dave dropped flat on his back, drew back his legs, and timed it perfectly, ramming both feet into Cos's meaty belly. It took the last of Dave's waning strength to push the big man up and over his head. Cos's head hit the rocky ground with frightening force. The knife clattered away. The big man lay unconscious, perhaps even dead.

Dave stared at him. Cos moved. He tried to get up. He placed his hands flat on the ground and forced himself up onto his knees. He slowly rose to his feet before Dave's unbelieving eyes. The fall would have killed the average man.

This time it was Dave who charged. He hit him in the gut and in the groin. He banged away at both sides of the jaw. Blood sprayed back onto Dave's sweating face. Cos shook his head. He made no effort to defend himself. His sight was blurring. He could hardly see his savage opponent moving in, always attacking, chopping away with every ounce of strength in his lean and powerful body.

Cos retreated. Dave kicked his bad leg. Cos swayed sideways and staggered backward toward what appeared to Dave to be a sharp line of shadow on the ground. Dave threw everything he had into a right cross. It was enough to tilt the balance. Cos fell backward and vanished before Dave's startled eyes. Cos screamed hoarsely. The impact of his body far below sickened Dave.

Dave sat down. Sweat dripped from his face. His undershirt and shirt were soaked with it. His breathing was fast, erratic, and painful. His chest rose and fell spasmodically. He buried his face in his bloody hands, then suddenly turned aside and retched until he could do it no more.

"Dave!" Ash called out, from cover, of course. He had a healthy respect for the big Sharps rifle.

"Where the hell have you been?" Dave demanded.

Ash stared at him. "What happened to you?"

"Cos Leach showed up. I lost my Colt and couldn't reach my Sharps. He didn't have a gun. Only a knife. We fought it out. . . ."

"Where is he?"

Dave jerked a thumb toward the deep cleft. "Down there."

"You threw him over?" Ash asked incredulously.

Dave shrugged. "Let's say I helped him go over."

"Just like that?"

"Just like that."

"You had a rough-and-tumble with *him* and *you* won?"

"Who's down there and who's up here?" Dave asked dryly.

Ash grinned. "Beg pardon. It does sound like a whopper, though, doesn't it, Davie?"

Dave nodded. "That it does. There was a burro with him. Look for it."

Ash looked down the trail. "Ain't no burro on the trail." He leaned farther over. "There's something 'way down there. Maybe he tried to get back down and didn't make it. You want to go down and see what we can salvage?"

"That silver won't be going anywhere," Dave replied dryly.

Ash stumbled over Cos's canteens. He picked them up. "Well, here's something we need worse than silver."

"Cos dropped them. He was probably pulling foot on the others and picked the wrong place to get out of the canyon."

Ash unstoppered one of the canteens and offered it to Dave. "Strange," he observed. "You killed the two of them at their own game. Vic with a Colt. Cos in a rough-and-tumble. That leaves Denton. He ain't good at either one."

"But he's smart, Ash, and because of that he's the most dangerous."

Ash nodded. "No question about that. Supposin' you do

get him? That leaves the woman. That should be the most interesting part. What about her, Dave?''

"I'll wait until it happens," Dave replied quietly. "I may have to wait a helluva long time, *but I will wait*. . . .''

Ash Mawson had been around. He had seen the elephant, but he had never experienced anything like this. Two deadly, hardcase fighting men beaten at their own game by a man whose vision was still faulty. Ash figured, on that basis, Denton would not likely survive a showdown with Dave. It should be interesting, though. There was one thing Ash did not want to witness—the bitter vengeance of Dave Hunter on the woman who had played at love with him and then had betrayed him to such an extent that it had almost cost him his life.

CHAPTER 21

THE MOON WAS UP HIGH WHEN MATT FOUND THE burro Cos had taken. There was no sign of the big man. It was eerily quiet in the canyon. The burro must have fallen from a hairline trace of a fault slanting up to the rim bordering the canyon. Matt looked nervously about himself. Where was Cos? Perhaps he had started up the trail, lost the burro, and had gone on by himself. Matt looked up at the rim again. Perhaps Cos had met the same fate as Vic. He turned and walked swiftly back to Lila, glancing uneasily over his shoulder as he went. Lila was seated on a rock. She looked questioningly at him.

Matt pointed back the way he had come. "I've found a trail leading up to the rim. The only way we'll get out of this hellhole is to go high. I might be able to see the river gorge from up there."

"Where's Cos?" she asked quietly.

He had to tell her. "I found one of the burros below the trail. Evidently it had fallen. Cos must have gone on."

"Are you sure? Remember what happened to Vic."

"We have no choice," Matt said. "Ahvote is gone. We won't live another day in these canyons without water. I think the trip will be too much for you. You wait here. I'll try for the river and come back for you as quickly as I can."

She studied him, then nodded slowly. She knew he had no intention of coming back. "You're taking the last burro, of course?"

He looked away from her. "Of course. We'll need funds once we're out of here."

She nodded. "I can keep an eye on the silver. I can't run away with it. Take enough to pay your way. Besides, if you're coming back with water, you won't have to have all that silver with you."

"I have a recent memory of a money belt that vanished when you left Chloride," he said.

"Half of it was mine!" she snapped.

"So you took the whole lot," he accused.

She shook her head in disgust. "We're getting nowhere. Go on with your loot, Matt. I'll wait. God alone knows why."

Matt tied the lead rope of the last burro to his saddlehorn and led the horse up the canyon. He knew better than to leave the silver with Lila. Odds were he'd never see her *or* the silver again.

He picketed the burro at the foot of the trail rather than risk himself and both animals on the treacherous path at once. He led the claybank slowly up toward the rim. Once up there, he could return for the burro. he was fifty feet below the rim when he halted for a breather. His legs trembled with tension and fatigue. He was in no condition for this type of thing, but he had no choice.

A stone detached itself from the rim. Matt saw it vaguely in the moonlight. It struck the horse on the flank. The claybank reared and half turned with his hoofs at the very edge of the trail. Dirt and stones broke loose under the hoofs. Matt yelled and dragged at the reins. The horse panicked at the yell, reared again, and tore the reins from Matt's hands. There was a fraction of a moment's pause, then the claybank went over the edge of the trail. The crash of its impact was heard. Then it was eerily quiet again except for the occasional fall of a stone clicking and clattering down the steep canyon wall.

Matt peered over the edge. A gun roared and flashed. The bullet ricocheted from the rock a foot over Matt's head.

He turned and plunged recklessly down the trail, gaining speed until he was forced to take giant strides. Fifty yards from the trail bottom he missed a step, struck a rock with a boot toe, and slid down the remainder of the trail in a cloud of dust to end up in a clump of cat-claw brush. The burro tore its picket line loose and galloped back toward Lila.

Even in his fear and panic Matt could not forget the silver. "Catch that damned burro!" he shouted at Lila.

She picked up the line as it trailed past her. The burro dragged her. She dug in her heels and brought the burro to a halt. Neither one of them had the strength left for a sustained struggle.

Matt crawled away from the trail. "We've got to go back!" he cried.

She shook her head. "We can't! You know there's no water there!"

"What else can we do?" he demanded as he got to his feet.

She looked up at the rim. "That's Dave Hunter up there."

"He's dead, damn you!"

Lila shrugged. "Perhaps. But if it is him, why don't you try to make your peace with him? I think he's a reasonable man and not a killer by nature. For God's sake, Matt, talk to him!"

Matt wet his dry lips. "Hunter likes you. He might even *love* you. You go up there and talk to him, *if* he's there. Tell him anything. Make a deal with him. You know what I mean."

She saw his fear-haunted eyes. "I know what you mean," she said. "But what makes you think he'll listen to me any more than he would to you? Or even *want* me, for that matter?"

There was no reply from Matt.

Lila led her horse down the canyon and rounded a rock shoulder.

Brush rustled in the windless air. Matt drew his Colt.

"It is Ahvote," the Paiute called softly from the brush.

"Well?" Matt demanded. "What do you want?"

"You remember deal we made?"

Matt narrowed his eyes. "Yes?"

"Deal still good? Okay? Okay? I got some water for now."

Matt would have sold his soul to get out of that hellhole—with the silver, of course. "All right, Ahvote. A deal is a deal."

"Not go to river by up canyon. Killer white men up there. You let horses and burro go. I lead you to river."

"The horses, yes. The burro, no," Matt said.

The burro and the silver mattered not to Ahvote. He was more interested in the five horses. If they were freed, they might find their way to water and Ahvote could round some of them up in time. "All right," he agreed.

Matt walked to where Lila sat on a rock, holding the reins of the dun she had been riding. The other four horses had drifted partway down the canyon.

"We're going to turn the horses loose," Matt said.

Lila nodded. "You might as well." She looked beyond Matt, and with a sudden chill of apprehension she saw Ahvote leading the burro toward them. "He's come back," she said, almost as though to herself. "But *why?*"

"He's brought water," Matt replied. "He'll guide us to the river."

She stared at him. "And you *believe* him?"

"Damn you!" he snapped. "What else can we do?"

"What will you pay him with? The silver has no value to him. We're probably letting the horses go to their deaths."

"We can give him guns," Matt said.

She saw the moonlight shining dully on the barrel of the Winchester in Ahvote's hands. "He's already got guns, probably from Vic and Cos."

He shrugged. "I've still got mine."

She studied him. "You *are* stupid. How long do you think he'll let you keep them? The first chance he gets he'll put a bullet in your back or stick his knife into you."

"I'll have to take that chance. It's either trust him or die in here. One more day of this and we'll be through."

They unsaddled the horses, then cached the saddles, some of the supplies, and the silver ingots that had been carried by the horses. Matt stepped back and studied the canyon intently, as though impressing it on his memory.

Lila watched him. The fool thought he might be able to return for the silver cached in a canyon that was hardly distinguishable from any other canyon in Hell's Forty Acres.

Matt and Lila followed Ahvote up a branch canyon. Matt held the lead rope of the burro in his left hand. He gripped his Colt with the other.

Somewhere up the canyon the eerie, high-pitched wailing cry drifted in the quiet air. It died away, came again, then faded away once more. Then there was silence, broken only by the faint footfalls and pattering of the burro's hoofs on the harsh ground.

The dawn wind met them in the wide mouth of a canyon that faced the north. The terrain sloped down from the canyon mouth. The slopes were stippled with clumps of thorned brush and clusters of boulders and riven with gullies and arroyos.

Ahvote halted. He turned with the Colt in his hand pointing directly at Matt's belly. He cocked it. "River down there," he said quietly, jerking his left thumb backward. "Couple of mile, mebbe more . . ."

Matt looked uneasily at the pistol. "Thank God for that," he said.

Ahvote looked at Lila. "Now we finish deal, eh, Matt?"

Matt nervously wet his dry lips. "Well, now, I don't know. . . ."

"Ahvote keep deal. We shake on that. Now Matt keep

deal. River ahead, like I promised. Plenty water. I take deal and leave now," the Paiute insisted.

"What does he mean, Matt?" Lila asked quietly.

It was getting lighter. The sun would soon be up. Matt looked about the area with its silent heights and brooding canyons. That son of a bitch Hunter could likely kill at half a mile or more with that Sharps of his. Once Matt got across the river, he should be safe.

"Well, Matt?" Lila demanded.

Ahvote gave her what he thought was a winning smile. "I get you for leading Matt to water. Make deal. Keep deal. Oh, yes. Ahvote not lie. Not like Matt. He lie all the time."

Lila stared incredulously at Matt. He looked quickly away.

"Give me rifle from burro!" Ahvote ordered.

Matt freed the Winchester from under a kyack lashing. He held it out to Ahvote butt first. "Look, Ahvote. I'll give you anything else you want—whiskey, more guns, horses, money, anything at all. Just let me take the woman to the river with me. When I get back to Chloride, I'll give you all those things, maybe even another woman."

The Paiute shook his head. "Now you call me Ahvote all the time. Before it was Whiskey or 'that goddamned breed,' eh?" He grinned. "Money no good to me. I got guns from dead men hidden in canyon. Whiskey, too, I took from you. I get horses back in canyon. Ahvote don't want whore woman from Chloride." He pointed to Lila. "That woman. *White* woman! That deal!"

"Matt!" Lila cried.

It was worse than Matt had anticipated. He had thought he'd euchre the Paiute out of the deal one way or another. "What the hell can I do?" he shouted. He grabbed the lead rope of the burro and ran, limping, down the slope. He led the burro into an arroyo and vanished from sight. Thin dust rose from the arroyo, marking his panicky flight.

Ahvote looked at Lila. He pointed back into the canyon.

Lila shook her head.

Ahvote smiled. "Got nice camp in there. Hidden. No one but me know about it. Plenty water. Plenty food. Plenty whiskey. Go on."

She shook her head again.

The smile vanished. Ahvote moved so quickly she had no chance to evade him. He whirled her about and planted his foot in the small of her back. She staggered forward and went down on her knees. He kicked her full-force on the buttocks, driving her face downward on the harsh earth. He gripped her by the arm and pulled her to her feet, then shoved her forward. As she staggered on, he kept poking her in the small of the back. Blood trickled from a cut on her cheekbone. Her hair hung bedraggled in front of her face. Suddenly she seemed to have lost all hope and resistance. She trudged along with down-hung head.

Ahvote grinned. "You like Paiute woman now," he said with deep satisfaction. "You learn quick. Ahvote boss. You remember, eh?"

Ash focused his field glasses on the faint wraith of dust rising from a deep arroyo. "There he goes, Dave," he said over his shoulder. "Headin' for the river with his burro load of silver." He turned and held the glasses on the mouth of the canyon. "The Paiute and the woman are walking into that big canyon." He took the glasses from his eyes and looked at Dave. "What's your choice?" he asked quietly. "Vengeance and a burro load of silver, or the woman who double-crossed you? You choose. I'll take what's left."

Dave's sight was almost back to normal. He looked first toward the canyon and then toward the arroyo. There was no reply from him.

"Denton will reach the river. What then? He'll be down in the gorge with no way out. You can find him easy enough. The woman? She's as good as dead already. If the

Paiute doesn't murder her, she'll probably kill herself one way or another after he's through with her."

The sun was rising. The wind had died away.

She wore a wide Mexican skirt and a white, low-cut camisa that revealed the deep cleft between her breasts. She wore tiny leather huaraches on her small feet. The blouse bared her smooth, creamy-white shoulders. She whirled in a dancer's pirouette. Her wide, flaring, midcalf-length skirt rose and undulated to reveal her shapely legs to midthigh.

"If we wait much longer, you'll never find her again—alive, that is."

Her eyes were gray, calm, and big enough for any damned fool of a man to fall into and never, *by God, be able to get out of them. . . .*

Ash handed Dave his Winchester, the field-glasses, and the half-full canteen. "Take the bay," he said. "You'll need the Winchester more than I will. Watch your back, Davie. I won't be around to do it." He grinned and strode down the slope toward the distant river. He looked back. "After I take care of Denton, I'll come back to look for you and the woman."

"I didn't say where I was going!" Dave called out.

Ash turned. "You didn't? Well, I'll be gone to Hell!" He turned back and continued down the long slope.

CHAPTER 22

DAVE RODE THE TIRED BAY TOWARD THE CANYON mouth. A thin veil of dust rose behind him. He and the horse would stand out like a fly caught in amber on the open ground once the sun was up fully. He was two hundred yards from the opening to the canyon. He saw no signs of the woman and the Paiute. The rim rock was sharp-edged in the growing light.

The sound came of a giant shingle being cracked. A puff of smoke appeared up the canyon. A spurt of dust erupted twenty feet ahead of the bay. Dave rolled out of the saddle with his Sharps in hand. He ran for cover toward a gully filled with brush while dragging on the bay's reins. The rifle flatted off again. The slug ricocheted from a rock just ahead of Dave. A third report followed on the echo of the second. There was a sound as though a stick had been whipped into thick mud. The reins ran through Dave's hand as the bay went down. he shot a glance backward as he ran. The bay was down, thrashing, on the ground. The fourth bullet slapped into its head. It rolled sideways without out a sound.

Dave hit the ground, belly-sliding into the brush. A bullet tore off his right boot heel, sending a stinging shock up his leg. "Son of a bitch!" he shouted in frustration. He lay flat with his head down in a shallow depression in the brush. Bullets combed through the brush just overhead. Twigs and leaves drifted down. That Paiute bastard could shoot, if it was indeed him, and Dave had no idea who

206

else it might be, unless it was Lila. He couldn't help but grin at the thought.

Twenty minutes ticked past with no more shooting. Dave bellied to the edge of the brush and peered at the canyon. It was as it had been before: a great, high-walled trough already being filled with shimmering heat waves. Nothing else moved within it or on the heights.

Dave reached for the field glasses. He raised them to his eyes. A moment later, a bullet struck the ground in front of him, flinging back a shower of stinging gravel. Dave cursed and withdrew like a turtle back into its shell. He couldn't leave his cover without risking more rifle fire. Sand was running swiftly through the hourglass. He had to reach better cover near or in the canyon mouth. He'd need his canteen or he'd not survive if he did make it into the canyon. It might be a long haul tracking down the Paiute and Lila.

Dave peered out at the bay. The dead horse was lying atop the Winchester. The canteen was still attached by its strap to the saddlehorn. He closed his eyes, voiced a silent prayer, then leaped to his feet and sprinted toward the bay. He dropped flat behind it just as a bullet thudded into the bay's belly. He eased the strap off the saddlehorn. He raised his head and then quickly lowered it. The rifle cracked. The slug hummed just overhead. Dave leaped to his feet. He had just enough time for the Paiute to lever in a fresh round, then sight and fire. He hit the ground within the brush just as the rifle was fired. The slug sank into the hard ground just behind his feet. He squirmed deeper into the brush.

Minutes ticked past in slow, ever-so-slow procession.

There was another depression twenty yards closer to the canyon mouth, and beyond that a shallow gully that trended into a wide-spreading clump of what looked like crucifixion brush, which extended all the way to the canyon mouth.

He took off his bandanna, tore it into thin strips, then

tied the strips together to form a cord about ten feet long. He crawled to a bush and tied the end of the cord to it, then returned to his position closest to the depression that would be his immediate goal. He got up onto his knees, slung his canteen over his shoulder, and then raised his right leg, ready for his dash. He gripped his Sharps in his left hand and the cord in his right. Dave twitched the cord. The bush top swayed in the windless air. The rifle fired at the bush, clipping off twigs and leaves.

Dave sprinted, head down, for the depression. He hit the ground and squirmed into the brush just as the gun flatted off again. He bellied in deeper, then waited patiently for another twenty minutes or so. Slowly, he raised his hat on the muzzle of the Sharps. There was no instantaneous rifle report this time.

Dave moved at a crouch toward the canyon, pushing his way through the cruel crucifixion brush with its long, needle-tipped thorns. After a while he could move erectly. He reached the sloping cliff face to the left of the canyon mouth. The thorn punctures stung and itched. Blood trickled from the minute wounds. He waited for a time, watching and listening. Finally he risked working his way into the canyon proper, taking advantage of every scrap of cover. The sun was up high. The heat was gathering.

A sense of urgency overcame him, but he held it in restraint. There was no sight or sound of the Paiute, but that meant nothing. The devil could be biding his time with spidery patience, waiting for a clear shot or the chance to tumble a boulder over the rimrock right on top of Dave.

He made slow progress but managed to work his way deeper into the great, heated rock trough. Finally he took shelter behind a rock ledge that was already in shadow from the western wall of the canyon. He scouted the heights with the field glasses. His eyes burned and ached from the strain. He closed them for a rest, then suddenly opened them. He caught a slight movement on the wall of the canyon where it trended west. He refocused the glasses. Two distant figures were moving slowly up a transverse trail to the heights. Now and again the first and smaller of the two figures fell but was dragged up again and forced upward. There was no question as to who they were. If Ahvote and Lila reached the rim and then vanished out of sight on the heights along some devious route of the Paiute's, by the time Dave reached the rim they would be long gone and lost somewhere in the maze to the southwest.

There was now no chance for Dave to catch up with them. Even if he did, the Paiute might be watching and waiting for him to ascend the trail. Ahvote had already proven that he was a far better than ordinary marksman with the repeater.

They were within fifty yards of the rim.

Dave reached for his Sharps. There was a round in the chamber. He felt in his right-hand trousers pocket for the two extra cartridges he had placed there. His fingers went right through a hole in the bottom of the pocket.

Ahvote had stopped on the trail. Something flashed in his hands. The field glasses picked it out as a bottle. The Paiute raised it to his lips. He was looking directly at Dave although he probably could not see him. He waved the bottle as though in defiance.

The trail and Ahvote's position was an estimated three quarters of a mile, or 1320 yards. The Sharps was fitted with a vernier-scale tang sight graduated to 1300 yards. The rifle had originally been fitted with an interchangeable globe and split-bar front sight with wind gauge, but Dave preferred the long-beaded front sight for field use. The other sights, reloading gear, and extra cartridges were packed in one of the bay's saddlebags. Dave knew he could never hit Ahvote at that extreme range. There was only one thing to do: close up the distance between him and the Paiute and hope to God that Ahvote stayed where he was, or at least in sight.

Dave stood up. He walked in the open toward the foot of the trail. The sunlight flashed on something—Ahvote's field glasses. He was evidently watching Dave's puzzling approach. Dave kept his eyes on any available cover as he walked. The instant he saw or suspected Ahvote was going to shoot, he'd have to dive for it. Odds were that the Paiute couldn't hit him at that range, but it was a possibility.

Dave estimated the distance as he walked. He was good at it. His early years of deer hunting in Michigan and then during the war when shooting conditions had rarely been even fair now stood him in good stead.

Ahvote was forcing Lila on up the trail. She was on her hands and knees, making slow progress. Dave started to jog-trot. He couldn't move any faster because of the rough ground and his physical condition. They were still an estimated thousand yards away. Dave's legs felt as though they were made of wood.

Dave kept going, slogging on, his head down, his rifle in hand and seemingly growing heavier by the minute. He heard the far-off crack of the Winchester. Without hesitation, he turned aside and hit the dirt behind a ledge. The bullet struck far to his right. He raised his head just in time to see the puff of smoke come again from the rifle. Down went his head. The bullet ricocheted from the ledge about ten feet from his right. He looked up again. Ahvote was again forcing Lila upward.

Dave was up and over the ledge in an instant. He reached an estimated range of about half a mile, give or take a hundred yards or so. He ran on, knowing full well that he'd never get up to the trail top in time to catch Ahvote and Lila.

His breathing was erratic. His heart pounded. He was sweating a freshet. He looked up and stopped short in surprise. Ahvote had reappeared. He stood at the very top of the trail right on the rim. It was now or never. Dave would have to risk shooting. He rested the rifle on

a five-foot-high boulder. He cocked the hammer fully
and squeezed the rear trigger to set the front, or firing
trigger, with a small click. The tendency firing uphill is
to undershoot. He set the vernier-scale sight for nine
hundred yards. He sighted. The small-looking, heat-
shimmering figure of the Paiute seemed to float into the
front-sight aperture. Ahvote stood motionless. Perhaps
he thought Dave had been hit by his last shot. The sun
glinted from the lens of the Paiute's field glasses as he
searched the canyon floor.

Dave's sight was about normal now, give or take the
sharp acuity one needed for long-range shooting. He closed
his eyes for a few seconds' rest. They burned. They teared
a little, which seemed to ease the burning. He opened his
eyes. Ahvote was still there. Dave would have to shoot
now or lose the chance forever.

He drew in a deep breath and let out half of it. He aligned
the sights and then placed the flat of his right forefinger on
the front trigger for a steady backward squeeze. He tightened his right hand on the small of the stock. The Sharps
bellowed, spitting out flame and smoke. It drove solidly
back into his shoulder. Dave raised his head from the rear
tang sight. Ahvote sank to his knees and then rolled over
backward and out of sight.

Dave gripped the Sharps and rounded the boulder,
plugging as hard as he could for the foot of the trail. The
angle of the narrow path was steep and the going was
hard. His breathing was really a form of gasping. His
legs seemed to be almost asleep. He kept on, driven by
his intense will. Rocks and decomposed materials were
kicked over the side, rattling against the cliff face and
falling far below.

The rim was just above him. Sweat streamed down his
face, almost half blinding his burning eyes. Now was Ahvote's chance, if he was still alive. He did not stand up.
Dave reached the rim, swaying perilously close to the edge,

on legs trembling with exertion. His lungs burned and his heart pounded.

Lila rose from a clutter of boulders. She shouted at Dave and pointed to his right. Dave turned. Ahvote stood, swaying back and forth. Blood ran down his face from his hairline. He fumbled at his belt for his Colt. Dave charged just as the Colt came up. He dropped to the ground as the pistol was fired. The bullet passed just over his head. Dave stood. Ahvote wiped the blood from his eyes and raised the Colt again. This is it, thought Dave. He had no chance. A pistol cracked twice, but it didn't sound like the Colt. Ahvote stood staring at Dave in disbelief. His right arm hung at his side. There was a spreading stain of blood on his filthy shirtsleeve. He dropped the Colt.

"Now, Dave! *Now!*" Lila screamed.

Dave swung from the hips in a fluid motion packed with concentrated power from days of swinging a singlejack in the mines. The heavy butt of the Sharps smote Ahvote alongside the head. The Paiute went sideways over the rim and pinwheeled down, down, and down. He cried out once, then struck the rocks far below.

Dave looked at Lila. She stood there, white-faced, holding her still-smoking double-barreled derringer in her right hand, her left hand at her throat. He walked to her and took her in his arms. She put her arms around his waist and placed her head against his chest. Her muffled sobs tore into him.

"You'll be all right," Dave promised.

She looked at him with a tear-streaked face. "He didn't search me," she said. "I didn't have a chance to use the derringer until now. I would have used it on myself if he had gotten away from you."

"All I can say is that was one helluva shot with that stingy gun from that range," he said. There was no question in his mind that in saving her own life, she had saved his.

Ahvote's Winchester lay on the ground. It was empty.

Dave picked up the Colt and checked the cylinder. It still had four rounds in it. He thrust it under his belt.

She looked over the rim and shuddered. "Your rifle shot struck a rock near him. A rock shard hit him alongside the head and felled him." She turned and looked at Dave with a faint smile. "Speaking of a helluva shot," she said.

They descended the trail together.

CHAPTER 23

MATT DENTON DROPPED THE LEAD ROPE OF THE BURRO and plunged down the steep, V-shaped arroyo that slashed down from the gorge heights to the river. The river there had formed a large eddy around an outthrust part of the gorge wall. There was a sort of beach extending back from the eddy piled high with a jackstraw tangle of logs, driftwood, and clumps of brush washed up there in times of flood over a period of many years. A narrow beach line extended downstream to another, smaller eddy, and beyond that the gorge wall was steep to the water. The far shore was barely a few feet wide and backed by vertical walls extending many feet high.

Matt clambered over the pile of logs and driftwood until he reached the water's edge. He splashed into the shallows and scooped the frothy, turbid water into his mouth. The sun glinted sharply on the churning waves. The roaring of the current resounded from the gorge walls. A hot wind swept through the gorge. There was no sign of life other than the lone man and the burro. The burro trotted toward the driftwood, clambered clumsily over it, encumbered as it was with the heavy, silver-laden kyacks, and drank from the river.

Matt crawled back into the hot shade. The river wasn't very deep, but the current was all-powerful. He'd have to get a move on before too long. Dave Hunter might be somewhere behind him and closing in for the kill. Matt

knew he'd never be able to buy his life from Hunter, even
with a burro load of silver.

Matt was almost dead beat, but he could waste no time.
He dragged material from the driftwood to the shallows to
make a crude raft. He laid out logs about twelve feet long
to form a raft averaging about five feet wide. He unloaded
the burro and used its picket line, a lariat, and the pack
ropes to lash the raft together. He found a slim, straight
pole from which he cut off the branches to use in guiding
the raft.

"You'll never make it, Denton," a cold voice said from
behind him. "Keep your hands up. Turn slowly."

Matt raised his hands and turned. A sickening feeling
came over him as he looked into the hawklike face of Ash
Mawson. Ash stood on the driftwood pile more than five
feet behind him. His pistol was cocked and ready in his
right hand.

In his younger days as a gambler on the Mississippi,
Matt had been involved in more than one shooting scrape.
He had survived by guile and speed. He worked the spittle
in his mouth together, then spat it full-force directly into
Ash's eyes. He moved with his right hand over, reached
inside his left shirt cuff, gripped the double-barreled derringer held there by a spring clip, ripped it free while at
the same time cocking both hammers, dropped his right
hand, and fired both barrels point-blank into Ash's belly.
Ash doubled over with the powerful impact of the two .41-
caliber slugs. He dropped his Colt. He went down heavily
and lay still. Matt dragged Ash by the heels to the water
and into the shallows. He shoved the body toward the racing current. It took hold of Ash. The last Matt saw of him
was one of his arms rising from the water in a sort of
laconic farewell, and then he was gone.

Matt wasted no time. He dragged the kyacks to the raft,
partially emptied them to lighten them, then manhandled
them onto the raft. He then replaced the ingots he had taken

from them and passed a lashing about them to hold them
securely in place.

Now and again Matt shot a fearful glance up at the empty
heights behind him. If Hunter caught up with him, there'd
be no warning, just the mad bellow of that fearful Sharps
of his, signaling the violent and bloody death of one Matt
Denton.

Lila went down at last. Dave knelt beside her. "Come
on," he urged. "It can't be more than a quarter of a mile
to the river."

She shook her head. "Go on," she said. "Get water.
I'll be all right, then."

"I'll carry you," he offered.

"No! Go on!" she said huskily.

He dragged her into the shade of some scant brush. He
turned away and jog-trotted stubbornly on. He held the big
Sharps in his left hand. It was empty, but he'd not part
with it. He looked back once. She waved him on.

He heard the muffled double report of a gun somewhere
ahead and down in the gorge. He placed the Sharps under
some brush and slogged on at a half-run, half-walk until
he saw the mouth of an arroyo leading down toward the
river. If that had been Ash doing the shooting, there'd be
no danger at the bottom of the arroyo; if it had been Matt,
which was hardly conceivable considering Ash's reputation, Dave would have to use the utmost caution. A cor-
nered rat is the most dangerous.

Dave went to ground twenty feet from the gorge rim,
then bellied to the rim and looked down through a screen
of thin brush. There was no sign of anyone at first. All
Dave could see was an immense pile of driftwood on the
shore of an eddy. Then he saw a head moving about just
beyond the driftwood right at the water's edge. He could
not tell whose it was, as it bobbed up and down too quickly.
He would have to take his chances.

Dave worked his way quietly down the arroyo. As long

as the driftwood was between him and the man, whoever
he was, he was safe enough. Once he was on the level,
open ground between the driftwood and the base of the low
cliff, he'd be in danger. He drew the Colt and cocked it.
He cat-footed toward the driftwood. A gun cracked on the
other side of the pile. The slug whipped Dave's hat from
his head. He hit the ground. It was no use firing into that
tangle unless he could see his antagonist. What the hell had
happened to Ash?

Dave bellied closer to the driftwood pile. He couldn't
hear any movement beyond the pile. The muted roaring of
the current drowned out most lesser sounds. He got up onto
his knees, then cautiously stood. Matt Denton seemed to
pop up like a jack-in-the-box, pistol in hand. He fanned
his Colt. Dave hit the dirt. The Colt cracked three times.
Dave crawled closer to the pile. He picked up a short chunk
of driftwood and threw it with all his power to his left. It
thudded against a log. The Colt seemed to echo the sound.
Dave crawled to his right. He threw another chunk behind
him. The Colt cracked again. Six rounds wasted, Dave
thought. Up and at 'em! He thrust his Colt beneath his belt
and clambered up onto the pile, plunging clumsily and
recklessly toward the river. His right leg became wedged
between two logs just as he saw Denton trying desperately
to pole a raft out into the shallows. Dave pushed down
with his hands to get his leg free. As he did so, his Colt
butt caught on a dead limb, was pulled out from under his
belt, and dropped down through the interstices of the driftwood.

Dave looked at Denton. He had stopped poling, and
while the raft drifted in the eddy, he was cramming cartridges into his Colt. Dave forced himself to pull his leg
free, ripping his clothing and scoring the flesh. He rolled
over and over atop the driftwood and fell onto the beach
just as Denton snapped the loading gate of the Colt shut.

The burro had been idling beyond the end of the driftwood. She looked up and saw Dave sprawling on the beach.

She brayed frantically and pounded along the narrow strip of shoreline toward him. Denton raised and aimed his Colt for a sure shot at thirty feet. Just as he cocked the hammer and pressed the trigger, Amiga rammed into Dave just as he was trying to get up on his feet for a dash to cover. The Colt cracked. The slug thudded into the side of Amiga's head and she went down as though poleaxed.

The current caught at the raft. Denton had recocked the Colt but turned to grab his pole to control the raft. That was enough saving grace for Dave. He hurdled the dead burro and splashed into the shallows. Denton turned and aimed the Colt with his left hand. Dave dived into the waist-deep water just as the Colt was fired. He swam underwater with his belly scraping the rough bottom. He surfaced within five feet of the drifting raft. Denton had turned again to get control of it.

Dave placed his hands on the edge of the raft and pushed himself upward to the full length of his arms. He rolled onto the raft. It sank beneath his weight, throwing Denton off balance. He pressed the pole hard against the river bottom to stabilize the raft. Dave stood up. The raft rocked perilously, shipping water alternately over both sides.

Denton turned, his mouth squared like that on a Greek mask of tragedy, and screamed hoarsely, "You'll drown us both!"

He might as well have appealed to the insensate river itself.

They grappled, straining together, knee against knee. Some of the ingots fell from a kyack and into the river. The raft was now pitching, bobbing, and swaying in the powerful current. Matt stared into Dave's face, still somewhat blackened, his eyes reddened from the explosion. It was like looking into the eyes of a demon come straight from Hell itself to claim the body and soul of Matt Denton for Satan.

The raft pitched heavily, breaking Dave's hold on Matt's right wrist. Matt drew his sheath knife. Dave threw himself to one side. The knife grazed his shoulder. The raft tilted and both men fell into the churning waters. They went under and came up again. Dave reached out with powerful hands to grasp Matt's throat.

"For God's sake, Hunter!" Denton screamed. "Take the silver *and* the woman! Just let me go!" His voice was cut off by an implacable constricting grip as both men went under again. It was as though Dave cared not whether he lived or died as long as he could kill Matt Denton.

They struck bottom. Dave's grip was broken. The wild current flung them sideways into an eddy cove. They stood face-to-face in waist-deep water battling like savage beasts. Denton fell backward and was torn from Dave's grasp by the river. Dave, was forced to struggle against the current to get back into the eddy. He turned as he reached waist-deep slack water.

Denton's head bobbed to the surface. He stared wide-eyed at Dave and shouted something unintelligible, drowned out by the roaring of the river. His head went under again. Then, fifty yards downriver, an arm came up as though reaching for the sky and then was gone. The raft was nowhere in sight.

Dave waded ashore and fell flat on his face with his legs still in the water. He heard footsteps and looked up. It was Lila.

"Are you all right?" she cried breathlessly.

Dave sat up. He nodded. "It evidently wasn't for me to finish him off," he said quietly.

"I heard the shooting and was afraid for you," she said.

He looked up into those unfathomable eyes of hers. "Everything is gone. Vic, Cos, Matt, and probably Ash. Even Amiga. *And* the silver," he added, almost as an afterthought.

"There's bound to be more silver in that mine," she said.

Dave shrugged. "Perhaps, perhaps not. Maybe this is the way it was supposed to be."

She touched his face with her hand. "It doesn't matter now, Dave. We can go back in time and maybe it will be like it was before they came and ruined everything." Her voice died away as she saw the look on his face.

"Dave! Dave! Dave!" Ash shouted from downstream. He hobbled toward them with his hand clasped over his belly. "Where the hell is Denton and the silver?"

Dave pointed to the river. "They went in there together."

Ash shrugged. "So he'll have some spending money in Hell."

"What happened to you?" Dave asked.

Ash unclasped his hands. His big brass belt buckle was neatly dented in the middle. "Denton put two derringer slugs against the buckle. An inch higher or an inch lower and he would have had me. Knocked the wind out of me and the sense as well. Denton must have dumped me in the river. Saved my life. I came to and had enough sense left to work my way ashore about half a mile down. Well, we've got a long walk to Stone's Ferry. The lady can ride my bay or the burro."

Dave shook his head. "Ahvote got the bay. Denton got the burro."

Ash looked strangely at Dave. "Why did he do that?" he asked curiously.

"It was my burro Amiga. She saw me. Came to me. He fired. She took the slug in her little head." Dave turned away.

"Will we go back to the mine after we reach Stone's Ferry?" Lila asked.

Ash looked at her. "In our condition? Besides, the mine has been buried. It would take weeks or months to reopen it. Further, we've no idea how much silver might be in there."

"If any at all," Dave added dryly. He was watching the expression on Lila's face.

"There are some ingots lying back in the canyons," she said eagerly.

Dave stood up. "We'd best get on our way," he said.

"Are you planning to come back to look for them?" she asked.

Dave shrugged. "They'll keep. When and *if* Ash and I come back, we might track them down."

She narrowed her eyes. "You and Ash?"

Ash nodded. "We're partners now, at least in the mine."

She looked quickly at Dave. "You always insisted you didn't need a partner. Why him?"

"He saved my life. We made a deal. It's as simple as that."

"But you haven't consulted me about that," she said.

"Why should I do that?" he asked curiously.

"Because we made a deal, damn you! Remember the money belt? Oh, you didn't want a partner, but you took the money quickly enough when you needed supplies. Well, David Hunter, that money you used was my collateral for a partnership in your venture at the mine, win *or* lose."

Ash whistled softly. "She's got you there, Dave."

Dave nodded. "*If* I go back to the mine."

"You'll damn well have to!" she shouted shrilly.

Dave studied her for a moment with those icy blue eyes of his. After a long pause, he shook his head. "No, I don't," he said quietly. "I'm not sure I'll ever go back there. It's said there's a curse on that damned canyon. I saw a warning left by the Spaniards well over a hundred years ago: Go back, stranger. There is nothing but death here."

She laughed. "And you believe it?"

"You've been witness to it. You saw what the silver did to the minds of men, turning one against the other."

"You talk like a fool!" she cried. She looked at Ash. "What about you? Do you have the guts to go back and mine that silver?"

Ash shook his head.

"You mean you believe that curse?" she demanded.

Ash shrugged. "I've got no real reason *not* to believe it, lady. I've lived too long in the Southwest and Mexico not to credit such things. Why, the stories I could tell you . . ."

"You're as loco as he is," she said shrilly.

Ash bowed a little. "Maybe that's why we became partners. Birds of a feather, eh?" He grinned lopsidedly.

She turned on her heel and walked away from them.

Ash looked at Dave. "Well, partner?" he asked quietly.

"How far to Stone's Ferry, partner?" Dave asked.

"Maybe a day or a day and a half."

Dave nodded. "We'd best be on our way then."

They grinned at each other.

CHAPTER 24

THE STERN-WHEELER *Cocopah* BLEW HER WARNING whistle at Yuma Landing to summon late passengers. She was about ready to cast off for the downriver run to the Colorado River delta and the Gulf of California. There, seagoing steamers discharged cargo from Puerto Ysabel to be reloaded into shallow, draft Colorado River steamers and then picked up cargo and passengers departing from Arizona Territory. The sonorous blast echoed along the high riverbanks and died away.

Dave Hunter stood beside Lila Denton on the upper deck. She had booked passage to San Francisco. The last passengers were hurrying along the wharf to board the steamer. Roustabouts were getting ready to swing the gangplank aboard as soon as the last passenger was aboard.

Lila looked up at Dave. "You eyes are all right now?" she asked.

Dave nodded. "An army surgeon at Fort Yuma checked them out. It was only a temporary condition."

"Thank God for that," she murmured. "You've still got your mind made up?"

"It is. San Francisco is no place for me. You understand?"

"Yes, I remember you saying, 'You can't buy your way into this life-style of mine'; and later, 'So here I stay, come hell or high water, and take my chances against this country, and Paiutes, and whatever else fate throws against me!' I asked you what would be the end results and you replied,

223

rather dramatically, I recall: 'A fortune, perhaps, or death.'
Do you remember?"

He looked into her eyes. "I do. Do you remember what
you said at the time?"

She shook her head.

Dave smiled a little. " 'There's always me, Dave,
whether or not you make a strike.' "

She was almost certain then that she had lost him because of her apparent greed back in the gorge of the Colorado. She looked upriver at the brown flood surging down
from the north. "I tried to buy your life from Matt by
revealing the silver ingot cache to him. I recall all too
vividly how you looked at me when you thought I had
planned to give Matt the silver all along. Do you know
what that did to me, Dave?"

Dave shrugged. "How was I to know? Besides, all I
have is your word that it was so."

She turned and looked into his eyes. "And that is not
enough for you?" she asked quietly.

It was his turn to look away from her.

"You did save my life from Ahvote," he admitted finally.

She smiled faintly. "In order to save my own."

He looked down at her. "Is that all?"

It was her turn to remain silent.

The whistle blasted again.

Lila placed her hands on Dave's shoulders, stood on her
tiptoes, and kissed him. There was no response from him,
but she'd never know how she stirred him with that tender
little act.

"Good-bye," Dave said quietly. He walked toward the
stairs to the lower deck.

She nodded. "I'll be in San Francisco until the end of
the year at least. If I can't find a position by then, I'll likely
return to New Orleans."

He was gone down the stairs.

"Cast off forward!" the mate shouted from the pilot-house.

The heavy lines thumped on the foredeck. The gangplank was being slowly drawn in. Dave ran along it lightly and leaped the gap to the landing.

"Cast off aft!" the mate commanded.

The paddlewheel began to turn as the *Cocopah* started to drift out into the main channel while churning up bottom silt. She swung out into the current with an increased thrashing of the paddlewheel. A muted *sssooo-hhhaaa, sssooo-hhhaaa, sssooo-hhhaaa* came from the long-stroke engines coupled with the rhythmic coughing of steam from the stack exhausts.

Lila stood at the rail. "Where will you go?" she called in her high, clear voice.

Dave shrugged. He took off his hat and swung it in a semicircle from the south to the east and then north. *"Más allá!* On beyond!" he called.

The *Cocopah* reached a bend in the river channel. Dave could just make out Lila standing on the upper deck. Then the steamer was gone from sight. Her whistle blew again, fainter this time.

Dave walked toward the shore.

Ash Mawson was seated on a barrel cutting a chew of Wedding Cake.

"I thought you were taking the *Gila* north to return to your marshal's job and the livery-stable business in Chloride?" Dave asked.

Ash shrugged. "I was waiting to see what you'd do today. The *Gila* doesn't leave until tomorrow morning."

Dave reached inside his coat and took out his ticket for Puerto Ysabel on the *Cocopah*. He tore it to shreds and cast it to meet the hot wind. The bits of pasteboard fluttered out over the river and then floated down to the surface. The current caught them and drew them out into the main channel, where they soon disappeared from view.

Ash stowed the chew in his mouth. ''Changed your mind, eh?''

Dave shook his head. ''I don't think I ever really intended to go.''

Ash chewed for a while. He looked up at Dave sideways with his bright, sharp green eyes. ''Wasn't easy, though?''

Dave looked downstream. ''Can't say that it was.''

''Maybe you'll forget her in a year or so.''

''Maybe. What are your plans, Ash?''

Ash stood up. He reached inside his coat and unpinned his brass Chloride marshal's badge from his shirt. He scaled it far out into the river. ''I'm like you in a way, Davie,'' he said quietly. ''We're like the bear that went over the mountain to see what he could see. There's a helluva lot of the Southwest I ain't seen yet.''

''I'll buy you a drink, Ash,'' Dave invited.

Ash nodded. ''I was wonderin' when you'd ask.''

They grinned at each other.

Far, far down the river, the *Cocopah*'s whistle sounded, ever so faintly.

Más allá . . . On beyond . . .

ABOUT THE AUTHOR

GORDON D. SHIRREFF's fascination with the American West began in 1940, when he was stationed with the army 39th Artillery Brigade at Fort Bliss, Texas. In World War II he served as a captain of anti-aircraft artillery in the Aleutian Campaign, then as a ship transport commander in the European Theater, concluding his service as a military historian. After World War II he took up writing. HELL'S FORTY ACRES is his eightieth novel. Previous books set in the West include the Lee Kershaw, Manhunter series; THE UNTAMED BREED, BOLD LEGEND, and GLORIETA PASS, which chronicle the adventures of mountain man Quint Kershaw, and THE GHOST DANCERS, which features Major Alec Kershaw. Mr. Shirreffs is also the author of many short stories, several television plays, one T.V. series, and four films. He lives in Granada Hills, California, with his wife, Alice.

JIM MILLER'S
SHARP-SHOOTIN' ST⊙RIES
O' THE WAYS
O' THE WEST!!